gears & gateways

A Cozy Fantasy

Tales from the Broken Claw
Book Nine

don jones

Copyright © 2026 by Don Jones

All rights reserved.

No part of this book may be reproduced in any form or by any electronic or mechanical means, including information storage and retrieval systems, without written permission from the author, except for the use of brief quotations in a book review.

❦ Formatted with Vellum

contents

Chapter 1	1
Chapter 2	11
Chapter 3	27
Chapter 4	37
Chapter 5	45
Chapter 6	61
Chapter 7	69
Chapter 8	79
Chapter 9	89
Chapter 10	99
Chapter 11	111
Chapter 12	125
Chapter 13	137
Chapter 14	147
Chapter 15	159
Chapter 16	169
Chapter 17	181
Chapter 18	193
Chapter 19	205
Chapter 20	213
Chapter 21	223
Chapter 22	237
Chapter 23	247
Epilogue	255
Afterword	263
Award-Winning Fiction	265
About the Author	267
Also by Don Jones	269

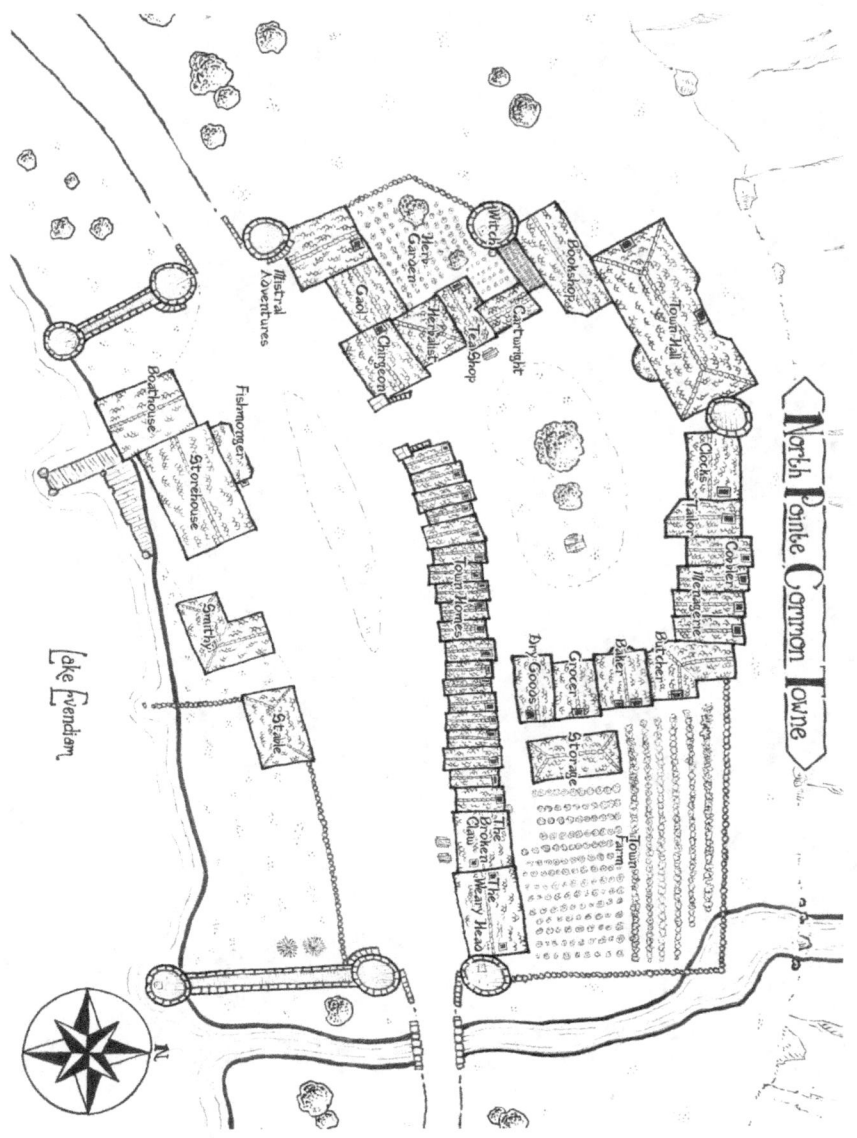

one
. . .

THE GRASSY SQUARE of North Pointe Common Towne had a habit of keeping its own time. Some said it was the town's well-appointed bell tower, always a little fast at sunrise and a little slow after midday. Others, less generous, blamed the Clockmaker's. The Clockmaker's shop squatted at the back of the square, a tidy slate-gray structure that huddled between its neighbors, whose windows bulged with elaborate timepieces, brass-wound orreries, and the occasional piece of machinery so confounding that children dared each other to stare at it for ten whole heartbeats.

Inside, the air was sharp with Number Seven Machine Oil, hot brass, and Finnian Springdale's unique brand of nerves. Finnian took his morning like clockwork: tea, two biscuits, one of Makota's thick slices of honeyed toast, and a stroll down the trade road and back. After three sennights of clear weather, the trade road's dirt was packed hard, raising only the barest hint of dust as travelers trundled through in their carts and wagons. Today, like every day, he was the first to unlatch his shop door, sweep away the night's accumulation of moths and ill-omened beetles, and settle in at his workbench.

His hands—nimble, lined, and just short enough to never catch in the gears—rested lightly on the battered rosewood surface. On the bench: a mantel clock for a client passing through, a cartographer by the name of Timme. The clock's face was mother-of-pearl, the numbers hand-lettered in deep blue, and the mechanism inside was a new design Finnian had been aching to try. Somewhere on the other end of the bench was a confusion of cogs, flywheels, and the beginnings of what he insisted would be the world's first Self-Buttering Toast Machine.

He would get to that.

First, Timme's clock. Finnian carefully lifted the clock's glass dome, his fingers leaving perfect smudges that only he could see. He set a final, garnet-studded pallet onto the escapement. The tick-tock, once limping and irregular, smoothed into a crisp rhythm. He allowed himself a small smile. Nothing, not even the infernal ticking of the bell tower, sounded as sweet.

The bell over the door jangled.

Timme stepped inside, boots damp from the rain, shoulders set in a way that suggested she could snap a yardstick over her knee without slowing her stride. Her satchel bulged with rolled parchment and, from the look of it, a couple of copper-capped canteens. Her hair, black and wild, was already halfway to dry from the walk across town. She eyed Finnian over the tops of her spectacles.

"You're early," she said.

Finnian dabbed at his forehead with a rag, then smiled with his entire face. "So is your clock. Which means it works." He turned the timepiece to face her, watching for the telltale narrowing of her eyes. Some clients could spot a deviation of half a minute; Timme was one.

She advanced on the clock, rolled a finger over the dome, and peered at the mechanism through the beveled glass. "Mother-of-pearl face," she mused. "Fancy."

"It's a gift," Finnian said, "for your ownself. From you to you, I gather."

"Did you adjust it to the local bell?" she asked.

"Indeed," Finnian said, holding up a small brass key. "You'll see the lever at the back. If you slide it to the right, you can adjust it. Slide it back to re-engage the mechanism. There's a detent to prevent accidental switch, so you don't—"

He broke off. Timme's finger brushed the clock face, and the world stuttered.

It wasn't a noise, not exactly, but the air seemed to snap taut and then quiver. Finnian's vision doubled. For half a heartbeat, he saw the shop as it was, and overlaying it, something cold and rushing and blue—he and Timme both tumbling down a wild, churning river, her precious satchel streaming parchment like the tails of a fleeing kite. Then, just as quickly, the world righted itself. The only sign of the interruption was Timme's hand, frozen on the clock, and Finnian's own pulse, racing as if he'd just chased a runaway clockwork hound down the road.

He coughed lightly. "I do apologize. There's a...strange effect on timepieces so near to the Mistral Mountains. Something about the ley lines, or perhaps the magnetic strata. If you notice anything...unusual...with the clock, just give it a firm tap on the base. That'll settle it."

Timme's eyes flicked from the clock to Finnian. "You felt that, too?"

He cleared his throat and straightened his vest. "Feel what?"

"The—" She stopped. Something in Finnian's expression, or perhaps the ghost of that river-vision, made her reconsider. "I suppose you'd know best. Local knowledge."

He decided it would be undignified to agree too enthusiastically. "I've lived here only a couple of seasons," he offered, "but I can say with confidence that time does run a little funny, on occasion. If you're heading through the mountain passes, you may wish to...tether your maps."

She nodded slowly, then reached for her coin purse. "The price was six-fifty?"

"Six even. It's not every day I get to build something with a pearlescent face." He wrapped the clock in oilskin, then again in brown paper. As he worked, Timme reached into her satchel, checking each map tube and wax seal, her movements precise. Finnian caught the faintest hint of magic—something in the way the runes on her case flickered when the clock came near. He filed it away. Timme might need her timepiece more than she let on.

She set six bright coins on the counter. Finnian noticed the particular way the coins were minted—foreign, but real, and likely dear to her.

"Tell you what," he said, "I'll throw in the winding key, free of charge. And a tip: if you absolutely must cross the pass, keep north of the standing stones. The weather's better, and you'll avoid the worst of the mudflows. The Mistral has been...energetic, this moon."

Timme looked at him, eyes softening just a fraction. "I don't have a choice, actually. What I need to map is past the stones." She hesitated. "Thank you, Finnian."

He nodded, watching as she tucked the clock into her bag. Before she left, she thumbed the catch on her map tube, triple-checked the wax seal, and only then set her shoulders. By the time the door jingled shut behind her, Finnian could already hear the mother-of-pearl clock tick-tocking in perfect time, fading down the lane.

He leaned back, the bench creaking in protest. Another satisfied customer, even if she didn't realize it yet. The flash of the river vision had left a chill in his chest. He shook it off. That sort of thing was better handled by the Púca or Leota, not a man with butter on his waistcoat and a backlog of repairs.

Still, he lingered on the feeling, the strange certainty that the clock had tried to warn its new owner. Maybe that was his own nerves. Maybe not.

He squinted across the workbench to his true obsession—the Self-Buttering Toast Machine. This was the real business of the day. He eyed the pile of brass cogs, bent forks, and several feet of surgical tubing with giddy affection.

"Back to the work of gods," he muttered, and reached for his best screwdriver.

The Self-Buttering Toast Machine had not been Finnian's first foray into unnecessary breakfast improvement, but it was, by any metric he cared to measure, the most spectacularly ambitious. He slid the nearly completed chassis onto the main work table, angling it for the best possible morning light. It was a contraption of pipes, springs, and polished copper, with a line of silver-plated gears running down the middle like a parade of mechanical ants.

Step one, as always, was to admire the thing.

Step two: recount, from memory, the many small victories and glorious defeats leading to its present state. There was the regrettable incident of Toast Machine Mark Zero, which had set fire to an entire loaf and blackened the ceiling above Finnian's bench for a fortnight. Mark One had succeeded in browning the bread, but the "buttering" component dispensed jam at random intervals, sometimes with explosive force. Mark Two, today's model, was leaner, hungrier, and engineered to deliver melted butter at exactly the optimal temperature and velocity. It boasted a teakettle-powered bread carriage, an oil-lamp-heated butter pump, and a lever-pulley system guaranteed to apply the melted butter 0.05 seconds before the toast cooled.

Every improvement, as Finnian liked to say, had been hard-won.

He was filling the water reservoir of the bread carriage with a pipette, tongue tucked firmly in cheek, when the shop's front door shuddered open. In waltzed a Púca—one of the managerial variety, judging by the green velveteen vest, starched white cuffs, and the tiny slate hung around its neck on a length of bright ribbon. The Púca's ears twitched in time with its quick, appraising gaze, and its hands were already clasped behind its back in an attitude of patient expectation.

"Morning, Handy Púca," Finnian called, deliberately getting the title wrong. The Púca's ears twitched again in mild offense, but it grinned nonetheless.

"Project Manager, if you please, Mister Springdale," the Púca replied, each word bouncing along the syllables like a lamb down a grassy hill. "Heard tell you'd have something needing a grand debut this candlemark?"

"I did, and you're just in time." Finnian gestured to the bench. "May I present: Toast Machine, Mark Two."

The Púca whistled. "Sure, it's a beauty, so it is. That's copper, is it?"

"Only the finest, reclaimed from an old still down by the Market Lane. Polishes up a treat." Finnian puffed out his chest, then motioned the Púca closer. "You're here for a demonstration?"

"I'm to fetch a timer for the jewelers' kiln, but I'll not say no to a slice." The Púca settled onto a high stool, legs swinging, and folded its hands neatly in its lap.

Finnian set to work. "All right. We'll need a thick slice of yesterday's rye, and—" He checked his pockets. "Butter, measured to the grain." He produced a pat of butter from a small tin, placed it into the brass reservoir, and double-checked the line of ceramic cups meant to catch any stray drips.

He cleared his throat for showmanship. "Initiating process."

He wound the main spring with a flourish. Instantly, the bread carriage creaked to life, shunting its lone slice of rye down a tiny ramp and into the waiting jaws of the toasting cage. The oil lamp beneath it flared to a steady blue-white, heat shimmering upward to brown the bread in short, even bursts. A bell dinged. The lever-and-pulley system engaged.

For a few glorious seconds, everything worked as intended. The smell of browning bread, then of butter just beginning to melt, filled the shop. The Púca's eyes shone with hope.

Then, a click. Then, a snap. A fine detent spring—decorative, not strictly necessary, but Finnian liked the symmetry—gave way with a sound like a cricket's curse.

The brass-and-copper assembly went full rebel. The butter pump, freed from its restraining spring, overcompensated and ejected the entire pat of butter at once. It struck the toast, then ricocheted, glancing off the Púca's slate and splattering the wall in an impressive, circular blot. The bread carriage, unbalanced by the sudden loss of mass, overshot its trajectory and launched the slice of toast in a shallow, parabolic arc directly at Finnian's prize display: a grandfather clock with an extra-tall spire.

The slice clipped the spire, spinning off a crumbly crescent, and continued its flight.

Finnian, prepared as ever for such events, snatched an oversized fishing net from behind the counter. With one swift motion, he swept the flying toast out of the air.

The Púca clapped politely. "A flawless save, and only a wee bit of damage to the wall."

"Progress!" Finnian crowed, inspecting the toast. "It's only the third airborne incident this sennight, and this time the crust held."

He offered the toast to the Púca, who accepted it gravely. "You have the soul of a poet, you do," said Project Manager Púca. "Perhaps next time it'll land butter-side down."

Finnian made a note on his pad, jotting "REDUCE SPRING TENSION" and underlining it twice. "Next time, I'll have the jam injector working as well."

The Púca shuddered. "Ah, that's how it is, then. You're breeding them for warfare."

Finnian snorted. "Only until I get a better offer from the bakery."

They both watched as the toast machine shuddered to a stop, leaking a small, sad rivulet of melted butter onto the tabletop.

"Would you like some tea with that?" Finnian asked, already reaching for the battered enamel kettle. The Púca grinned, hopping down from its perch.

"Don't mind if I do, but best get to the reason I called, eh? The jewelers are after a timer for the kiln—needs to measure exactly one candlemark, no more, no less."

Finnian nodded, butter still dotting his shirt, and set the net aside. "You may be in luck. I believe I've got just the thing." He rummaged under the counter, then frowned. "Hmm. I'll need to hunt it down. Come back in a bit? I'll need to clean up, first."

"O'course, o'course. Shall I send Custodian Púca over to assist?"

Finnian chuckled. "It's just some crumbs and butter. I think I can handle it."

"I'll see you in a trice, then."

Project Manager Púca was not gone long. In North Pointe, the passage of time could be often measured in how quickly the Púca came calling for repairs, improvements, or the occasional sympathetic ear. The Púca returned before Finnian had finished reassembling the Toast Machine's errant spring, already dabbing at the butter-blotched wall with a handkerchief and a spritz bottle of lemon water.

"Any luck finding the timer? The jewelers are on edge—if they overcook the gold again, there'll be smoke from here to the river."

Finnian nodded, pleased to change gears. "Indeed. One moment."

He knelt to the lowest drawer behind the counter, withdrew a velvet-wrapped case, and set it with reverence on the workbench. He lifted the lid to reveal a wind-up timer, the face glazed in deep blue enamel, the numbers crisp and bold. The case was brass, but polished so smoothly it reflected the shop's light in soft halos. "It was hidden in the back along with bins of parts. Don't know what I was thinking. Meet the Horologue Mark One," Finnian said, voice low with pride. "Wind it to your mark and the hand glides as true as any clock."

The Púca reached for it, fingers surprisingly gentle. "Lovely, so it is. But what makes it special?"

Finnian smiled. "It's the spring. I wound it myself from a single strip of iron. Tension is constant, even if you wind it while it's already running. No skipping, no catching." He demonstrated, turning the key until the minute hand swept to a precise, satisfying stop. He flicked the release, and the timer ticked down, smooth as water.

The Púca was transfixed. "How long will it run?"

"Up to one candlemark, exactly, if you trust the calibration. I measured it against the bell tower for a full moon."

"Sure, you did." The Púca beamed. "You're a marvel, Finnian Springdale."

He felt the compliment like a warm loaf, fresh from the oven. "Thank you. It's a pleasure, truly."

As the Púca tucked the timer into its pocket, Finnian hesitated. "If I may make a small proposal... The old units—candlemarks, bells—sound like they belong to a world of candles and bells. But horology, the study of time, is what gives us...well, order. Shouldn't we call the time a clock measures an hour?"

The Púca's ears twitched. "Hour, you say?"

Finnian shrugged. "I read it once. It stuck with me."

The Púca tried the word on its tongue. "An hour." Its smile broadened. "It has a bite to it, doesn't it? I'll bring it up at the next Púca meeting."

Finnian bowed. "Let's see if it catches on." Then he gave a shy smile. "And I'll admit I could use some help cleaning up, if the offer is still good. It's all crumbs behind the large clock and I can't shift it myself."

"Consider it done." The Púca doffed an imaginary hat, then paused. "Do you want the cleaning bill sent to your home or your shop?"

Finnian laughed. "Surprise me."

With a nod, the Púca vanished, a faint scent of lemon water lingering in its wake.

For a long moment, Finnian listened to the ticks and tocks of his clocks, each measuring time in its own careful way. The Toast Machine Mark Two waited on the workbench, already promising trouble and delight in equal measure. The world outside would keep on spinning, even if North Pointe marked time a little differently than the rest.

Finnian sipped his tea, savoring the quiet. He made a mental note: Horologue Mark Two, next market day. Perhaps he'd ask Leota to test it. Or maybe, just maybe, he'd finally get the jam injector to work without incident.

There was, after all, always next time.

two
...

THE CLOCKMAKER'S shop had a rhythm all its own, and in the hour after dawn, it was more anticipation than actual business. The hush inside was never complete, filled as it was with the gentle, overlapping tickings of three dozen clocks, each measuring time in its own slightly stubborn way. In this chorus, Finnian always found a peculiar contentment, as though even the machines he made couldn't quite agree on reality and chose instead to negotiate.

He spent the first hour of every day setting each clock as true as he could—never perfectly, but close enough that the differences could be measured in a matter of heartbeats. This morning, the workbench was already swept clean, the Toast Machine Mark Two had been corralled to a far corner, and the wall above the mantel shone where Finnian had scrubbed away the traces of yesterday's butter incident.

He was just aligning the minute hand on a wall clock with an inlaid dial when the bell over his door gave a tired jingle. Finnian didn't look up at first; it was always the traveling sort who visited this early. Locals were busy at this time, and trusted the bell tower for their timekeeping, but a man with a journey ahead liked to set his own pace.

This traveler wore a battered felt hat, its brim weathered pale. His coat, patched at the elbows and shoulders, showed signs of hard use, and his boots were caked with two distinct colors of mud—one a bright red from the east, one slate-gray from the Mistral pass. A satchel hung at his hip, the leather gone soft and shiny with age.

He stood in the doorway for a breath, letting his eyes adjust. "Are you open?" he called, polite but wary.

Finnian wiped his hands on a chamois and beamed. "Always, for a fellow outpacing the bell." He motioned the man in. "Come to browse, or is there a particular need this morning?"

The traveler hesitated, then stepped fully inside. "Looking for a sturdy timepiece," he said. "One that can stand a wagon ride to Starling, and maybe another year on the road after that."

"Pocket or wrist?"

The man fished a battered watch from his coat and displayed it on a broad palm. "Had a wind-up like this, but the last frost got inside. Stopped ticking halfway to the pass."

Finnian considered the old watch, eyes narrowing with professional respect. "She's seen some miles, hasn't she? Most would have given up after the second soak."

"Gift from my grandfather," said the traveler. "But I need something that works, not just looks the part."

Finnian gestured toward a glass-fronted case on the back wall. "I can do you better than works. Got three models right here, all tested for dust, water, and shock. They're as tough as winter and twice as reliable." He unlocked the case, hands steady and confident. "Would you like to see the movements?"

The man nodded, and Finnian lifted three watches from their velvet cradles, setting them on a patch of deep-blue felt. He lined them up with the care of a man arranging chessmen.

"This one," Finnian began, tapping the leftmost, "is steel-cased with a full hunter cover. The chain's brass, but I can swap for steel if you prefer." He popped the cover, exposing a white enamel face with gold numerals. "Keeps time to a tenth of a minute, unless you take it up a mountain, then it runs just a hair fast. It's a quirk of the alloy."

He tapped the center. "Here, we've got a double-wind design. Bit heavier, but it compensates for changes in temperature. The chain's integral to the casing, so you won't lose it even if you break the fob." He demonstrated the wind, the click audible even through the clamor of wall clocks.

"And the last is silver, pure enough to fetch a coin if you ever need to barter it. The glass is crystal, shatter-resistant, and the movement's my own design. It ticks like a heartbeat, steady and just a touch slow at altitude. If you don't mind carrying a little extra weight, it'll see you through a siege."

The traveler took his time, lifting each in turn. He listened to the tick, rolled them in his palm, measured their heft. "What's the price on the silver one?"

Finnian named it, the number high but not greedy. "Comes with a guarantee, too. You break it, I'll fix it—unless you drop it off a cliff, in which case I'll sell you a replacement at cost."

The man chuckled. "That's fairer than most I've dealt with."

"Would you like it engraved?" Finnian asked, already reaching for a slender tool.

A pause, as if the man hadn't expected such courtesy. "Could you mark the back with a compass rose? Just the four points."

"I'd be insulted if you didn't ask."

While Finnian worked, he caught the traveler scanning the shelves, taking in the odd assortment of devices. "You make all these yourself?"

"Most of them," Finnian said, not looking up from the delicate etching. "Some are gifts from friends or bartered for repairs. It's a living, though sometimes I think the clocks are better company than most people."

"You're not from here," the traveler observed.

"Does it show?" Finnian allowed himself a smile. "I grew up on the coast, where the tides mattered more than hours. North Pointe is home now, though."

"Good place for a fresh start," the traveler said, voice distant.

Finnian slid the finished watch across the felt, the compass rose gleaming. "There you are. If you wind it once every morning, it'll never lose time."

The customer reached for the watch, and as his fingers closed around the silver, Finnian felt it again—a twist in the air, a flicker just behind the eyes. For a heartbeat, the shop melted away. Instead, there was a porch, sun-drenched and worn smooth by generations of feet. The traveler, younger, cleaner-shaven, ran up the steps to a cluster of waiting arms. Laughter, tears, a woman and two children. A sense of return so sharp it stung.

Then it was gone. The clocks ticked on. Finnian steadied himself, making sure his smile didn't falter.

"Thank you," the traveler said, voice tight.

Finnian nodded, as if the vision had been only a check of his own handiwork. "Safe travels," he said. "May you always be right on time."

Money changed hands. The man tucked the watch into his pocket, and for a moment, the weight of it seemed to root him to the spot.

"I'll keep it wound," he promised, and stepped out into the morning, his stride just a little surer.

Finnian watched the door swing shut, listened as the echoes of the man's boots faded. Alone again, he let his gaze rest on the empty spot in the velvet case.

He didn't question the vision; he never did. Most days, the future was best left to clocks.

But sometimes, it was nice to know the seconds really did lead somewhere good.

Finnian had a particular fondness for the bakery, and not just because Makota's Hearth was the only establishment in town that routinely measured time to the quarter-mark. The real draw was the smell—a tide of warm, yeasty air that swept out the door every time it opened, laying a trail all the way to his shop if the wind was right. It was the kind of scent that knew just how to find the gaps between Finnian's ribs and nestle there until surrender was inevitable.

Today, he surrendered early.

The bakery's front room was a deep rectangle, heavy-beamed, with three tables wedged together lengthwise along one wall. The windows were strung with hand-tatted lace, catching the late morning sun in an intricate net, painting white-on-gold patterns over every table and face. The counter itself was a marvel—three slabs of river-polished granite, pieced together with such precision that not a crumb could slip through. On display: heaps of rolls, stacks of honeyed brioches, and a row of scones glistening under the glass with what could only be described as weaponized sugar.

Finnian sidled in behind a pair of farmers arguing quietly about the difference between rye and spelt. The line moved with practiced efficiency, and soon he found himself face-to-face with Makota herself, wiping her hands on a blue-striped apron. She wore a dab of flour on her chin, and there was a streak of dough clinging to her left whisker.

"Mountainberry muffin, fresh from the oven," she said, before Finnian could even open his mouth. "Or was it the sweet cheese braid this time?"

"Muffin," Finnian said, the word escaping as a sigh of contentment.

Makota grinned, sharp teeth barely showing. "I thought so. You look like you could use a pick-me-up." She turned to fetch one, flicking her tail behind her in a manner Finnian found endlessly entertaining.

He was halfway through counting the ticks of the bakery's wall clock—never quite as accurate as it should have been, he noted—when Makota returned, muffin in hand. She also set down a cup of hot barley tea.

"On the house," she said. "That way I can keep your veins full of pastry."

Finnian hesitated, then sat at the counter, careful to dust the flour from his sleeves before touching the mug. "A fair exchange. How are the new timers working out?"

Makota's ears flicked, pleased. "Like a charm. Sora's not managed to burn a loaf all week, which is a record. I did have a visit from one of the Púca yesterday, though—Production Assistant, I think it called itself. Said you built a timer for the kiln, and it was the talk of their shop." Her eyes were bright with mischief. "You wouldn't happen to have one for the ovens, would you?"

Finnian grew bashful, brushing a crumb from the countertop and avoiding Makota's gaze. "I did, actually. Made it months ago, but I wasn't sure it would be…received. Everyone seems so attached to the old marked candles, and—"

Makota laughed, a sound that rattled the muffin trays. "Finnian Springdale, you're talking to a woman who started putting cheese inside bread just to see if anyone would riot. I'm as progressive as they come. Show me your invention."

Finnian blinked, then nodded. "It's in the shop. If you have a moment, I can show you."

"Let me corral my kits," Makota said, calling over her shoulder. "Sora, Kene! Hold the front. I'll be back before you can eat the profits."

A muffled "Yessss, Mama!" sounded from the kitchen, accompanied by a brief thud and the high-pitched yelp of a flour sack going airborne. Makota rolled her eyes, then motioned Finnian out the door.

The walk to Finnian's shop took less than a minute, but Makota filled it with questions. "What sort of timer? Can it be set for multiple loaves? Does it make a sound or just a movement? I have to know."

"It's adjustable," Finnian explained, "with six independent levers. You pull one down for each oven, and they count down. Well, the lever goes up, all at a specified rate of speed. When the cycle's complete, each chime sounds with a different tone. I made the gongs from scrap—one's brass, one's iron, the rest are a mix."

Makota's whiskers quivered. "And the settings?"

"Calibrated for your ovens," Finnian said, a little pride sneaking into his voice. "I watched the bread cycles for two weeks. Not that I was loitering, but—"

"—You were loitering." Makota gave him a look, but it was affectionate. "Come on. I want to see."

Inside the shop, Finnian led her past the public display and into the small back room he reserved for repairs and prototypes. Here, the air was sharper with oil, and every flat surface held a small forest of clock cases in various states of disassembly.

The timer occupied a place of honor on the back wall. It was a slab of polished walnut, mounted vertically, with six evenly spaced brass levers arrayed beneath a row of hand-etched dials. Finnian gestured to it with a sheepish flourish.

"It's not much to look at, but it's reliable," he said.

Makota approached, running a careful paw along the wood. "May I?"

"Please," Finnian said, his voice so earnest it almost startled him.

Makota gripped the first lever, pulled it down a bit, and watched as the corresponding dial began to turn, counting off the increments. After a few moments, the chime sounded—a sharp, cheerful note. The next lever gave a lower, bell-like ring. The third sang out bright and clear, almost musical.

Makota's tail swished with delight. "You made it sing."

Finnian ducked his head. "I thought it would help in the morning rush."

"It will," she said, testing each lever with increasing excitement. "And you called these hours and minutes, you said?"

Finnian nodded. "I know candlemarks have their charm, but if you want precision…"

Makota interrupted. "I want bread that doesn't burn." She turned to face him, face all smiles. "You're a genius, Finnian Springdale."

He found himself wishing he'd worn a cleaner vest.

"I'll send one of the kits to fetch it after closing," Makota promised, still playing with the timer. "But only if you'll stop by for the next test batch."

Finnian smiled, feeling a warmth that had nothing to do with the shop's radiator. "I wouldn't miss it."

As she left, timer still on her mind, Finnian surveyed the little shop. For once, the clocks all seemed in harmony. He allowed himself a moment to believe the world could be improved, if only in tiny increments.

Maybe he'd even start wearing a watch himself, just to keep up.

———

The afternoon sun turned the glass of Finnian's shop window to honey, bathing everything inside in a mellow, golden syrup. It was the slowest part of the day, and Finnian always used it to catch up on the repairs that never seemed to stop arriving. He was hunched over a carriage clock with a stubborn mainspring when a measured, hesitant knock tapped at the glass.

He looked up to see a man outside, mid-forties perhaps, the sort of customer who wore his best jacket for a visit downtown. The stranger's hair was cut close, shoes shined to a soft glow, and his fingers fiddled constantly at the lapel of his coat. Finnian set the clock aside and waved him in.

"Come on in, the door's open," he called, dusting his hands off on a cloth.

The man entered with the careful gait of someone raised to mind his manners. "Are you Mister Springdale?" he asked, voice as precise as his grooming.

"In the brass and bone," Finnian replied, offering a smile. "How can I help?"

"My name is Orley. I'm here on the recommendation of Vamir." He hesitated, then added, "From the bookshop. Said you might have something... special, as a gift."

Finnian's eyebrows rose. "I'm flattered. Who's the lucky recipient?"

Orley seemed to choose his words with care. "My mother. She's been a collector all her life. Anything finicky. Automata, music boxes, that kind of thing. Now her hands are...not what they were, but her eyes are sharp as ever. I want to bring her something she can enjoy, even if she can't wind it herself."

Finnian's mind leapt immediately to his few self-winding pieces, but he slowed himself, letting the man's tone guide him. "Would she prefer something ornate, or simple but precise?"

Orley looked around, taking in the myriad clocks and baubles, then pointed to a shelf near the window. "That one. With the bird on top."

"Ah, the Chirp-Chirp." Finnian stepped over, plucking the clock from its perch. It was a handsome piece—mahogany case with brass fittings, the lacquered finish set off by a delicate filigree. The clock's face was ringed by painted flowers, and a tiny wooden bird perched above the numerals, its beak caught in mid-song.

"I engineered the movement myself," Finnian explained, winding it with a small brass key. "Every hour, that is to say every candlemark, on the dot, the little bird pops out and sings. No winding needed, if you keep it where it can catch a bit of sun or lamp-light; the interior mechanism is powered by a spring, but the bellows recharge themselves on the cycle."

He set the clock gently on the counter, facing Orley. "Would you like to see it work?"

Orley nodded, wordless, his fingers knitting together in anticipation.

Finnian waited, checking the angle of the hands, then at precisely the next hour, the clock whirred softly. A panel above the face slid aside and the bird jerked forward, head bobbing. It opened its beak and let loose a soft, musical trill—far more melodious than the raucous birds of the forests, Finnian thought, but still enough to make you smile. The song lasted five heartbeats before the bird retreated and the door slid shut.

Orley's smile began as a quirk of the lips and grew, unguarded, into something pure. "She'll love it," he said, almost to himself.

Finnian grinned. "I can polish the case, or add an inscription on the base, if you like."

"Could you engrave it with her name? Ethelredia. She always hated it, but it suits her now, somehow."

"It's a lovely name," Finnian said, and meant it.

As he fetched his tools, Orley drifted around the shop, fingers trailing over glass cases and dusty curios. He paused by a domed automaton, the little figure inside endlessly raising a cup of tea to its lips, then shaking its head in disapproval. "Did you make this one, too?"

Finnian looked up from his bench. "The automaton? That was a joint effort with a fellow down south, in Clockholm. He made the case, I did the movement."

"It looks…lifelike, somehow. Almost like it's thinking."

Finnian nodded. "Sometimes I think all the best machines have a bit of soul. Or maybe they just borrow it from their owners, over time."

Orley smiled at that. "That would explain a lot, actually."

While Finnian worked, silence settled in, but it was the companionable kind. He finished the engraving—her name, in a neat arc along the clock's brass base—and wiped the piece with a soft cloth. "There. Would you like to try the winding? Just to be sure it suits you?"

Orley accepted the clock with a reverence usually reserved for newborns and rare books. He turned the key, set the time, and watched as the bird performed again, trilling a perfect note.

Finnian waited for the moment—the small, unmistakable shift that signaled approval. It came when Orley exhaled, the tension gone from his shoulders. "She'll like this," he repeated, but his voice had gone softer, more fragile.

"Would you like it boxed, or…?"

"Boxed, please," Orley said. "But I'd like to pay first."

Finnian named the price, and Orley counted out the coins with slow precision. As their hands touched over the counter, Finnian felt the shift again—the jolt of a vision, this one clearer and more poignant than the last.

He saw a sun-drenched parlor, windows open to a garden in late spring. The woman—Ethelredia, older but with the same sharp eyes as her son—sat in a high-backed chair, the Chirp-Chirp clock at her side. Her hands, gnarled by time, trembled as she stroked the wooden case. When the bird popped out, she clapped, the joy radiant on her face. Behind her stood Orley, his expression proud and unbearably tender.

Then Finnian saw the shadows creeping at the edge of the vision—a sense of time running thin, the visits growing fewer. The clock, though, continued to sing, defiant and bright against the hush of a fading life.

The vision receded, leaving Finnian blinking. Orley's eyes were damp, but he stood tall. "Thank you," he said, voice barely above a whisper.

Finnian nodded, finding his own words slow to return. "It's an honor," he managed.

They stood in silence as Finnian wrapped the clock, placing it in a box lined with soft felt. He tied the package with a length of twine, then pressed it into Orley's hands.

"If it ever needs service, just bring it back," Finnian said. "No charge."

Orley lingered a moment longer, then offered a thin, genuine smile. "Vamir said you were the best. He was right."

As the door closed behind him, Finnian listened to the sound of the clocks, each marking time in its own way. For a fleeting moment, he wished his machines could run backward. Just a little.

But the trilling of the Chirp-Chirp clock lingered, sweet and persistent, and he took comfort in knowing that sometimes the best a clockmaker could do was measure out the happiest moments, one song at a time.

———

There was no better way to close out a day than a stop at the Broken Claw. For Finnian, it was ritual: one hearty meal, a pint of whatever the barrels had yielded that week, and—most importantly—a change of scenery from the ever-watchful ticks and tocks of his own shop. The Claw was perpetually half-full, and always seemed to glow with a hickory warmth, whether from the fire in the hearth or the laughter that rolled out in bursts from behind the bar.

Finnian claimed his favorite table, a small round affair that had seen so many elbows over the years its edge was worn to a buttery smoothness. From here, he could see everything: the line of ale kegs along the wall, the old dartboard over the fireplace, the battered pianola in the corner—whose keys Finnian had, more than once, re-leveled in exchange for a free drink. Light filtered through the smoke-hazed windows, and it was easy to imagine that time passed differently inside the Claw—measured not in hours or even 'marks, but in the number of stories told before last call.

He'd just settled in with a plate of bread and sharp local cheese when Sam herself appeared, wiping her hands on a towel tucked into her belt. "You're early," she said, but the smile in her voice said she was pleased to see him.

"Decided to close the shop on time, for once," Finnian replied. "There was a rush on gifts for the solstice, and I figured I'd earned it."

Sam regarded him, one eyebrow arched. The jagged scar across her cheek made her seem stern, but Finnian knew her smiles could still split a man in half. "Solstice is a month away."

"Preparation is everything," he countered. "Besides, I'm here for the company. And the ale."

Sam vanished and reappeared with a tankard, the foam capped in perfect symmetry. She set it in front of Finnian, then pulled up a chair, spinning it around and straddling it backward. "On the house, as always, if you'll tell me about the latest disaster in Clockmaker's Row."

Finnian sipped, savoring the first cold tang. "Nothing exploded today," he said, feigning disappointment. "Though I did send a slice of toast into low orbit yesterday."

"Progress," Sam said, and raised her own glass. "You know, most people would just use a knife."

Finnian grinned. "Where's the fun in that?"

Sam tilted her head, eyeing him with an affection that was half amusement, half concern. "You ever take a break, Finnian? Not just physically, but up here—" she tapped her temple "—where the ideas are always going."

He shrugged, picking at his cheese. "If I stopped thinking, I'd lose the thread. There's always another improvement, another problem to solve." His gaze drifted across the tap system behind the bar, its copper lines running in tangles. "Take your keg line, for instance."

Sam groaned, mock-exasperated. "Don't you dare redesign my pub."

He couldn't help himself. "It wouldn't be a redesign. Just… refinement. I could meter the pours with a ratcheting spigot. You'd get the same amount every time, no more foamy overfill, less waste—"

"And none of the drama when two locals start arguing over who got the larger pint," Sam finished for him. "I know your tricks, Finnian Springdale."

He tried to look wounded, but his heart wasn't in it. "At least let me fix the flue on your stove. Last week the place nearly smoked itself out."

She rolled her eyes, but her tone softened. "You do that, and I'll never hear the end of it. Next you'll want to automate the inventory, or track how much bread we use per day."

He considered, eyes brightening. "Actually, I've been working on a—"

"Stop," Sam said, laughing. "Eat your lunch."

He did, relishing the soft bread and the sharp bite of the cheese. Sam watched in comfortable silence, scanning the room for anything out of order. The regulars filtered in and out, a constant churn of faces and stories, but Finnian noticed that Sam always made time for anyone who sat alone, or who looked like they needed it. She'd even once chased off a pair of traveling ruffians with nothing but a glare and a pointed question about their manners.

When Finnian finished his plate, he pushed it aside and reached for a napkin, beginning to sketch out a schematic for the keg meter he'd proposed. Sam peered over his shoulder, then shook her head. "You're unstoppable."

He shrugged. "Idle hands are wasted potential."

A moment of comfortable silence stretched between them. The fire crackled, the pianola played a few bars on its own, and outside, the town square rang with the distant sound of the bell tower. Finnian took another sip of ale, feeling the day's worries soften at the edges.

Sam's voice was quiet. "You ever wonder if it's okay to just… let things be? Not improve them, not optimize. Just live with them a while."

Finnian thought about this, gaze drifting to the old dartboard, the battered tables, the mismatched chairs. He thought about the clocks in his shop, each imperfect in its own way, and the people who came for repairs not always needing a fix so much as a reason to chat.

He smiled, meeting Sam's eyes. "Sometimes I wonder. But then, I remember it's the little improvements that make a place feel like home."

Sam nodded, a glint of approval in her gaze. "As long as you don't try to automate me out of a job, you're welcome here."

Finnian raised his glass in a silent toast. "I wouldn't dare."

As evening crept in, the Broken Claw filled with laughter and light, and Finnian found himself content just to listen, making quiet mental notes on how to make the next visit even better. He let the warmth of the pub settle into his bones, grateful for the company and the stubborn, beautiful imperfection of it all.

Evening in Finnian's apartment was a study in gentle contradiction. The upstairs rooms were as plain as any in North Pointe, the furniture spare and the walls painted a pragmatic white, yet everything from the battered desk to the humble bedstead carried a subtle undercurrent of invention. The place was quiet, but never silent; the hush was shaped by a soft quilt of sound, dozens of clocks from below keeping time in a thousand overlapping harmonies.

Finnian's nightly routine was as measured as any of his mechanisms. First, he set the water for tea. The kettle was fitted with a clockwork timer of his own devising—a slender metal whisker would flex when the water reached the perfect temperature, tapping a ceramic bell with a tone so clear it could be heard over the soft debate of wall clocks. Finnian waited for the sound, eyes closed, breathing in the faint metallic promise of steam. When the bell rang, he poured the water, and the scent of bergamot unfurled through the apartment.

While the tea steeped, he did his rounds in the shop below, resetting any clocks that had drifted during the day and checking on the Self-Buttering Toast Machine—which, this late, mostly served as a shelf for notepads and broken pencils. There was a peculiar pleasure in winding down his own creations, a quiet intimacy that felt almost like tucking in old friends for the night.

Back upstairs, Finnian sipped his tea by the window, watching the square empty of travelers and locals alike. The bakery's lights were out, and the bell tower across the way stood silent and dignified against the dark. He wondered if Makota had tried the new timer yet, or if Sam had discovered the sketch he'd left on her bar, tucked discreetly under the napkin.

He finished the tea, washed the cup, and wound the last of his own timepieces—a slim, silver watch that had never left his apartment, a relic of the past and a reminder of why he'd started making clocks in the first place.

His bed was a simple cot, but the quilt was a masterpiece of hand-stitched squares, each dyed a different hue and sewn by a local seamstress who had, for a while, been the light of Finnian's life. He ran his fingers over the seams as he lay down, the fabric cool and familiar.

In the hush before sleep, Finnian's mind did what it always did—worked. It cycled through the day's events, refining and improving. The vision with the traveler flickered up: was there a way to measure the weight of reunion, to record it in gears or springs? He thought about Orley's mother, her hands too weak to wind a key—what about a clock that wound itself from the gentle touch of a fingertip? For the bakery, a timer that chimed in the voice of a singing cat, just to see if Makota's kits would notice.

His thoughts unspooled, tangled and bright. Even in dreams, the world spun with invention. He dreamed of gears that meshed with the stars, of clockwork birds that carried the hour from house to house, of a place where every tick and tock stitched people closer together.

In the early hours, just before dawn, Finnian's apartment was silent for a single moment. Then the first clock struck the hour, and the rest followed, each adding its own voice to the chorus. Finnian slept on, a gentle smile creasing his face, as the world around him continued its beautiful, imperfect negotiation with time.

three
...

THE MORNING after solstice was unusually bright, even for North Pointe. Sunlight hit the clock shop's window at just the right angle to scatter gold across every countertop, dial, and glass dome. It lit up the interior like a treasure vault, dust motes drifting in lazy orbit around the dozens of ticking clocks that lined the walls. Finnian, who had already lost two hours to fine-tuning the escapement on a customer's wall clock, barely registered the effect—he was elbow-deep in springs and his mind was three problems ahead.

The door creaked open and let in a wedge of light, followed by a figure with the compact build of someone accustomed to long days in the saddle and longer nights hunched over parchment. The man paused just inside, gaze sweeping the shop as if mapping its terrain, then advanced with purposeful strides to the workbench.

Finnian looked up, pushing his spectacles into place with an oil-smudged thumb. "You've the look of a man measuring his steps," he said, voice bright with curiosity.

The customer grinned, lines around his eyes sharpening. "Guilty as charged. Are you Mister Springdale, the clockmaker?"

"In the brass and bone," Finnian said. "What's the project?"

The man unslung a battered satchel from his shoulder and withdrew a thick roll of parchment. "Name's Fell," he said, flattening a bundle of drawings and half-finished maps onto the counter. "I make routes for the river guild. Surveying the new cut-through to the east ridge. The Púca told me you might have a knack for... specialized devices."

"I try," Finnian said, hands hovering over the diagrams. "What's the specification?"

Fell jabbed at a sketch with an ink-stained finger. "I need something that can measure distance, but not by time or map. By steps—paces—directly off the harness of a draft horse. There's a baseline I'm supposed to follow, see here?" He pointed to a tangle of lines annotated with minuscule numbers. "Each stride is about eight hands, but it varies. I need something that can click off the distance, mechanically, and tell me when I've run a league."

Finnian's eyes widened a fraction; the glass of his spectacles caught the sunlight and flashed. He bent closer, voice dropping to a reverent hush. "You want a mechanical step counter. For a horse."

"Exactly."

A long silence. Then, Finnian let out a giddy laugh and pressed both palms flat to the bench. "That's the best thing I've heard in a month." He spun the sketch around and examined it, index finger tapping at the notched wheel Fell had drawn. "I take it you've tried the old ways—chalk marks, tick marks on the yoke, counting aloud?"

"Sure," Fell said, "and every one of them is useless if you hit a pothole or get distracted by the weather. The Púca said you made a bread timer for the bakery that never drifts by more than a minute. Thought maybe you'd have an idea."

Finnian was already in motion, reaching for a fresh sheet of vellum and a stub of charcoal. "What sort of terrain?"

"Mostly flat, but the ridge is rutted. I can show you the course on the map."

"Show me, yes, but I'll want the stride length and, if you can recall, the gait at your average speed. Was it a walk, canter, or...?"

Fell laughed. "Mostly a resigned plod."

"Perfect." Finnian began sketching, lines crisp and purposeful. "You need a ratchet mechanism keyed to the vertical movement of the harness—here, see? If you mount a cam at the girth, it'll pivot with every step, rotate this axle..." He was muttering to himself now, already lost in the machine taking shape under his fingers.

Fell watched, bemused, as the abstract gears and levers became a real apparatus. Finnian finished the sketch in under a minute, then began annotating it with dimensions and guesses for materials. He glanced up, eyes shining. "I can make this. Brass, maybe, if you want it weatherproof."

"I need it to work in rain," Fell said.

Finnian nodded, jotting a note. "I'll seal the housing. The counter—do you want it to display in steps, or should I calibrate it to read leagues?"

"Steps," said Fell. "I can do the conversion. But if you make the face big enough to read from the saddle, I'll buy you a drink next time you're in the Claw."

Finnian gave a bow so dramatic it nearly toppled his spectacles. "You have my word. Can you leave the harness here, or at least the mounting band? I'll want to test the fit."

"Got a spare in the wagon. I'll bring it in."

As Fell turned to go, Finnian's mind was already ticking off the tasks ahead. He called after the cartographer, "Wait—do you need the step counter to account for backwards steps? Sometimes a horse, if startled—"

Fell snorted. "If my horse goes backwards for a league, I'll have bigger problems than my maps."

The door closed behind the surveyor, and Finnian stood for a moment in the hush, only the layered tickings of the clocks keeping time. He allowed himself a grin—this was the kind of commission that made him wish for an extra set of hands.

He cleared the workbench, set the wall clock carefully aside, and pulled out his small tray of gears and miniature cogs. Sunlight painted a bright circle over the wood as he laid out the pieces. The smell of Number Seven Machine Oil—sharp, almost sweet—drifted up as he opened a fresh bottle.

Already, Finnian could see the completed mechanism in his mind.

He flexed his fingers, whispered the measurement to himself, and got to work.

The first step was always the same: clear the mind, clear the bench. Finnian's fingers were quick and sure, but he had learned that a clean workspace was worth an extra hour in the end. He lined up his favorites—a pair of soft-jawed pliers, a battered set of jeweler's screwdrivers, and the bone-handled awl he'd used since apprenticeship—then took inventory of the raw parts. Brass sheet for the gears, a tangle of wire for the linkages, three different grades of clockwork spring. The glass dome would come last, if the thing survived prototype.

He sharpened a pencil, rolled up his sleeves, and began.

The main drive wheel, he decided, needed to be lighter than he'd guessed. A steel pinion would wear down the softer gear teeth and rattle itself to pieces by week's end. Brass, then—fine-cut and polished, with the edges smoothed so as not to fray the pawl. He scored the blank, set it in the vise, and began to file. The sound was music: a dry, gritty whisper underlined by the pulse of clocks all over the room. Each sweep of the file released a curl of sunlight, as if the metal itself was giving up its shine.

He lost himself in the work, shifting gears—literally and figuratively—without pausing for tea or even a proper breath. His mind ran parallel to his hands, always one problem ahead. If the counter was too sensitive, it would double-count on rough ground; too stiff, and the smallest steps wouldn't register. Fell's draft horse was not known for precision, but Finnian meant to make the device foolproof.

He checked the first gear for wobble, pinched the axle with a strip of felt, and spun it. The tick-tick-tick it made was off by a hair—a resonance he didn't like. He reset the bearing, sanded the axle down half a whisker, and tried again. The noise disappeared, replaced by the clean, confident click of a thing done right.

He built the cam next, bending wire around a carved mandrel until the curve matched the sample harness Fell had dropped off. The cam would rock with every step, turning the main shaft in tiny increments. Finnian marked out the anchor points with a dot of blue wax, then fixed them with minuscule screws. He tested the fit, clamping the mechanism to a broomstick and mimicking the jostle of a walking horse. Each step moved the counter one click forward, exactly as intended.

Finnian grinned, then frowned, then grinned again—he wasn't used to a first attempt going so smoothly. There was always a catch, and he waited for it like a man expecting thunder after lightning.

It came when he tried to fit the escapement. The ratchet he'd borrowed from a discarded wall clock was too large, and it fouled the smaller gears. For a moment, irritation fluttered in his chest. But rather than curse, he set the part aside, reached for a blank, and began to file. This time, he went slower, thinking about the math. If he changed the ratio, would it drift? Would it count too quickly on a downhill slope?

The numbers whispered to him: eight hands per stride, one thousand paces per mile, ten thousand per day if Fell's stories could be trusted. He tuned the escapement, feathered the spring tension until the motion was crisp but forgiving, then anchored the reset lever to the side of the frame.

He tested it again, this time mounting the entire mechanism to a leather strap and buckling it to a weighted bag. He dragged the bag in a slow circle around the shop floor, counting aloud under his breath. Each thunk against the boards was met by a satisfying click from the device. After ten laps, Finnian checked the dial and saw he was short by only two paces—a margin smaller than the error on most city bell towers.

The sunlight through the window had shifted, painting the shop's far wall in a buttery orange. Finnian blinked, startled by how the hours had vanished. He wiped his brow, then dabbed a drop of oil onto the mainshaft and watched it wick into the joint. He gave the device a final once-over, then reset the dial and set it on the bench.

He allowed himself a moment to just look at it. The brass shone, the levers all lined up in neat, stubborn rows, the numbers etched clean and bright. Finnian felt a small pride, the kind that ran deeper than applause. He flexed his hands and reached for the final step—a leather housing, stitched to protect the works from dust and rain. The fit was snug, and as he pressed the lid closed, the machine gave a tiny, almost grateful, tick.

He set it under the bell jar and leaned back. The clocks on the walls ticked in counterpoint, and Finnian realized he hadn't noticed their music for hours. He smiled, weary but content.

When the sun hit the device directly, it glowed as if powered from within. Finnian nodded to himself, and let the clocks keep watch.

Fell returned at midday, punctual as a town crier and every bit as eager. He ducked through the door and thumped the spare harness onto the workbench, scattering a regiment of screws and wire clippings. "Is it ready?" he asked, before even catching a breath.

Finnian, who had anticipated this moment for most of the morning, retrieved the device from under its bell jar with a flourish. The brass gleamed, every surface free of tarnish, and the dial at the center caught the sun and doubled it. "Behold," Finnian said, trying for solemn but ending up with barely contained glee. "The Automated Step-Measuring Clock, Mark One."

He fitted the device to the sample harness in three practiced motions, buckled the straps tight, and anchored the cam so that it rested just below the shoulder piece. Then, with a careful hand, he lifted the harness and gave it a gentle shake, imitating the stride of a heavy draft horse.

The machine responded immediately: with every dip, the cam rotated and advanced the counter, each motion punctuated by a clear, musical click. The numbers on the face ratcheted up, clean and crisp.

"Each click," Finnian explained, "is precisely ten paces. The dial here—" he tapped a brass window at the top "—counts up to one thousand before it resets. I've calibrated it to one revolution per mile, within a margin of error no greater than four lengths of a standard yardstick." He shot a look at Fell. "Depending, of course, on the average stride of your horse, which I admit may have a personality all its own."

Fell leaned in, eyes bright. He flicked the dial back and forth, then thumped the harness again. "And if the horse shies or doubles back?"

Finnian shook his head. "One-way only. There's a catch in the escapement. If the step is reversed, it doesn't register."

Fell grunted, but it sounded approving. He tried to peer into the case. "And if it rains?"

Finnian unlatched the side and showed the customer the tight fit of the leather gasket. "Oiled and sealed. The works are all brass or ceramic—no rust to worry about, but it would appreciate a quick towel-off at the end of the day." He gave Fell a measuring look. "If you want it waterproof, I could fit a glass cap, but the fog may cloud the readings."

Fell waved this off. "Better it work at all than work pretty."

Finnian nodded, pleased. "I think you'll find it does both."

Fell buckled the harness closed around his own waist, as if testing the weight. He jogged in place, grinning as the device counted up with every step. "Brilliant," he said, after a quick burst. "How much do I owe you?"

Finnian considered, but only for show. "No payment, yet. You take it on your survey, and if it counts you home again, you can return and settle up. If not—well, I'll want to know why it failed." He hesitated, then added, "And maybe a quick note if you find any flaws. I'd rather get it right before the next iteration."

Fell's grin softened. "A man who stands by his work. Fair enough. If it lives through the ridge, I'll be back in a sennight." He left the shop in a flurry, already strapping the device to the worn leather harness on his cart outside.

Finnian watched from the window as the cartographer mounted up, adjusted the dial, and set off down the trade road. The device ticked over with every stride, and from this distance, Finnian fancied he could hear the faintest echo of its progress.

He returned to his workbench and found, for the first time in a while, that there was nothing pressing. He filled the shop's battered kettle, set it on the small coal stove, and dug through his supply of teas for the good stuff—rare, faintly floral, perfect for the aftermath of a job well done.

As he waited for the water to boil, Finnian looked around the shop. The sunlight was stronger now, painting everything in a thin gold leaf. He picked up the bone-handled awl and twirled it, mind drifting.

He realized, suddenly, that he hadn't experienced a single vision or premonition during the build. When he'd handed over the device, there was no flash of future for Fell, no rush of memory or destiny. Only the steady, certain promise of gears and numbers and distance.

It was only the timepieces—watches, clocks, anything that measured hours and minutes—that triggered his peculiar flashes. But not devices that measured other things: steps, bread, or even the rhythm of a bellows in the forge. It made him wonder about the nature of North Pointe's magic, and whether it obeyed the same rules as his own clockwork.

He poured the tea, watched the steam rise in slow, ribboned plumes, and allowed himself to savor both the drink and the absence of ticking thoughts in his head.

It was enough, for now, just to enjoy the silence and let the clocks keep perfect time.

The slow hour before sunset brought the last customer of the day: a merchant with a traveler's stoop and the gentle, persistent cough of someone who'd spent too long on river barges. He stepped into the shop with the careful tread of a man who'd learned to respect fragile things, and waited by the counter as Finnian boxed up a repair for delivery.

"Mister Springdale?" he asked, voice rough but polite. "I'm here for the clock. The one with the cherrywood case."

Finnian recognized the name from his ledger. "You must be Borven. I have it finished, just as promised." He slid the box across the counter, then drew out the clock and set it gently on the mat for inspection. "I tuned it myself this morning. Keeps time to within a minute a sennight, and the chime is mellow but clear."

Borven ran his hands over the polished wood, tracing the grain with almost reverence. He was silent for a long moment, lost in the reflection of the shop's lamps on the glass dome. "My wife—" he started, then coughed, then tried again. "She always wanted a clock like this. For the mantel."

Finnian smiled, but he understood the gravity that sometimes clung to these exchanges. "I hope it brings you both luck and peace."

They exchanged payment and receipt, and as Borven hefted the clock—careful, cradling it like a sleeping cat—their hands met over the casing.

For a heartbeat, time stuttered.

Finnian saw—no, felt—a parlor lined with sun and shadow, the clock ringing out a deep, sweet tone. A woman with hair pulled tight, face lined by more laughter than years, sitting at a table with Borven. There was bread, and soup, and the unspoken comfort of home. The vision sharpened: a girl, perhaps twelve, running in from the garden, and Borven rising to greet her, the clock's chime threading through their reunion.

The vision faded as quickly as it came, leaving a fragile hush behind.

Borven looked up, eyes suspiciously bright, and Finnian realized the man had seen it too. They shared a nod, the kind that acknowledged something inexplicable and agreed to never speak of it.

Borven tucked the clock into the crook of his arm and left, a little straighter than when he'd come in.

Finnian watched the door settle, then stood in the fading afternoon light, hands clasped behind his back. He'd never understood why the visions only came with timepieces. Maybe it was the town, or the mountains, or maybe just himself. But in those moments, the world felt bigger, and his place in it just a little more meaningful.

He locked up early and stepped into the street.

The light outside was honey-thick, pouring over the trade road and the muddy ruts between the buildings. Finnian strolled past the bakery—Makota's youngest waving from the window with jam on her nose—and headed for the lakefront. The air here was a swirl of fresh bread, distant coal smoke, and the sharp brine of the fish shop.

Calder Seaherder's storefront was a storm of activity: the man himself slicing filets with a precision Finnian could respect, his three children arguing over the size of a bucket. Finnian paused to watch, already outlining an improvement to the scaling process—a rotary brush, maybe, or a water-driven conveyor that would spare Calder's knuckles on the busy days.

He nearly called out the idea, but caught himself. Calder was a man who liked the old ways, and besides, invention was sweeter when it arrived unannounced. Finnian waved instead, and was rewarded with a flash of teeth and a friendly salute.

He continued down the lane, past the stables and the small cluster of vendor stalls closing for the day. The clang of Warren's forge carried on the breeze, deep and rhythmic, as if the ogre-smith was forging not just tools, but the tempo of the whole town.

Finnian smiled at the memory of the mechanical bellows he'd designed for Warren last winter—a gift, never delivered, because Warren had insisted on "doing it by muscle, or not at all." He made a mental note to try again, maybe with something less intrusive. An automatic ore-sifter, perhaps, or a heat indicator for the anvil.

The last rays of sunlight caught on the brass weather vane above the Broken Claw, the alehouse windows already warm with lamplight and laughter. Finnian reached the door, hesitated, and looked back at the skyline of North Pointe: the tower, the bakery, the sweep of rooftops leading to the lake. Every inch of it familiar, every routine newly precious.

He took a deep breath, the air tinged with yeast and iron and the coming night, and stepped inside the pub.

The warmth hit him like a memory, and for a rare moment, Finnian let himself stop measuring. He ordered bread and cheese, and raised a glass to time itself—imperfect, inexorable, and, sometimes, just right.

four
. . .

FINNIAN PREFERRED THE EARLY MORNING, before the world had gotten up a head of steam and started churning out all the little emergencies that would fill his shopbell hours. In the cool air, the smell of dewy grass tangled agreeably with the ever-present hints of coal smoke and yeast that made North Pointe Common Towne so distinct among the lakeside settlements. He walked the gentle curve of the trade road in his usual measured gait, but today there was a new awkwardness: a crate, awkwardly lashed with canvas straps, bobbing like a stubborn toddler at his hip.

The crate contained the Automatic Bellows System—v1.9, according to Finnian's own bookkeeping, though only two versions had made it outside his back room before today. He had to admit this was a little silly. Warren, the town's smith and Finnian's friend, had never actually complained about pumping the bellows. "If hands too weak, bring child to do," Warren had once said, deadpan, before winking in Finnian's direction. But the ogre had been the first to repair Finnian's own shop sign after a roofslide, and so Finnian felt compelled to reciprocate with some sort of clockwork solution, which was his personal idiom for affection.

The forge was already roaring by the time Finnian arrived.

Warren's silhouette blocked the open smithy door—a dark, hulking green against a backdrop of white-hot fire, black iron, and the fizzing staccato of hammer on steel. The ogre wore his hair tied back with a length of what looked like tanned shoelace, and his sleeves were rolled all the way up to boulderlike shoulders. Finnian caught, not for the first time, the simultaneous thrill and mild terror of seeing a creature so mythically huge that it seemed to bend the rules of reality just by standing still. It was easier to focus on the details: the expertly braided white hair, the spotless leather apron. The ogre's ears stuck out sideways, like the fins of some river beast.

Warren noticed Finnian's approach with a grunt and set down his hammer. The air inside the smithy tasted like pennies and burnt toast. "Good morning, Finn," he called, the words emerging with more warmth than the furnace itself. "That time again?"

"'Tis," Finnian replied. He set the crate on a scarred trestle table by the wall, dusted off his hands, and affected an air of mock seriousness. "But this time, I believe I have solved the oscillation."

Warren's eyebrows went up. "No more shaking like tiny earthquakes?"

"In theory, no."

A second shape moved from the shadowy interior—Susan, the smith's wife, her hair up in a red kerchief and her hands already flour-dusted from the morning's baking. She offered Finnian a mug of coffee and the sharp look of a woman who had known both men since they were less wrinkled. "You're late," she said. "The bread's already done."

Finnian accepted the mug with gratitude. "I came for the company, but I won't object."

"Liar," Susan said, slapping him gently on the shoulder as she strode toward Weary Head Inn. "Warren, don't be late for lunch today. Minnie and I are putting on a whole spread. I'll be right back with some bread."

Warren nodded agreement as he approached the crate, giving it a nudge with his enormous finger. "Heavy this time. You put weights in, or just more gears?"

"Only two gears more than last version. And a governor. And a failsafe. And, ah, a small brass cam." Finnian hesitated, then gave a sheepish shrug. "But it will save you five—no, seven—seconds per hour."

"Time is money," said Warren, deadpan, but his wide mouth curled into a smile. "Let's see."

The ogre lifted the crate with one hand and set it on the anvil as if it weighed nothing. Finnian followed, chattering with instructions as Warren untied the straps and revealed the mechanism.

The Automatic Bellows System was a masterpiece of overcomplication. Its core was a set of triple-linked leather bladders, connected by rods and counterweights, with a brass flywheel and a ratcheting lever that could be triggered by a single heavy stomp. Finnian had also added a small, spring-driven ticker to count the cycles—entirely unnecessary, but the effect was pleasing. Most of the parts were rescued from broken clocks

Warren turned it over in his hands with all the delicacy of a mother cradling a newborn. "Pretty," he said.

"I even polished it," Finnian said. "Now, if you'll allow me—"

Warren set the device in place next to the forge, attaching the intake nozzle to the existing bellows with a leather collar. It fit perfectly. Finnian waited, breath held, as Warren loaded the release lever with one massive finger. The ogre looked at Finnian with a theatrical show of caution.

"Ready?"

Finnian nodded.

Warren pressed the lever.

There was a faint, springy *clunk*, then the entire bellows system began to shudder rhythmically. The clockwork governor ticked and whirred. The leather bladders filled, contracted, filled again. The airflow was, Finnian had to admit, beautifully smooth. He stood back, arms folded, to savor the rare taste of success.

"See?" he said.

"Nice," Warren agreed.

They watched together. After about thirty seconds, the governor began to tick more loudly.

Finnian's smile faded just a touch.

The bellows started cycling faster, then much faster, like a hiccuping heart. The ticker began to whirr. The bladders pulsed in an almost obscene rhythm. Then, with no warning, the central bladder exploded with a sound like a horse sneezing into a barrel. A thick, wet *POP* echoed through the smithy. A fine mist of coal dust, brass filings, and clock oil sprayed out in a shimmering fan.

Susan, who had returned with a loaf of bread, was caught in the blast radius. Warren took the brunt, his entire chest and face suddenly soot-blackened, two enormous white eyes blinking from a mask of machine oil and damp dust.

Silence.

Finnian said, "Well, the seal integrity could use—"

Warren burst out laughing, a sound as deep and resonant as a kettledrum. "Finn, you say seven seconds saved—this costs you three hours cleaning."

Finnian, to his credit, bowed in defeat. "You are, as ever, the master of the practical arts."

Susan coughed, then grinned. "At least your eyebrows are still attached, Warren."

The ogre inspected his reflection in a cooling pan, then left the soot on for effect. "You make a new improvement, Finn?"

"Oh, certainly," Finnian said, already mentally sketching out the next iteration. "With a reinforced valve and, ah, less… optimism in the spring tension."

Warren handed him back the battered remains of the bellows. "Maybe next time you can just bring bread," he said.

Finnian managed a laugh, even as he wiped at his spectacles with a slightly oily kerchief. "If I did, you'd complain the crust was too thick."

Warren turned serious, just for a moment. "Truth, Finn: I like the work. Not hard for me. But you bring good company, and that's rare." The ogre's huge hand engulfed Finnian's in a gentle shake.

"I'll try to explode less of your equipment next time," Finnian promised.

Warren's face split into another grin. "Please do. Or Susan will start charging you by the mess."

Susan, already at the door, wagged a finger at him. "I keep a tab, Finnian."

He smiled. "And I wouldn't have it any other way."

He left the forge with the remains of the invention tucked under his arm, and the peculiar satisfaction of a social call well spent. The town bell rang in the distance, eighth mark already, and Finnian hurried his step: he had repairs waiting, and possibly, somewhere in the house, a clean shirt.

Finnian's clock shop came alive as the morning bell rang, the room warming in increments as the early sun angled through the eastern windows. It was a small shop by the standards of Evendiam's lakeshore, but Finnian had a gift for cramming infinite detail into finite space. Every shelf, every stretch of wall was thick with timepieces: some practical, some whimsical, all of them ticking in their own private conversations. If you sat perfectly still, you could almost hear the distinct syllables of each mechanism, like a congress of insects reporting on the progress of the day.

Finnian wore a clean shirt, but had kept the soot-stained one from the morning's adventure on a hook by the door—a badge of honor, or perhaps a warning to potential customers. He set the battered Automatic Bellows System on his workbench, made a note about "bladder seals—critical," and poured himself a second cup of coffee. The world felt comfortably in order.

He was halfway through restoring a pocket watch when the door bell tinkled. The effect was subtle, but the room seemed to chill by two degrees and the clocks along the east wall hesitated for a fraction of a second. Finnian straightened his spectacles and looked up to see Leota Harbinger in the doorway, black dress as ever, her face paler than he remembered from last sennight.

"Good morning, Finnian," she said, voice clear and direct as always.

"Leota!" he answered, rising. "I'd have put on the good tea if I'd known."

She let the door close with a sound like a breath exhaled, and glided to the counter. Even now, there was something a little unearthly about the way Leota moved—her steps seemed to stir less dust than anyone else's, and when she leaned in to examine a clock, the entire object stilled in her presence.

"You're up early for a visit," Finnian said, fetching the battered tin of Queen's Leaf from beneath the counter. "What brings you out?"

She did not answer immediately. Instead, she studied the Grandfather Clock—a monstrous, unfinished thing that loomed over the rest of the inventory from its place in the corner. Finnian had inherited the shell from a watchmaker in a far-off city, but the internal mechanism was his own innovation: double escapement, redundant pendulums, even a secondary drive to track lunar phases. He'd been working on it in secret for months, mostly at night, and he had started to think of it as more companion than project.

Leota turned to Finnian and said, "You built that to keep time, yes?"

Finnian flushed, which he tried to hide with the tea strainer. "To keep time, and perhaps... regulate certain anomalies."

Leota arched an eyebrow. "You know it is not working as intended."

He grimaced. "I thought the secondary pendulum would stabilize the phase drift, but it's just introduced a different sort of—"

"I am not speaking of drift," she interrupted gently. "That clock is not a regulator. It is a prison. And it is not a well-made one."

Finnian felt a small, precise fear prick along his spine. "I haven't wound the mainspring yet. The movement isn't even calibrated."

Leota shook her head. "It's already ticking. I can hear it. And more than that, I can feel it." She leaned close to the case, then placed a single finger against the grain of the wood. "Do you not feel it?" she asked.

Finnian hesitated, then joined her. He pressed his palm to the side of the case. There was the expected vibration of clockwork, yes, but beneath that was something else: a quivering, nervous thrum, almost as if the brass and steel had a pulse.

Leota's voice was soft. "It is very clever. I have never seen such an overabundance of balance wheels. But sometimes too much cleverness draws attention." She looked up at him. "Do you remember the old legend about the Seven-Chime Bell in Marrowfield?"

Finnian considered, then nodded. "The clocktower that summoned back the dead, yes?"

Leota smiled faintly. "No, not the dead. The potential. Marrowfield was famous for its clocktower because it kept perfect time. But it also measured possibility, not just minutes. When the bell was wound too tightly, it broke—not with a snap, but with a flowering. And the entire town was suddenly every possible version of itself."

Finnian thought about that for a while. "Sounds... lively."

"It was for a moment. Then it wasn't. My point is, do not over-wind your clocks, Finnian."

He took the advice with a sheepish smile, but privately he could not bring himself to regret the design. There was something beautiful about complexity, about each gear depending on the next in an intricate braid of consequence.

Leota, watching him, seemed to know what he was thinking. "You do not need to make everything more complicated, you know. Some things are beautiful because they are simple."

"My customers like the complications," Finnian said. "And, honestly, so do I."

She gave a small, genuine laugh. "I suppose you would."

They lapsed into silence, listening to the ticking of the room. Even the most ordinary clocks seemed to hush themselves when Leota was present.

After a moment, she spoke again, "I came for a different reason. Do you have a crystal pendulum? A long one, perhaps as long as my forearm?"

Finnian brightened. "I do! At least, I think I do." He disappeared into the back room, leaving the shop to Leota and the Grandfather Clock. It did not escape his notice that her gaze drifted back to the timepiece the moment he was out of sight.

Finnian's storage was, if possible, even more tightly packed than the showroom, and filled with all the things he had not yet found an application for. He rummaged among dusty bins, passing over a glass eel clock—never worked, but made an excellent nightlight—a pair of matched birdcage timers, and a box of beetle-guts for an insect clock he'd abandoned after the third time it tried to escape. Finally, he found the right bin: a set of crystal rods, each of which could serve as a pendulum.

He returned to the front. "These are the best I have," he said, setting out three crystal pendulums of differing lengths.

Leota bent to examine them, but her attention wandered back to the unfinished clock. "Finnian," she said, "promise me that if it starts to sound strange—or if you see anything odd—you will tell me?"

"I promise," he said, then thought about it. "Or, at least, I will try not to fix it alone."

Leota selected a pendulum and weighed it in her hand. "This one will do," she said. "How much?"

"For you? A song's worth of advice," Finnian replied, then blinked. "Or, perhaps, some warning before North Pointe turns into a garden of possible towns?"

Leota laughed, this time a true one. "Very well. You will be the first to know."

She left with the pendulum, and the chill in the shop faded as quickly as it had come. Finnian watched her go, then turned back to his Grandfather Clock. He stroked the side of the case with something like affection. "She means well," he said to the machine.

The clock, as always, kept its own counsel.

With a satisfied sigh, Finnian got back to work, humming the measure of a waltz whose second movement he was sure he'd heard before but couldn't place. All around him, the clocks of North Pointe kept on ticking.

five
...

THE SUN SEEMED to rise a little early in North Pointe that morning, and the clocks inside Finnian's shop seemed to sense it. Before the first customer of the day, before the bread carts rattled up the street, before even the bell tower had finished its first chime, a faint, eager energy pulsed through every pendulum and mainspring. Finnian felt it, too, a kind of anticipatory itch that sent him tidying the shop to a higher standard than usual and polishing every glass dome until it shone like a lighthouse lens.

The first to arrive was a merchant, the type who never left his own reflection alone. He stood tall enough to stoop at the doorframe, his coat a shimmering emerald cut of silk, and his boots so lustrous Finnian wondered whether he'd paid a cobbler to buff them while he slept. The merchant's smile was wide, deliberate, and Finnian clocked it for the practiced move it was.

"Good morning," the merchant said, voice like well-oiled leather. He removed his hat with a flourish and set it on the counter, where it promptly rolled onto the floor.

Finnian, still dusting the face of a twelve-day regulator, looked up and grinned. "Good morning. You're out and about early."

"In my line of work, it's the only way to stay solvent," the merchant replied. "And, I spent the night in your lovely inn, giving me a head start or sorts." He extended a hand as though to measure Finnian's character by the firmness of his grip, but Finnian took a sidelong approach and offered a mug of coffee instead.

The merchant accepted. "Name's Wystan," he said. "Word is, you're the one builds clocks."

"I do my best," Finnian replied. "Are you here for a repair, or is there a particular need?"

"Both, maybe." Wystan set the mug down, drew a pocket watch from his vest, and spun it across his palm. "My old one's been slow since the Mistral crossing. Something to do with the altitude, the jeweler said, but I'm not a man to trust excuses." He flicked his wrist, and the watch's lid snapped open. The face inside was gold, engraved with a pattern of ivy leaves; the hands were bent, and the seconds ran with a visible limp.

Finnian examined it. "Nothing wrong with the movement. There's a tension here…" He wound it, listened, and then shook his head. "It's not the altitude. There's a trick to these old regulators. Sometimes the mainspring forgets what it's meant to do."

Wystan leaned in, crowding the counter. "Have you anything in stock that runs a bit truer?"

Finnian gestured to a case behind him. "All tested, all guaranteed to the mark. But if you want something built for long roads and hard knocks, I'd suggest brass over gold. The gold looks nice, but it's soft as a butter slab in midsummer."

Wystan weighed his options, then pointed at a heavy brass watch on a chain. The case was burnished to a mellow glow, and the face bore only the numbers, no decoration, save a faint, swirling filigree.

"May I?" he asked.

Finnian nodded, and the merchant picked it up. He turned it over in his hands, then thumbed open the lid. The tick was steady and confident; the weight was right. Wystan closed his eyes, and for a second, Finnian saw the muscles of his jaw relax. Then the merchant frowned, as if startled by a phantom, and placed the watch down.

Finnian, who'd seen this before, asked, "Everything all right?"

Wystan hesitated. "It's silly, but for a moment I had the oddest vision. Like I was standing at a market stall, somewhere far south. People crowding in, coin raining into my palm. Then just as quickly, it was gone."

Finnian studied the man's face. "Not so silly," he said. "Happens to many who try a new clock. Timepieces are like shoes. Some need a day or two to fit." He gave the merchant a look, gentle but direct. "If I had to guess, you're about to have your best trading season yet. But watch for the first hot day of spring. Markets can turn on a dime—or on a weather vane, if you're unlucky."

Wystan, perhaps unnerved by how closely Finnian's words echoed his own ambitions and worries, grinned. "If I end up richer, I'll send a cask your way. What do I owe you for this?"

Finnian named the price, which was fair but did not cut too deep. The merchant paid in silver, took his old gold watch as backup, and left with a brisk tip of the hat.

Finnian, alone for a moment, let out a breath and looked at the brass watch's vacant spot in the display. Some clocks, he knew, worked on more than just springs and cogs. Some ran on longing, or hope, or dread.

The bell over the door jangled again. This time, it was a woman in a broad-shouldered tweed dress, her arms full of neatly bundled books and her hair braided into a crown. She was in her late twenties, maybe thirty, with a scattering of freckles across her nose that made her seem younger than her bearing suggested.

She cleared her throat and addressed Finnian with the clarity of one used to maintaining order among chaos. "Are you the proprietor?"

Finnian, who had been both the shop's only staff and its chief janitor for years, said, "That's me. How can I help?"

"I'm here about a clock for our schoolroom," she said. "The candles have made the ceiling black, and I promised the mayor I'd have it cleaned before next sennight. I'm Lane. Lane Paddock, from Nethistown, a few 'marks east down the road." She set the stack of books on the counter with a satisfying thump.

"Schoolmistress?" Finnian asked.

She nodded. "And sometimes, apparently, clock repair technician. But I'd rather leave the complex work to experts. I mainly come to see Vamir for new texts, but saw your window display and thought I'd stop in."

Finnian could tell from the way Lane handled her books—never letting them tilt or slip, always squared at the corners—that she would not tolerate a clock that drifted even a few minutes. "I have two wall clocks that might suit. One is a twin-bell, the other a weight-driven pendulum." He lifted both from the shelf and set them before her.

Lane inspected them, then pointed to the latter. "That one. It looks... authoritative."

"It's a good timekeeper," Finnian said. "Mahogany case, clear numerals, and I tuned the chime to be soft, not shrill. Would you like to test it?"

She nodded, and Finnian set the pendulum in motion. The clock's sound was deeper and more pleasant than most—almost like a grandfather clock's voice, but scaled down for the attention span of children.

Lane's eyes softened, and she watched the hands move for a few seconds. When she touched the face, Finnian saw her pupils widen. A faint flush rose to her cheeks.

"Did you see something?" he asked quietly.

Lane looked up, surprised. "I—I saw myself in the Town Hall, not the schoolroom. All the students were there, and I was at the front, speaking, but I couldn't hear my own words. They were all smiling, and someone was clapping in the back."

Finnian smiled. "Sounds like a fine future to me."

Lane returned the smile, more hesitantly. "Is that normal? To see things like that when you touch a clock?"

"In my shop, more often than not," he said. "Consider it a small bonus. I can have this wrapped up for you in ten minutes, if you're on your way to class."

"I am. Thank you, Mister Springdale." She hesitated, then added, "You'll come to our next exhibition, I hope? The students have been working on something... unusual, and I think you'd appreciate it."

"Wouldn't miss it," Finnian said, and meant it.

Lane left with her new clock under one arm, her books balanced atop. Finnian watched her go, then set to dusting the shelf she'd browsed, finding it easier to breathe when the shop was filled with the small echoes of other lives.

Midday crept in, warming the room and sending slats of sunlight crawling across the tile floor. Finnian used the lull to repair the merchant's old gold watch, gently coaxing the hands back into alignment. He had just finished and was testing the movement when the next visitor arrived—a hooded apothecary, hands stained with ink and fingers bandaged in two places.

The apothecary did not introduce herself at first. She scanned the shop's offerings with a critical eye, then drifted toward the counter, keeping her hands mostly hidden inside her sleeves.

"I was told you have clocks that travel well," she said, her voice quiet but edged with something sharp.

Finnian set down the gold watch. "For travel, I'd suggest a wind-up alarm. They're small, sturdy, and loud enough to wake the dead—or, at least, the moderately hung over."

The apothecary pulled back her hood, revealing a thin face and quicksilver eyes. "I don't sleep deeply. That's not the issue. I need a timepiece that can be trusted to mark out exact intervals. I do a lot of tinctures and steeps. If the timing is off, the result can be… unpredictable."

"Understood." Finnian reached under the counter and produced a small, silver-cased alarm. "This one's been calibrated for accuracy. Set it to any interval, and it'll wake you—or remind you—to the minute. The hands are phosphor, too, so you can read it in the dark."

The apothecary took it, her bandaged thumb tracing the ridged edge of the casing. She seemed satisfied, but a moment later, her face tensed. Finnian recognized the look: another vision.

She set the clock down abruptly. "That's… That's not possible," she said.

Finnian didn't press, but gave her space to explain.

"I saw myself in my workshop, and there was a fire," the apothecary said. "Not a big one, but enough to ruin everything on the main shelf. I saw a jar roll off the table and smash, and the floor was covered in…" She shook her head, visibly rattled.

Finnian considered. "Best take extra care with the lamp, then. I could add a fire bell to the alarm, if you like. It's loud, but it might save you a mess."

The apothecary nodded, subdued. "How much?"

He quoted her a fair price, and she paid in coin that bore traces of blue powder. As she left, Finnian watched her walk a little faster than she'd entered.

By late afternoon, the shop was flush with the smell of brass polish and the gentle clamor of clocks running in happy disharmony. Finnian sat by the window, cleaning his spectacles and feeling the ache in his fingers—a reliable indicator that business had been good. He was contemplating a second cup of tea when the bell chimed again.

This time, it was a young man in a guard's uniform—breastplate buffed to mirror-bright, hair cropped so short it was more memory than presence. The guard's eyes were wide, earnest, and perhaps a little too blue for his own good.

"Mister Springdale?" he asked.

"That's me," Finnian replied, waving the guard in. "What's the need?"

The guard removed his helmet, tucking it awkwardly under his arm. "I was hoping for a desk clock. The kind you can keep in a guard house. They said you make ones that ring the mark precisely, and I… Well, I need that."

Finnian cocked his head. "Rough nights on patrol?"

The guard blushed, which clashed oddly with the uniform. "Sometimes. The bells in the town square echo funny, especially in the fog. If I miss my rotation, my captain will… let's just say he'll notice."

Finnian gestured toward a row of smaller clocks. "Take your pick."

The guard lingered over the options, then selected an iron-faced clock with blocky hands and a sturdy build. He held it in both hands, as if it might leap away.

For a moment, he just stood, staring at the second hand as it swept a clean arc. Then, without warning, the guard's eyes went glassy. Finnian saw the muscles in his jaw tense.

"Something?" Finnian prompted.

The guard nodded, but seemed reluctant to speak. "It was like a dream, but sharp. I saw myself at our gate, middle of the night. There was a lot of shouting, and I... I couldn't get the gate open in time. My hands were shaking."

Finnian reached across the counter and set a steady hand atop the clock. "Sometimes, the future tries to warn us," he said. "Or just nudge us to take care. If you trust your training, and keep this wound, you'll be ready. But stay vigilant on the mark after midnight. That's when most trouble tries to walk through a door."

The guard exhaled, then gave a short, grateful bow. "Thank you, sir. For the clock, and the advice."

Finnian smiled. "It's part of the service."

When the shop emptied again, Finnian watched the light lengthen along the wall. Four clocks lighter, and the day had passed with nothing more than ordinary oddness. He thought of Wystan, and Lane, and the apothecary, and the young guard—each with their burden, each choosing a clock like a charm against fate. He wondered, as he often did, whether the visions were a gift of the town, or something peculiar to himself.

But it hardly mattered. So long as the clocks kept ticking, and the people who took them found their way a little more surely, he'd call the work good.

Finnian wound his own pocket watch, the one he never let out for sale, and felt the weight of it in his palm. He closed his eyes and waited to see if there would be a vision for himself, but as always, there was only the memory of his old mentor's workshop: sunlight, laughter, and the endless, stubborn beauty of time refusing to stand still.

He tucked the watch back into his vest, smiled at the thought, and set about sweeping the floor in time to the rhythm of his favorite clock.

———

The bell over Finnian's door gave a warning growl before Dardrad Pebbleblade even stepped inside. It wasn't that the bell was old or poorly mounted—it had just learned to anticipate Dardrad's approach the way a cat learns to brace for an overenthusiastic toddler.

Dardrad entered with a stomp that rattled the panes. The dwarf's boots were caked with brownish grit, his beard freshly combed but already trying to escape its own neatness. Today's shirt was a muted ochre, clean at the collar but already showing signs of flour dust near the cuffs. Finnian suspected a visit to the bakery had been on the morning's agenda.

"Springdale," Dardrad rumbled, sounding mildly disappointed to find the shop in such perfect order.

"Pebbleblade," Finnian replied, not bothering to stand. "If you've come to borrow the toast machine, you'll have to forgive me."

"Bah," Dardrad said, with a dismissive wave. "I prefer honey on my toast. No, I'm here about a clock."

"Oh?" Finnian set aside his tiny screwdriver and looked at Dardrad, genuinely curious.

"We prefer a water-clock, of course," the dwarf grunted. "But it's cracked. Dalossalda says I can just make another. She's probably right. But if I have to rely on the town bell, I'll go mad before the next moon. And I don't fancy glasswork."

Finnian could understand the sentiment. The town bell tower was notorious for running a mark slow on rainy days, and a mark fast on busy days, as if it had a personal stake in the town's well-being.

"What are you looking for? Wall clock? Pocket?"

Dardrad eyed the shelves. "Something with heft. Something… reliable. None of that willow-wood, not for me. Stone or metal."

Finnian wiped his hands and came out from behind the counter. He led Dardrad to a row of clocks on the far wall, each more robust than the last: a squat granite clock with a bronze face, a blacksmith's timer built from a melted-down horseshoe, and a barrel-shaped number wound with a heavy iron key.

"Take your pick," Finnian said, watching Dardrad's eyes settle on the granite model.

Dardrad hefted it in one hand, nodding approvingly at the weight. "This'll do. Reminds me of home. Never did care for clocks, truth told. In the old caves, we kept time with water—real time, not marks and bells. But…" He hesitated, and Finnian saw the moment of pride turn to something softer. "Makota's bakery got that new timer of yours. The one with the singing chimes. She says it works better than any candle or water basin she's used."

Finnian grinned. "She's got a knack for precision. You see the look on her face when the bread comes out right on the first try?"

Dardrad's own face creased in something like amusement. "She was insufferable for a day. Sora and Kene said she danced around the ovens. I think she named the timer. 'Clocky.'" He said it with the disdain only a dwarf could muster for a nickname so lacking in gravitas.

Finnian ran a hand along the side of the granite clock, checking the alignment of the numerals. "It's a good model. If you're looking for something similar, I could fit a chime. Or leave it as is. Entirely up to you."

"Chime's fine. But not too shrill." Dardrad's eyes flicked to the hammer inside. "Nothing worse than a clock that wakes the dead."

Finnian popped open the back, adjusted the tension on the chime's spring, and set the mark to the current time. "There. Should be mellow enough. You want to test it?"

Dardrad nodded. Finnian pressed the chime, and it sounded a rich, rounded note—not a jangle, but a gentle reminder. Dardrad gave a single, approving grunt.

He took the clock, set it on the counter, and then hesitated. Instead of coins, Dardrad reached into a pocket and produced a palm-sized bag of something dense and fragrant. He set it next to the clock with deliberate finality.

"New blend," Dardrad said. "Makota's idea. Rye flour, ground fine, mixed with dried berries and a pinch of smoked salt. She says it's best in the morning."

Finnian recognized the payment for what it was: a barter among craftsmen. "I'll try it with my first cup of tea," he said. "Thank you."

"Thank you." Dardrad picked up the clock, gave it an experimental shake, and squinted as if expecting a loose gear to leap out and bite him. When none did, he tucked it under his arm.

As Dardrad turned to go, Finnian noticed something odd—a lack of the usual prickling at the base of his skull, the sense that something else hovered around the moment. No vision, no whisper of future or possibility. Just the faint scent of rye and stone dust.

He wondered aloud, "Funny. I don't think I've ever sold a clock without at least a flicker of a vision."

Dardrad turned, eyebrow arched. "Maybe it's not a sale. Maybe it's a trade. Or maybe you're just low on magic today."

Finnian chuckled. "Could be."

The dwarf considered. "You want a prediction? Makota's kits, they follow her mixer like clockwork. But come next moon, I'll have a better timepiece than she does. I'll set it next to the bread basket and let the whole bakery see who keeps truer time."

"Competitive, are we?" Finnian said, delighted.

Dardrad grinned, and it was a good, toothy dwarf grin. "We'll see."

He left with the granite clock under his arm and a purposeful stride, leaving behind a faint echo of stone on wood and the scent of honest trade.

Finnian set the bag of flour on his workbench, opened it, and inhaled the aroma—nutty, faintly sweet, just as Dardrad had said. He thought about the absence of visions, and found he didn't mind. Sometimes, a clock was just a clock, and a day could be measured in good work and good barter.

He wrote "Granite Model—Dardrad" on a slip of paper, taped it above the workbench, and got back to his repairs, the hum of stone and metal still resonant in the air.

Dardrad had scarcely cleared the stoop when Vamir Oakkin ducked in, moving with the fluidity of someone who'd spent more years among shelves than trees. The elf's white hair caught the morning light and refracted it in faint rainbows along the window glass, and even his footsteps seemed more suggestion than noise.

"Finnian," Vamir said, his greeting as smooth as poured honey. "Busy day, or is that just the impression of passing through?"

"Dardrad just left," Finnian replied. "If you're here to buy up all my stone clocks, I'll have to commission the quarry."

Vamir smiled, but his eyes were already drifting around the shop, cataloging details. "Not today. My need is more… public." He leaned in, lowering his voice as if sharing a minor scandal. "The town hall has been without a reliable clock for a full sennight. The children in the schoolroom cannot keep their eyes off the sundial, and the adults can't agree when the meetings begin. I promised Jen I'd see to it."

"A civic clock?" Finnian said, immediately intrigued.

"Yes, and with a proper face. Something large, easily read from anywhere in the hall. The bells are fine and all, but we need something that we can glance at, not remember when the last bell rang."

Finnian considered the shelves. "I can modify a wall clock to fit, but for a large room, you want size and legibility." He plucked down a sturdy oak clock, examined its mechanism, and frowned at the tiny numerals.

Vamir followed Finnian into the workroom, peering over his shoulder as Finnian began to unscrew the back plate. "If it's not too much trouble," Vamir ventured, "could you fashion the numbers in black, against pale oak? Something even a child might read from the far bench."

Finnian grinned. "If I made them any larger, you'd hear the children counting in their sleep."

"That is the dream," Vamir replied, hands folded, watching with open fascination as Finnian dismantled the old face and sketched out a new one on a pale veneer. Finnian's penmanship was precise and purposeful; the numerals marched in a perfect circle, bold and clear. He set the new face in place, aligned the hands, and double-checked the tension. "This will be the most accurate in the square, for at least a moon. If it drifts, bring it back and I'll recalibrate."

Vamir admired the finished piece, tilting it so the sunlight struck the fresh black numerals. "You do beautiful work, Finnian."

"It's my pleasure," Finnian said, and meant it. He carefully wrapped the clock in a towel for safe transport. "You want it delivered, or can you manage?"

"I'd rather carry it myself," Vamir said, taking the clock as if it weighed nothing. "Let it be known that the north shore of Evendiam keeps better time than anyplace else."

Finnian couldn't help but beam at that. "And someday, maybe we'll even move beyond candlemarks and bells."

Vamir's smile was all delight. "One hour at a time, my friend. Do you know how my people traditionally keep time in the forests?"

"I assume not candles."

The elf chuckled. "Certainly not. No, we listen to the whisper of the leaves."

Finnian raised an eyebrow. "Is that… accurate?"

Vamir laughed. "Absolutely not." He hefted the clock. "I much prefer this approach."

The elf departed, clock under his arm, already humming a tune Finnian recognized as one of the more complicated rounds the schoolchildren liked to sing.

Alone again, Finnian dusted off his hands and looked around the shop. With each clock that left, the room felt less cluttered, more purposeful, as if the passage of time had found its own rhythm and was gently coaxing everyone along.

He leaned back in his chair, savoring the lingering satisfaction of a job well done, and waited for the next visitor. He had the sense that the clocks would not be idle for long.

If the clocks marked out the rhythm of North Pointe, Minnie Trulast was its pulse. She bustled through Finnian's door at half-past noon, arms laden with a covered basket and her trademark energy riding ahead of her like a vanguard of good cheer.

"Finnian! I brought you lunch, and not a crumb too soon, I'm sure." She deposited the basket on the counter, ignoring the featherduster Finnian tried to conceal behind his back. "Sit. Eat. Don't make me fetch Susan to force-feed you like a goose."

He obeyed, mostly because he'd learned resistance was futile. Minnie's bread was dense, seeded, and always cut thick enough to withstand even the most aggressive butter. The cheese, sharp and a little salty, paired with pickled root vegetables wrapped in a waxed paper twist.

"I was just about to take a break," Finnian said, mouth already full.

"Liar," Minnie retorted, wagging a finger. "You'd work yourself into a grave if the bell tower let you."

He shrugged, grinning. "How's business at the Weary Head?"

"Lively!" Minnie's eyes sparkled. "Three caravans in by noon, and the new girls can barely keep the flagons straight. Trevor's growing like a weed and keeps telling guests you once built a clock so loud it rattled the bottles off the shelf."

Finnian winced. "Only the prototypes."

"Speaking of," she said, "I need a favor."

He knew that tone; she was winding up for a pitch. "Name it."

"I want a clock for the main lobby," Minnie said, the words tumbling out all at once. "Something everyone can see, with a chime loud enough to chase the lazybones out before the midday rush. You know, a friendly reminder, but with... authority."

Finnian finished chewing, then wiped his hands. "Not a problem. Did you have a style in mind?"

Minnie tilted her head, considering. "Something classic. The town's always had our candles, but if you say hours and minutes are the way of the future, I'll trust you."

He beamed. "Hours, definitely. I can set the chime to ring two hours before noon, which gives guests a full mark to pack and shuffle out. Want it to play a tune, or just a single note?"

"A tune! But not too fancy." She leaned in, lowering her voice. "Remember, this is North Pointe. Some of the regulars can barely count past ten. If it's too clever, it'll just confuse 'em."

Finnian sketched a quick diagram in his mind, then started rummaging through his shelves. "I've got a cherrywood case I was saving for something special. Big, open face, the hands painted red so they're easy to spot. I'll tune the chime to 'Up and At 'Em'—it's catchy, and nobody can forget it."

Minnie's smile lit up the room. "You're a treasure, Finnian. And if you have any little ones, the kind for guest rooms, I'll take a dozen next fortnight. Only stipulation: they all match."

He made a note. "One big clock, and a dozen siblings. Got it. You want to test the prototype when I finish?"

"If I don't, Trevor will never let me hear the end of it." Minnie lifted the bread basket, reclaimed a heel for herself, and popped it into her mouth with a satisfied hum.

Finnian watched her for a moment, feeling the quiet happiness that came from being useful in a place where every hand knew its trade. "Do you ever get tired?" he asked, genuinely curious.

She finished chewing before answering. "Tired? Maybe by sundown, but I sleep like a stone and wake up ready for more." She wiped the crumbs from her apron. "I like to think we're all parts in a big clock, Finnian. You keep the hours, I keep the people, and somehow we all keep moving."

He couldn't have put it better. "I'd be lost without your bread, Minnie."

"Flatterer." She pointed at the remains of lunch. "Don't forget to eat every bite. If you die of starvation, I'll never forgive you."

"I'll pace myself," Finnian promised, already plotting the main lobby clock in his head.

Minnie gathered up her basket, gave a quick squeeze to Finnian's shoulder, and bustled back toward the inn. The air seemed a little emptier for a moment, as if even the clocks missed her when she was gone.

Finnian tidied away the crumbs, sat at his bench, and began laying out parts for the promised clock. As he sanded the cherrywood and polished the brass, he found himself humming "Up and At 'Em" under his breath.

It was only when he reached for his pencil that he caught the subtle, insistent tick coming from the far corner of the shop.

He froze. The grandfather clock, the one with the locked movement and the too-clever escapement, sat silent and inert. But as he listened, Finnian heard the faintest heartbeat of metal on metal, too faint for anyone else to notice.

A cold shiver ran through him. He checked the case—locked, mainspring unwound—and the ticking stopped.

Just a clock, he told himself, and pushed the feeling away.

But even as he resumed his work, Finnian knew that tomorrow, or the day after, the clocks would once again set the rhythm for every hour, every chime, every breath in North Pointe. He hoped the ticking would always bring comfort. And if it ever grew too loud, he would meet it head on, armed with tea, tools, and—above all—the knowledge that in this town, nothing ever happened alone.

He finished the rough sketch, set the cherrywood piece in the window, and let the clocks keep time. The world outside marched on, one hour at a time, and Finnian, for the first time in a long while, let himself just listen.

six
...

FINNIAN WAS NOT the type to ignore good advice, except when it ran contrary to the demands of curiosity. He had spent the next morning in a sort of philosophical wrestling match with Leota's words. They stuck, as her words always did, like a burr under his collar or a misaligned gear in an otherwise immaculate assembly. Sometimes, Finnian wondered if the witch's real magic was the ability to plant ideas that gnawed at you until you did something about them.

By third bell, he'd tidied his shop twice, sorted the same box of fractured mainsprings three times, and resisted the Grandfather Clock not at all. He loomed beside it now, a little self-conscious, as if the hulking mechanism might scold him for ignoring its warnings.

The day outside had grown overcast and pressed flat against the shop's windows, but the interior was alive with the layered ticking of clocks and the persistent, subterranean hum from the unfinished behemoth in the corner. That hum was new—Finnian was certain of it. More than just the vibration of gears and levers, it was almost a resonance, a low tone that seemed to ripple through the wooden floorboards and make Finnian's own bones vibrate in sympathy.

He had convinced himself, in the intervening hours, that the issue was simple: a fractional drift in the main spring's tension, perhaps compounded by temperature fluctuations or a slightly out-of-true ratchet. He told himself, quite logically, that the solution was a micro-adjustment, nothing more, nothing less. He just needed to take a tiny, incremental risk.

Finnian rolled up his sleeves—clean shirt, still, thank you—and sat at the base of the Grandfather Clock, eye-level with the swinging dual pendulums and the layered complexity of escapement wheels. He had built and repaired clocks for over half a century, and he had never felt nervous before a repair, not even when handling the three-thousand-part minute repeater in the Duke's collection, nor the delicate hour-glass automaton gifted to the town's mayor on account of his spectacular, if inadvertent, ability to make time disappear during council meetings. But this clock felt different. It was as if the whole shop was holding its breath, waiting for him to move.

His hands found the tension screw with unerring certainty. He'd fabricated the thing from his own stock of extra-hardened steel, its threads as fine as spiderweb. He rested the tip of his jeweler's screwdriver into the slot, feeling the anticipation thrum through his fingertips.

Finnian took a steadying breath. The scent was a blend of machine oil, dust, and distant, fresh rain. He twisted the screw one half-turn, then another, the minute clicks masked by the greater, living rhythm of the clock's mechanism. With the third turn, a vibration ran through the casing, and the tension screw seated with a near-silent but decisive click.

For a moment, nothing happened. Finnian waited, exhaling slowly, as if he'd just convinced a dangerous animal to sit. Then, without warning, the chime mechanism snapped awake. The Grandfather Clock began to chime.

It was nothing like the test chimes he'd triggered before. Instead of the familiar, soothing peal, the sound that issued from the clock's brass tubes was a discordant, impossible symphony: high-pitched metallic shrieks, the deep moan of a foghorn filtered through the innards of a cathedral, and a background hiss like wind rushing through a distant canyon. It layered and folded, each tone tripping over the next, and all of it underscored by the insistent, pulsebeat tick of the main escapement. Finnian was seized by the conviction that the clock was not marking time, but calling out—to what, or whom, he had no idea.

The brass face of the clock, already shiny from Finnian's compulsive polishing, began to warp. At first it simply rippled, as if made of something less than solid. Then, in a spectacle that both awed and terrified him, the brass seemed to liquefy, sloughing away from the casing and running downward in slow, viscous streams. The numerals peeled away like overripe fruit and pooled at the base, revealing behind them not the clock's wooden core, but a window—no, a portal —of swirling indigo and silver. The colors had depth, impossible to focus on, and within the vortex danced lights and darks that never quite held still. It was like peering into the mechanism of the world itself, the inside of some cosmic geartrain.

Finnian staggered backward, bumping into a side table and upsetting a trio of carriage clocks, which hit the ground with a trio of unfortunate clangs. But he barely noticed. His every sense was devoured by the phenomenon in front of him.

He was not alone.

There was a customer in the shop, Finnian now realized—the sort of customer who could enter and stand for minutes unnoticed, especially if you were lost in the inner workings of a machine. Finnian remembered only a vague impression: a merchant's traveling coat, pockets bulging with coin and invoice slips, a face as lined and weathered as a wind-struck cliff. He'd been standing at the counter for who knew how long, apparently rooted there by indecision. Now, the man turned slowly toward the portal in the clock's face, and his expression transformed from polite impatience to something like bone-deep recognition.

"By the stones," the merchant breathed. "It's real."

Finnian wanted to speak, to warn, to apologize—he wasn't even sure for what—but the words caught in his throat. He could only watch as the merchant stepped forward, almost reverently, as though drawn by some invisible cord.

"Always wondered," the man said. "If I'd know the right time."

He reached out and touched the liquid brass at the edge of the clock's casing. His fingers did not burn; the metal parted for them, and the swirl beyond seemed to lean in, hungry or welcoming or both. Finnian watched, paralyzed, as the merchant put his whole hand through, then his arm, then his whole self. For a moment, the merchant's shape was silhouetted against the vortex, thrown into impossible relief by the indigo-silver chaos beyond.

Then, with a sound like a bell struck underwater—a dense, shivering *BOOM*—the portal snapped shut. The brass returned, solidified, flowed back into place like water drawn up by a thirsty sponge. The clock's face was whole again, unblemished except for the faint, oily shimmer left on the numerals.

The shop was silent, except for the clocks. Finnian could hear each one individually now, their ticks and tocks no longer lost in a crowd. It was as if the very air had been wrung out and replaced with something thinner, hungrier.

Finnian staggered forward and touched the Grandfather Clock's case. No hum. The low resonance was gone, replaced by a tingling, residual static. The mainspring inside was still wound. The hands ticked on, marking out the minutes with a sort of cruel indifference. He tried to open the front panel, but it was stuck fast, as if fused by the event. His heart raced.

He cast about, scanning the shop for the missing merchant, for evidence, for something to make sense of what had just transpired. On the countertop was a small, neatly folded piece of paper—the only sign the man had ever existed. Finnian picked it up with shaking fingers. It was a receipt, unsigned, for an order never completed. At the bottom, a single line in a spidery hand: Thank you, Finnian. Time well spent.

Finnian sat down hard on the nearest stool. He felt suddenly older, wearier, as if he'd skipped a few steps in his own aging process. The world had not ended, but it had certainly shifted, and he suspected nothing in North Pointe Common Towne would ever feel quite normal again.

All around him, the clocks of his shop kept on ticking, each one now a little reminder that there was more than one way to measure time, and more than one way to get lost in it.

He lasted half an hour, if that, before the urge to find Leota became overwhelming. The memory of the merchant's disappearance played over and over in Finnian's mind, each time with some new horror: what if he'd been sent to some random when, rather than some where? What if, on the other side of that shifting, silvery void, the man was simply... unmade? Finnian's hands trembled as he locked up the shop, twice forgetting where he'd left the door key and once nearly leaving without his boots. Outside, the late afternoon was wrapped in a heavy, expectant silence. Not even the blackbirds dared make a racket.

Leota's house was less a house and more a warning in architectural form: three narrow stories of black-bricked severity, set behind a bristling iron fence and fronted with a door so perfectly centered that Finnian always felt off-kilter approaching it. The house sat at the far corner of the town square, perfectly aligned to watch both the lake and the main road. Its windows were always shuttered, its garden comprised entirely of blue-green herbs that Finnian could neither name nor tolerate for more than a few moments' proximity.

He rapped on the door with more force than intended. There was a long, breathless moment before it swung open, not with a creak, but with the soundless efficiency of something that resented being disturbed.

Leota herself appeared, framed in the gloom. Her black dress absorbed the last traces of daylight, her hair and skin a study in deliberate, unyielding contrast. She wore no adornment save a single silver ring, and the only color on her person was the faint pink in her cheeks, as if she'd just finished a brisk argument with a stubborn spirit.

"Finnian," she said, voice neutral but edged with curiosity. "I take it you did not spend the day reading as planned."

He hesitated, then, with a visible effort, decided honesty was his only hope. "Something happened."

She opened the door wider. "Come inside. Mind the threshold."

He'd been inside Leota's home exactly twice before, and the experience was consistent: the entrance hall was neither cold nor warm, neither inviting nor hostile. It simply was, like a waiting room in a palace where the king might or might not exist. The walls were covered in bookshelves, the floor swept clean enough to shame the town's entire cleaning guild. A faint odor of dried lavender and old, crackling paper filled the air.

Leota gestured to a pair of battered armchairs near the parlor's hearth. Finnian sat. He realized, belatedly, that his hands were still shaking.

She perched opposite him and waited, like a patient predator.

He blurted, "I may have opened some sort of… gateway? Portal? In the shop." He braced for mockery, but Leota only raised an eyebrow.

"Describe it."

So he did: the tuning of the mainspring, the uncanny chime, the brass melting away, the vortex of color and light and sound, the merchant's singular reaction, and the way the world had grown suddenly thinner in the aftermath. He did not embellish. He didn't need to.

Leota listened in silence. When he was done, she said, "That sounds about right."

Finnian sputtered, "About right for what?"

She folded her hands in her lap. "You've lived in North Pointe long enough to know about the houses, yes? The traditions?"

He nodded, uncertain. "Every shop is a legacy," he recited. "Inherited along with the building. Gifts, sometimes, or… oddities."

"Exactly," she said. "Most are harmless. Warren's forge is old as dirt and stubborn as its owner, and it sends him dreams to tell him what to forge; Minnie's inn always mends itself after a particularly boisterous night, and it sends guests dreams of their destinies. Yours —" she gestured at him "—is perhaps a little related. Have you ever thought about what your shop's gift is, Finnian?"

He blinked, thrown by the question. "Making clocks? Fixing things? There's not much magic to it."

"Don't be obtuse," she said, gently, not unkind. "If you prefer, I can tell you what I've noticed."

He didn't answer, so she continued, "People walk out of your shop with more than just a timepiece. Sometimes they leave with an answer to a question they never asked, or a memory they'd lost, or a sense of purpose that wasn't there before. I've seen it happen. You don't sell clocks; you sell… possibility. Not unlike the Weary Head."

Finnian tried to process this. "I've noticed people remember things, sometimes. Or say the clock 'spoke' to them, in a sense. But that's just —" He shrugged helplessly. "Coincidence. Or I assumed so."

"Not coincidence. Your shop amplifies potential," Leota said. "It helps people see what they could be, or what they've forgotten they are. But—" she paused, eyeing him as if deciding whether to continue "—the Grandfather Clock is an anomaly. You brought the frame with you, correct?"

Finnian shook his head. "Yes. I built the mechanism it myself. From scraps. Some from old stock, some imported. A few pieces I… found."

Leota nodded, as if that explained everything. "Sometimes, when enough potential energy builds up in one place, it stops being theoretical. It becomes literal. What you made, Finnian, is not just a clock. It's a threshold. A tool for sending possibility—people, maybe even things—somewhere else. Or somewhen."

He stared at her, blankly. "I just wanted to see if I could get the lunar phase to sync with the secondary drive," he muttered.

A faint smile touched Leota's lips. "And you did. Perhaps too well."

Finnian exhaled, a long, shuddering breath. "What do I do now?"

"Close the shop for a day or two," she said, with more authority than he'd ever heard from her. "Let the energies settle. I will help you ward the Grandfather Clock tonight, if you're willing. But you must not, under any circumstances, adjust the tension screw again."

He nodded, too grateful to question her.

Leota stood and crossed to a bookshelf, returning with a thin volume bound in iridescent blue. "Read this," she said, handing it to him. "It explains, in… roundabout terms, what you are dealing with. Come see me at sundown."

Finnian accepted the book. It was heavier than it looked, the cover cold to the touch. He wondered if it had ever been read by human eyes.

As he rose to leave, Leota regarded him over her shoulder. "You did nothing wrong, Finnian. Curiosity is a virtue. But so is caution." She paused, then added, "And the man who went through? I think he found what he was looking for."

Outside, the rain had started in earnest, drumming the town square into a silvery blur. Finnian hurried through it, book tucked beneath his shirt, feeling simultaneously lighter and more laden than before. His mind spun with possibility: the gateway, the lost merchant, the potential for more miracles—or more disasters.

He reached his shop and stood a long while in the doorway, listening to the honest, unassuming tick of a hundred clocks. For the first time in a long time, he wondered what else his hands might be capable of.

And in the center of the room, the Grandfather Clock sat silent, its face restored, its hands precisely aligned. It looked almost innocent, as if it had never harbored a secret at all.

Finnian smiled, in spite of himself. He locked the door and went to find a towel for the rain.

Tomorrow, he would take Leota's advice. Tonight, he would read.

seven

. . .

THE SIGN Finnian made for his shop was not, strictly speaking, necessary. North Pointe's morning crowd tended to be both literal and loyal, and if a clockmaker failed to open on time, customers would simply return at the next bell. Nevertheless, he fussed over the cardstock, trying out three different pens before settling on a thick, unforgiving ink that bled into every word. He taped the sheet—TEMPORARILY TEMPORALLY UNSTABLE. DO NOT ENTER.—to the inside of the door, just below the painted hours. Then, for good measure, he locked the deadbolt and tried the handle twice.

A minute later he was striding down the lane, nerves strung tight as a regulator spring. He ignored the bakery, ignored the tempting scent of melting sugar wafting from Makota's, and aimed straight for the only establishment in town that served ale before second bell.

The Broken Claw had a talent for feeling full even when empty. The moment Finnian stepped inside, the rush of warm, yeasty air and the wash of conversation hit him like a friendly blanket. Only three patrons clustered around the scarred oak tables: a pair of travelers nursing last night's regrets, and a solitary woman in a faded wool coat hunched over her notebook. Jen, the town's constable, ran the bar with a soldier's economy—polite to locals, suspicious of strangers, and immune to every story short of manslaughter.

Sam stood behind the bar, refilling the tiny oil lamp that kept the polished brass tap array glowing even in the morning gloom. Her white hair was bound in its usual tight braid, and the puckered scar that scored one side of her face looked almost rosy in the lamplight. She caught sight of Finnian, nodded once, and jerked her head toward the corner booth by the hearth.

"Bad morning?" she called.

He hesitated, then found his usual perch at the booth's end. "Not the worst," Finnian said, though he looked it. He ran a hand over his scalp, which seemed to have picked up an extra inch of shine overnight. "But complicated."

Sam wiped her hands, then poured him a mug of black coffee without asking. "You're three bells early for lunch. Or is it a new time standard I missed?"

He started to answer, but Jen beat him to it, slipping out from behind the bar with the grace of a woman who never allowed a stumble, even when tipsy. "You look like a man about to confess to murder," she said, easing onto the bench across from Finnian. She poured a shot of something clear and set it in front of him, then kept the bottle for herself. "Spill it, Clockmaker."

Finnian took a sip of the coffee, then the shot. The burn helped. "I had a customer vanish," he said. "Right there in the shop. He touched the Grandfather Clock and—" Finnian pantomimed a hand through empty air. "Portal, vortex, some kind of—"

"Freak accident?" Sam offered, brows arched.

"Dimensional collapse," Finnian said, not quite joking.

Jen's face settled into its "wait for the nonsense to end" expression. "Was he pushed?"

"What? No!"

She leaned in, sharp gray eyes catching the firelight. "Did you see what happened, or did you just find the clock empty and the man missing?"

"I saw it," Finnian admitted. "He touched the face. The clock changed—chimed, opened up. It was like he… knew it was for him."

He looked down at the table, feeling suddenly foolish. "He stepped through. Willingly."

Sam poured herself a coffee, then set her elbows on the bar and regarded Finnian. "So, magic clock, magic man, magic result."

He grimaced. "I'm supposed to be the practical one here."

"That's a lie and you know it," Jen said, but her tone was almost kind. "You've lived in this town how many seasons?"

"Six?" Finnian answered uncertainly.

"And how many times have things gotten weird?"

He hesitated, then counted on his fingers. "Thirteen, if you include the time the entire bakery got turned into gingerbread for a night."

"Good," Jen said. "Because this isn't the first time a shop did something strange. Makota's pies? You eat one, you get dreams about your old family. Sometimes happy, sometimes not." She knocked the bottle on the table for emphasis. "And her bread? If she likes you, the crust never burns. If she doesn't, it comes out hollow."

Sam leaned in. "Point is, every business in this town has a trick. Yours is the clocks. What's new is that yours is now... upping its game."

Finnian considered this. "So the solution is to do nothing? Just hope it goes away?"

"Not nothing," Jen said, her voice like a calm wind against glass. "But don't try to fix it with a wrench. You want an answer, you ask the right people. Leota, for one. Maybe the witch has a theory."

Sam snorted. "She always has a theory. Half the time she's right."

Finnian splayed his fingers on the wood, feeling its familiar grooves. "She said the Grandfather Clock wasn't just a timekeeper. That it was a threshold. I didn't believe her, and now—" He trailed off, the words melting into the clatter of mugs from the other table.

Jen regarded him. "Did the man who vanished leave anything behind?"

"A receipt," Finnian said. "And a message: 'Time well spent.'"

Sam laughed, deep and honest. "There you go. He got what he needed."

Finnian closed his eyes, trying to savor the comfort of that idea. It didn't quite take. "What if the clock does it again? To a child, or someone who's not ready?"

Jen shrugged. "I suppose you'll have to pay closer attention, then." She finished her shot. "You're not closing the shop."

He gaped. "I was planning on it! I even made a sign."

"No," Sam said, her voice as gentle as it was final. "You close the shop, that's when something truly awful happens. The town is like—" she paused, searching for the metaphor, then grinned. "It's a circle of wagons. Every business is a spoke. You yank one out, the whole thing goes off-kilter."

Jen nodded agreement. "And if a clock wants to eat a merchant, who are we to say it's not for the best?"

Finnian let the silence stretch. Sam pushed another mug his way, and for a moment, the three of them just sat, listening to the creak of the fire and the low laughter from the far table.

He finally said, "If I keep the shop open, I'll need a witness every time I wind that clock."

Jen grinned, teeth flashing like a knife's edge. "Happy to volunteer."

Sam tapped her mug to his. "And if the clock gets you, you can haunt the pub. We could use a better timekeeper."

Finnian tried to smile. It came out weak, but true. "Thank you," he said.

"Anytime," Jen said, already sliding out of the booth. "Now go home and eat something. And read whatever Leota gave you. I guarantee it'll make less sense than you hope, and more than you want."

Sam added, "And take the back door. The bread delivery's due, and you know how Makota gets if you block the front step."

Finnian stood, feeling the warmth of the place seep into his bones. He hesitated, then looked back at the two women who, in their own way, kept the town running smoother than any clock.

"Thank you," he said again, and meant it. The regulars didn't look up, but he saw the solitary woman in the wool coat make a note in her book.

Outside, the air was cooler, tinged with the promise of rain. Finnian walked slowly, mind ticking over every word of the conversation. Maybe Sam and Jen were right. Maybe the shop—like the rest of the town—was never meant to be perfectly safe. Maybe the point was to keep time anyway, and trust that, when it mattered, someone would be there to catch you on the other side.

He reached his shop door, regarded the sign with a new eye, and decided to leave it up, just for tonight. He unlocked the door, went inside, and locked it again behind him.

Upstairs, he found the book Leota had given him. He poured a mug of tea, settled into his armchair, and opened to the first page.

The title was handwritten, in a careful, looping script: "On the Proper Containment of the Miraculous and the Damnable."

Finnian grinned. The world, for all its danger, was a very well-kept clock.

The next morning, Finnian expected dread to greet him. Instead, it was Makota, head baker of North Pointe and sworn enemy of all things imprecise. She waited outside his shop, arms folded, tail lashing, a loaf of sweet bread nestled in the crook of her elbow.

He was still fumbling with his vest buttons when she rapped on the window. "If you're closed for existential crisis," she called, "I'll need my clocks back."

Finnian fumbled the lock open and peered out. "You saw the sign," he said, unable to keep a sheepish smile from his face.

Makota's whiskers bristled with amusement. "I saw it. Then I came anyway." She brandished the bread. "Bribery, if needed."

He stepped aside, and she swept in, the familiar scents of flour and vanilla and wood smoke trailing after her. "Sora read the sign and thought it was a riddle," Makota said, setting the loaf on his workbench. "She's still guessing. Kene just wanted to see if you'd really locked the door."

Finnian found himself laughing, the weight of the previous day's strangeness already fading beneath the baker's force of personality. "They're good kids."

"They are, if you keep them on a timer." Makota tapped the side of her head. "Which, thanks to you, I now can." She drew from her bag a battered, flour-dusted version of Finnian's Multi-Timer. "It is perfect. Every bell rings on the mark, and the bells are loud enough to bring even Sora back from a daydream. I owe you a debt."

He shrugged, genuinely pleased. "I'm just glad it works. Bread is easier to please than brass."

Makota's feline face grew serious, which was always a little startling. "That's the thing. I want something... more. You see, the timer helps the bakery. But I want a clock for me. Something I can wear, or keep in my pocket. To remind me of the important marks."

Finnian blinked. "A personal timepiece. You'd be the first in North Pointe."

"Why not?" Makota said, tail flicking. "You make them for everyone else. Make one for me."

It felt like a challenge, and Finnian never shied from those. "Any features in particular?" he asked.

She considered. "Simple. Easy to wind. Something I can read without a fuss, even if my hands are in dough."

He led her through the green, sunlight just beginning to slant across the dewy grass, then past the tidy line of shops. A few children played at the fountain, while a gaggle of geese squabbled near the lakefront. The town was itself again—nothing surreal, nothing dangerous, just the usual tangle of personalities and chores.

Inside the clock shop, Finnian peeled off the sign and tossed it into the bin. The room felt cleaner already.

He motioned Makota to the counter, then unlocked the case of personal watches. There were three finished models: one in gold, one in steel, and one with a hammered brass casing, each with a distinct personality.

Makota leaned in, nose nearly touching the glass. "The steel one," she said instantly, paw tapping the case. "It matches my pans."

He handed it over. "The dial's extra bold, the numerals big, the glass a little convex for easy reading. The winding crown is textured, so you don't need claws." He smiled. "And it keeps time within two seconds a sennight, barring extreme misfortune."

Makota turned it over in her hands, eyes bright. "I love it."

He showed her how to wind it, how to set the time, and how to check the reserve. She practiced it twice, then snapped the case shut and slipped the chain around her neck. "What do I owe you?" she asked, knowing the answer.

"First breakfast, tomorrow," Finnian said, bowing. "No rush. I'll still be alive if the town doesn't swallow me whole today."

She purred, a low, amused sound. "You worry too much, Finnian."

"Habit," he replied.

Makota left, whiskers twitching, and the shop felt a little brighter for her passing. Finnian set the timer she'd brought on the shelf, gave it a respectful tap, and got to work. There were repairs waiting. There were customers waiting. There was life, tick by measured tick, waiting to be lived.

He made a note to arrive early for breakfast.

———

As dusk settled over North Pointe, Finnian found himself alone in the shop, surrounded by clocks in various states of readiness. The repairs he'd put off all morning were done, the counter was swept, and the "TEMPORARILY TEMPORALLY UNSTABLE" sign lay crumpled in the bin. He sat at his bench, Leota's blue-bound book open at his elbow, and tried to make sense of the line he'd underlined three times: "A thing contained may yet contain the world that birthed it."

He was contemplating this when the shop bell rattled. Jen stepped in, shedding a light spatter of rain from her shoulders. She looked around as if checking for threats, then locked eyes with Finnian and gave a single, sharp nod.

"Good. You're open," she said.

"For now," Finnian answered, not moving from his seat.

Jen prowled the displays, hands clasped behind her back. "I came to see if you'd blown up the town yet. Word gets around when a clock tries to eat a customer."

"I wouldn't say 'eat,' exactly—"

"You're here. That means you're not the next to go. But let's cut to it." She pulled a stool up to the counter and sat, boots braced. "You're worried you did something wrong."

Finnian considered the question. "I'm worried I can't fix what I started."

Jen shrugged. "Strange things happen here. Sometimes the bakery delivers loaves with the faces of lost pets. Sometimes the lake coughs up coins from towns no one remembers. We don't always get an explanation." She folded her arms. "You know why, right?"

He thought of Leota's stories, and of the townsfolk's easy acceptance of weirdness. "Because North Pointe isn't magic. It just works for the people who need it."

Jen grunted. "Exactly. The town's gifts—they're not some grand design of wizards or witches. They're the work of the God in the mountains. You've heard the stories?"

Finnian nodded. "The Whispering Peaks. The God of Possibility."

Jen grinned, the line of her mouth crinkling with humor. "And you thought you could out-invent a god. Don't feel bad. Half the town's tried."

Finnian tried to smile, and almost managed it. "He likes to make things… complicated."

"That's the point," Jen said. "People show up here looking for answers, or escape, or sometimes just a second chance. The town gives them what they need, even if it doesn't look like what they wanted. Usually, they go away better. Occasionally, they go away weirder. But always, it's on their own terms."

Finnian turned the page in Leota's book. "So when the Grandfather Clock opened up, and Silas stepped through—"

"That was Silas's choice. He probably didn't even know he'd made it until the last second." Jen looked at him, eyes steady. "You can worry about the next one, if you want. But don't close the shop. You're part of the town's plan, even if you don't see the shape yet."

He considered this in silence, listening to the steady tick of a dozen clocks. The air was filled with a gentle, layered humming—the sound of potential, if you were feeling poetic.

Jen slid off the stool. "If anything else happens, come get me. I'll stand in the doorway and catch anyone who tries to make a run for the next dimension."

Finnian grinned. "You'd make a very good bouncer for the multiverse."

She gave him a withering look. "Don't get cute, Finnian."

"Wouldn't dream of it."

Jen headed for the door, then paused. "One more thing. If things ever get truly out of hand, the bakery's cellar has a panic room. It's designed for bread, but it'll fit a clockmaker and a constable, if the world comes to that."

He saluted her with the handle of his awl. "I'll bring snacks."

She left, letting in a gust of wet evening air before the door clicked shut.

For a long minute, Finnian sat and listened. The clocks all ran in perfect disharmony, their tics and tocks overlapping in a way that was not quite music, not quite noise. Beneath it, or maybe within it, was a persistent, almost electric humming—the kind of thing you might mistake for your own heartbeat if you weren't careful.

He closed Leota's book, marked his place, and leaned back. Maybe this was what it meant to be part of something: to surrender a little, to trust that the whole was smarter than the sum of its parts, and to believe that every tick, even the weird ones, pushed the world forward.

Finnian closed up shop at midnight, and left the door unlocked for the first time in years.

If a god was going to drop by, he wanted to be ready.

eight
...

FINNIAN HAD BEEN UP since well before dawn—one of those rare, lemon-tinged mornings where every hour felt like a bonus just for being alive. It helped that his shop was thick with the aroma of Makota's breakfast basket: still-steaming bread, a wedge of Sam's sharp cheese (cut so thin you could see the light through it), and, the real showstopper, Dardrad's sausages, sliced into rounds and blistered on the stove just as Finnian liked them. He'd layered them all together on a slab of rye, perched the sandwich on the edge of his workbench, and only half-pretended to ignore it while he polished up the day's first repair.

He'd just finished the sandwich's crust and licked his thumb clean of the last streak of rendered fat when the shop door banged open. The handle was barely at knee-height, but Galhani, queen amongst the gnomes, made her entrances with such a burst of cheer that the door always seemed too small for her energy.

"Finnian!" she said, arms out like she expected a stage's worth of applause. "I see you're busy feeding the brain."

"Best way to keep the fingers nimble," Finnian replied, standing to greet her. "What brings you in so early? I haven't even wound the window clocks yet."

Galhani glanced up at the wall—twelve clocks, twelve subtle arguments about what time it truly was in North Pointe—and grinned. "I have an experiment. I need a timer, but not like the one you made for Makota. Hers is... wonderful, but perhaps too robust. Mine needs a gentler touch." She had, as always, a pouch over one shoulder, and from it she drew a battered notebook and a tiny glass bottle filled with a swirl of blue and gold. She set both carefully on the counter, standing on tiptoe to do so.

Finnian eyed the bottle. "Delicate work?"

"Delicate doesn't begin to describe it," Galhani said, voice lowering to a conspiratorial whisper. "Some blends must steep for exactly—exactly—one minute and fifty seconds. Any longer and the active property dissipates. Any shorter, and you're left with a rather expensive cup of leaf water."

Finnian's mind was already ticking. "You want a timer you can set to the second."

"Set, start, and stop, even with hands covered in tincture," Galhani said. "Oh, and it must be able to run at least six intervals at once."

"Six," Finnian repeated, raising an eyebrow. He glanced down at the sausage sandwich, already mourning its disappearance, then gestured to the far end of the workbench. "Which is what Makota's has."

"Yes! It works beautifully," Galhani admitted, "but I need greater accuracy, and perhaps a more musical chime. My clients—" and here she shot him a look both sly and shy "—they appreciate a bit of ceremony."

Finnian nodded, the design already percolating in the back of his mind. "Fine increments, elegant signal, resistant to oil and powder. I see it." He reached into a drawer and fished out a stub of pencil and a square of waxed paper. "What are you steeping these days?"

Galhani's eyes sparkled. "You'll see, if this works. There's a contest at the lakeshore next moon. First prize is a set of silver spoons—antique, from the Mistral dynasty."

"Motivation enough for anyone," Finnian said. He started sketching, the graphite tip flying over the wax paper. "How small do you want the increments?"

"Down to the second, if possible. For most, I'll use minute-marks, but in the best experiments…" She trailed off, obviously relishing the thought.

"Second-precision, six channels, resistant to spills and shocks." Finnian grinned, already seeing the contraption in his mind. "I can make it."

Galhani hopped onto the stool on the customer side of the workbench. "I'll wait."

Finnian's ears warmed. "It might take a little—"

"I'll wait," she repeated, settling in with a contented sigh. "The clocks are very friendly company."

And so they were. As Finnian measured and marked out the brass for the new gearing, the clocks kept a polite, layered chorus behind him—never quite in unison, but always harmonizing in that way only a shopful of well-tuned clocks could. He worked without distraction, hands moving with the surety of long practice, but his thoughts were running far ahead. Every time Galhani made a noise—a gasp of delight at the test ring of a bell, a small hum of interest when he clicked a lever into place—he absorbed the feedback, recalibrated, and improved the design a notch or two.

He lost track of time, as always happened with a promising project. He was dimly aware of Galhani's presence—the faint clink of her necklace against the counter, the scritch of her pencil as she annotated her notebook—but it was background, like the clocks or the soft light pooling over the workbench. He didn't even notice the morning had turned to late afternoon until a chime he hadn't set up himself sounded from the far wall.

Finnian blinked, and there it was: the Precision Tincture Timer, not even a full day from concept to completion. He was almost shocked by how tidy it looked—six lacquered brass levers, each with a tiny jeweled indicator, a clockface beneath each row marked in bold black ink, and a bell assembly so finely tuned it sang rather than rang. He polished the casing, wiped away the last fingerprint, and turned it toward Galhani with a little flourish.

"Shall we test it?" he asked.

Galhani was off the stool and at his side before the question finished leaving his mouth. "Show me."

He set each timer: the first for one minute, the next for a minute thirty, and so on, all the way up to six full minutes. He wound the main spring, then dropped all six levers in sequence. The effect was oddly hypnotic—each jeweled indicator began its circuit, gliding over the scale with exacting, almost balletic grace. The first timer hit its mark, and the bell chimed—a soft, crystalline note, bright but not harsh. The second followed, and then the third, each perfectly timed.

Galhani's delight was uncontainable. "That's it! That's the magic. Finnian, you've made it perfect."

He tried for modesty, but pride crept through his smile. "Glad to be of service."

Galhani gathered the timer into her arms—she had to hug it, just to hold all the joy at once—and set it carefully back into her pouch. "You've made my whole sennight," she said, and meant it. "I'll be the envy of every herbalist on the lakefront."

"Just send them my way," Finnian replied. "And bring me a cup of the winning brew, if you win."

She bobbed in agreement, then skipped out the door, trailing gratitude and the faintest hint of lemon balm behind her.

Finnian watched the door swing shut, then looked at the empty workbench and the dozen ticking clocks on the wall. His sandwich was gone, but his appetite for invention had only grown.

There would always be more timers to build. More moments to capture. More stories, waiting to chime.

After Galhani left, the shop felt curiously expectant, like a stage that had just seen its warm-up act and was awaiting the main event. Finnian eyed his now-empty workbench, the residue of lemon balm and the ghost of a sausage breakfast hanging in the air. His gaze drifted to the wall of clocks. One ticked a hair fast, the next a hair slow, but in their sum total, the room felt as perfectly timed as a heartbeat. It gave him an idea—one that wouldn't stop pricking at his mind.

What if, he thought, these timers weren't just an oddity, but the mainstay? Galhani's delight had been so real, and Makota's version was already on its second generation in the bakery. Finnian was suddenly seized by the image of every household in town with a timer on its mantle, every merchant with a custom job behind the counter. It could be... business.

He wiped down the workbench, found a sharp pencil, and started sketching. This time, the plan was for manufacturability: three levers instead of six, streamlined casing, stamped metal instead of hand-cut brass, a simple bell that still rang with authority. The ideas unspooled in neat, clockwork order. Within a quarter-hour, he'd filled a whole sheaf of graph paper with layouts and assembly diagrams.

He barely noticed the sun lowering behind the shop's leaded windows, or the way his own hunger returned, edging in on the corners of his focus. He was in the thick of optimizing the geartrain for the Multi-Timer II—perhaps a bit ahead of himself, considering he'd only just made the Mark I that morning—when a new sound cut through the ordinary background tick and tock.

It was a deep, arrhythmic thud, like a blacksmith's hammer slamming against a bell tuned for disaster. Finnian's head jerked up. The sound repeated, a mechanical thump overlaid with a shrill, whining tick that didn't match any clock in the shop. He froze, listening.

Tick-thud. Tick-thud. Tick-tick-thud.

It was coming from the back. Specifically, from the tiny washroom off his rear workshop, where he kept the only invention he truly regretted: the Self-Winding Toilet Roll Dispenser.

The device was a study in overindulgence, a glittering mass of silvered gears, chrome levers, and unnecessary complication that took up nearly half the wall beside the water closet. It was the sort of thing a clockmaker might invent in a fit of drunken self-loathing and then keep out of pride, despite the fact that it had never dispensed a single roll without a catastrophic jam. Finnian had left it alone for weeks, but now, as the thudding grew more insistent, he steeled himself for the worst.

He rushed down the narrow corridor, braced for the usual disaster —a burst spring, a mangled roll, perhaps a gentle dusting of confetti as the case exploded—but when he opened the door, the sight stopped him cold.

The dispenser was vibrating so violently it had migrated a good two inches along the stone wall. The air around it was shimmering, distorted, and there was a faint, salty tang—sea spray?—on the air. Finnian stared, mesmerized, as the roll of tissue spun faster and faster, the silver cage flexing under the strain.

A sound like a zipper ripped through the room, and just to the left of the dispenser, the wall bulged outward. The paint blistered, the plaster cracked, and then, with a sullen pop, a perfect oval portal irised into being, hanging midair with the casual indifference of a soap bubble. The rim shimmered between blue and green, flecked with gold, and beyond it was nothing but darkness.

Finnian's first, last, and only thought was: I am not being paid enough for this.

Before he could decide whether to run or call for help, the darkness on the other side of the portal rippled. Something—someone—tumbled through, knees and elbows first, and landed on the washroom floor with a solid, undramatic thud.

Finnian leapt back, grabbing a towel as his only possible weapon.

The figure lay still for a heartbeat, then sat up with the resigned, bone-deep weariness of a man who had, quite literally, come a very long way. He was human, broadly built, dressed in plain but expensive travel clothes. He looked around the room with a dazed sort of composure, as if popping through magical portals was an everyday nuisance. His hair was perfectly in place. His face was clean. The only strange thing was the small, battered leather satchel clutched in his left hand.

Finnian recognized him immediately. "Alred?"

The man blinked. "Yes?" he said, voice a perfect octave of calm. "Is this… is this the washroom?"

Finnian stammered, "It's my washroom. In my shop."

"Perfect," said Alred, and dusted off his knees. He looked around, eyes settling on the still-shuddering Toilet Roll Dispenser. "What is that thing?"

Finnian answered before thinking. "A failed experiment."

Alred nodded. "That would explain the vibration. I was aiming for a lakeshore, but this is fine."

The portal behind him began to shrink, the colors swirling inward.

Alred took this in stride. "Excuse me," he said, and stood with smooth, practiced grace. The satchel in his hand seemed to hum, and for a moment, Finnian saw a faint blue light leaking from the seam.

"Can I... help you?" Finnian said, towel at the ready.

Alred smiled, but it was a very small smile, the kind you might reserve for a beloved pet who'd just soiled your favorite rug. "No need," he said. "Just passing through." He regarded the closing portal and added, "A convenient, if unexpected, arrival. If anyone asks, I was never here."

The oval winked shut, leaving the room heavy with the smell of salt and pine needles and the faintest ozone tang. The dispenser, deprived of whatever residual magic had powered it, gave one last, heroic spasm, then exploded in a hail of silver gears and a soggy wad of half-dispensed tissue. The carnage was, even by Finnian's standards, impressive.

Alred regarded the mess, nodded once, and then quietly let himself out of the washroom, leaving a trail of clean footprints all the way to the shop's front door.

Finnian stood in silence for a full minute. He felt the strange, echoing sense of fate at work, the same prickle that always accompanied an especially meaningful clock repair or the rare, vivid vision. He half expected the walls to start ticking.

But nothing else happened. The air cleared. The mess remained.

He took a deep breath, put the towel away, and set about collecting the fragments of his failed experiment. He made a mental note to never again build a device with more than three independent mainsprings. Also, to stock up on mops.

There were questions—many, many questions—but for now, there was only the practical satisfaction of setting things right, and the knowledge that North Pointe was, and would always be, a little stranger than it appeared.

It took longer to clean the mess in the back room than Finnian would have liked. The shrapnel from the Self-Winding Toilet Roll Dispenser had embedded itself in a variety of unlikely surfaces, including a soap dish, a wall calendar, and (somehow) the ceiling. He methodically swept up every spring, gear, and sliver, and then, once the place looked more or less like a normal water closet, washed his hands three times just to be certain.

But it was the aftertaste of the event—the shivering, uncanny sense of having hosted something cosmic—that stuck with him. Finnian stood for a while, listening to the shop's ambient chorus, searching for any hint that another portal was forming. The clocks ticked in their normal, slightly smug counterpoint. Nothing seemed out of line.

He returned to the main room, but the nerves remained. He found himself compelled to touch every clock, every invention, every half-completed device on the shelves. It was more than a craftsman's check: it was the anxious patdown of a man who suspected Fate had left a fingerprint on his shop.

He started with the front counter—his pride and joy, the "Clockmaker's Array," a triptych of timepieces that kept local, lake, and town-square hours in perfect relation. He ran his hands across the lacquered cases, feeling for heat, vibration, any telltale sign of possession. Nothing.

Next came the "Automated Bellringer," a wall-mounted contraption that had once, briefly, synchronized with the actual town bell tower (until Jen had asked him to "cease and desist, for the love of reason, before someone dies of anticipation"). He listened for any off-kilter clank, but the bell rang only at the appointed hour, obedient as a schoolchild.

He moved to his personal favorites: the "Self-Tending Cactus Clock" (which regulated watering schedules, at least until it overwatered its prototype to death), the "Tea Chime" (which steeped and poured at precise marks, and had been responsible for at least three minor scaldings), and, tucked behind a battered ledger, the "Midnight Porridge Timer"—never deployed, because Finnian had never once in his life remembered to put oats in a pot before sleep.

He checked the lot, one by one, and then checked again. Each device met his gaze with the calm, familiar certainty of a pet that had done nothing wrong, and was vaguely offended by the implication. He laid his palm on each, willing them to betray some evidence of yesterday's or today's madness. But if Fate was lurking, it was content for the moment to stay hidden.

Still, Finnian couldn't shake the sense of being watched. It wasn't the sinister, creeping kind of watchfulness—it was more like the way a parent might observe a child, curious to see which way the next experiment might go. The sensation was strongest when he lingered at the Grandfather Clock in the corner, the one that had sparked this week of strangeness. Its face gleamed, its pendulum swung in a sure, steady rhythm, but behind the glass, Finnian thought he caught a glint of indigo, just at the very edge of perception.

He shut the case, locked it, and resolved to leave it alone until Leota's next visit.

By the time Finnian finished his full diagnostic, the sky was a deep, twilit blue. He felt spent but not entirely wrung out—a sort of nervous, forward-leaning anticipation lingered in his hands and his head. There was nothing for it but to let the clocks do their job, and to see what tomorrow would bring.

He straightened his vest, took a last look around, and closed up shop. The familiar walk to the Broken Claw felt more comforting than usual, the pub's lights a promise of warmth and sturdy food. He paused just once, at the shop's doorstep, to listen for any last tick or chime that might hint at further mischief. The world held its breath, then exhaled. All was as it should be, at least for now.

Finnian let himself savor the moment. He'd done all he could; the rest would have to sort itself out in the morning.

With a final glance back at the glowing clocks in his window, Finnian strode into the evening, eager for bread, for conversation, and for the next tick of destiny.

nine
. . .

LATE THE NEXT MORNING, Finnian found himself in a state that could only be described as "one tick off true," though he doubted anyone else would have noticed. The world had righted itself, more or less. The clocks kept their tune, his hands were steady, and the shop bell, when it rang, still sounded the clean silver note he'd tuned it to years before. But a memory clung behind his left ear: the sensation of possibility barely contained, the echo of yesterday's portal, and the uncanny certainty that, somewhere, a pair of eyes waited for his next move.

The morning's work was honest and unremarkable. He set about repairing a spring-wound timer for the seamstress across the green, then reassembled a second-hand carriage clock that, for some reason, only kept time if wound upside-down. He'd just finished re-aligning the escapement when the bell tinkled—a gentle tap, as if the caller were reluctant to disturb even the dust motes.

Leota Harbinger eased inside, all black dress and blacker humor, with the air of someone who had already observed the room for ten minutes and only now deigned to enter. She swept a glance across the shelves, registered the absence of disaster, and, with a half-smile, said, "You appear intact."

"I'm afraid so," Finnian replied, and realized he meant it. He set down his tools. "Not a single ripple in the air all morning. Unless you count the coffee."

She closed the door and leaned against the frame. "Coffee can be magic, given the right hands. May I?"

He waved her to the counter. "There's some in the pot. Don't judge my brewing; I haven't dared upgrade the machine since the last incident."

Leota poured herself a small mug, black, and sipped with a care that made Finnian's own nerves jangle. She was not a morning person, he suspected, but neither was she a creature of the night; she existed in the ambiguous borderlands, always slightly out of step with the rest of the town's circadian rhythm.

She looked him over as if checking for cracks. "You've recovered. Or at least, you pretend well."

He chuckled. "You can only be shaken so many times before you start to rattle as a matter of course." He paused, then, more quietly: "Has anything like that ever happened to you?"

She didn't answer right away. Instead, she examined the seam at the edge of the counter, finding some satisfaction in its flawless join. "I've seen thresholds before," she said. "Most are more subtle, though. Yours was... ambitious. Messy."

"Is it dangerous?"

She shrugged. "Potentially. Most things are, if neglected. But nothing more than the usual risk for North Pointe." She set the mug down with a click. "I came to see if you'd had another episode."

Finnian shook his head, still uncertain. "No more portals. Just a faint feeling like... like the shop wants to do something else. Like it's expecting a visitor."

Leota's lips quirked. "The town's gifts don't operate on your schedule, Finnian. Sometimes they have their own sense of timing." She lapsed into thought for a beat, then said, "Did Jen speak with you?"

He nodded, remembering the evening at the pub. "She did. Her advice was more practical than I expected."

"Jen is rarely wrong," Leota said. "Even when she's convinced otherwise." She peered at Finnian. "You should listen to her. She's more sensitive to the town's, ah, rhythm than anyone gives her credit for."

A silence stretched between them, companionable but fraught. Leota broke it. "So. Did anything else unusual happen?"

Finnian hesitated, not sure how much to share. Then, with a helpless shrug, "There was a... visitor. Yesterday. Not through the front door."

Leota's gaze sharpened. "Go on."

He explained about the self-winding dispenser, the portal's appearance, and the abrupt, wholly unmagical exit of Alred—his longtime customer and the only man in town who could out-bake a fire, but not out-run a clock.

When he finished, Leota made a noise that might have been a laugh. "Of all the people to drop out of the ether, I should have guessed it would be Alred." She looked faintly pleased. "Did he say why he was there?"

"Just 'passing through,'" Finnian said. He hesitated, then added, "He seemed to expect it."

Leota tapped her mug. "He would. Alred has... connections, let's say. To the world's less-tidy corners. I suspect he was on his way somewhere much more interesting. He's been fascinated with the legends of lost Elven tribes."

Finnian, emboldened, asked, "Do you think the portals are getting more common?"

"I think the icosagon has noticed you," Leota said, direct and unsentimental. "And now it's tuning you in."

He frowned. "The icosagon. That's the magic that binds the town, right? The twenty shops, the—"

She cut him off with a nod. "That, and more. It's the pattern that makes North Pointe what it is. Everyone here fits a spoke. Sometimes, when a spoke is well-aligned, the wheel spins a little faster."

He mulled that over. "And when it isn't?"

She smiled, a flash of dark amusement. "Then you get haunted bakeries and time-eating clocks."

Finnian reached for his own mug, cradled it, and admitted, "I'm not sure I want to be the cause of anyone's destiny. Jen said it's about setting travelers on their paths. What if the path is a bad one?"

Leota's reply was unexpectedly gentle. "We don't get to decide which journeys matter. Only that they're possible. Most people never walk through a door, even when it's open. You gave Alred a way out, and he took it." She paused, then, more softly, "He'll be fine. His gift is landing on his feet."

Finnian exhaled. "That's a relief. I had this terrible image of him falling into a bottomless void."

Leota's eyes glinted. "If he did, he'd turn it into a brewery within a year."

The thought made Finnian laugh, the tension melting from his shoulders. "Is there anything I should do differently? With the shop? With the clock?"

"Don't over-wind it," Leota said, but her tone was kind. "And don't stop making things. The world needs both." She stood, shaking out the chill that always seemed to cling to her. "On that note: I have a commission."

He blinked. "For you?"

She nodded. "I want a clock, but one that doesn't keep the same time as everything else. I want it... off. Not randomly, but according to a different standard. Can you make such a thing?"

Finnian's brain immediately latched onto the challenge. "A time-keeper that runs at a variable interval?"

"Precisely." Leota's gaze was steady. "I want it to track the movements of the stars—not the sun, not the town bells. A sidereal clock, if you know the term."

Finnian, who did, was already mentally sketching gears and ratios. "That's possible. But it might need recalibration, depending on the season."

"Even better," Leota said, with an approving tilt of the head. "Can you have a prototype by next week?"

He made a show of checking the shop, then said, "With luck, yes. But I'll need to see your reference data."

She handed him a folded slip of paper, inked with neat columns of numbers and a hand-drawn chart. "It's for a spell. Some things require more precision than mortal time allows."

He studied the figures, then looked up with renewed curiosity. "What does it do?"

She smirked. "If it works, you'll know."

He could live with that. "And if it doesn't?"

She reached the door, paused, and said, "Then I'll owe you a pot of coffee." She let herself out, the bell jangling in her wake.

Finnian looked at the numbers again, already imagining the arrangement of gears and weights needed to make such a clock run true to a different cosmos. There was a joy in that—an order to the world that could be coaxed out of chaos, if only you set your mind to it.

He fetched his ledger, cleared the workbench, and started making a parts list. This would be his best commission yet, and for the first time in days, Finnian felt the tick of his own mind in perfect step with the world.

The hours drifted by, measured in plans and promises and the secret, silent hope that the next time the clock called out, he'd be ready to answer.

The shop was thick with the smell of solder and oil, both hands wrist-deep in the most promising geartrain he'd ever designed, when Finnian heard the customer enter. He kept his focus for three more ticks—just long enough to finish setting the last jewel in the prototype escapement—before brushing off his hands and standing to greet the new arrival.

The woman who waited at the counter looked entirely ordinary, in the particular way that only someone who'd spent decades refusing to be otherwise could manage. She wore a traveling cloak, the hem singed and re-mended three times over, and carried a canvas satchel stitched with the crest of one of the outlake universities. Her face was unremarkable save for the eyes: alert, sharp, and already scanning the shelves as though plotting the most efficient escape route.

"Good morning," Finnian said, and meant it. "How can I help?"

She answered in a voice just a half-shade deeper than expected. "You carry folding clocks, yes? With alarms? Preferably ones that will wake the dead."

Finnian grinned. "The dead, the hungover, and the occasionally comatose. We have several models." He waved her toward the workbench, where three portable timepieces awaited final inspection. "Any particular features you're after? Besides volume."

"Reliability," she said, with a click of her tongue. "I'm on a schedule, and I can't afford drift." She slid the satchel onto the counter and unbuttoned the clasp with the practiced flick of a fencer. "I'm headed east, to the old manse at Dawnditch, and I need to travel an exact number of hours each day, and sleep precisely that number at night. Otherwise the, ah, schedule slips." She looked up at him. "You know how it is."

He did. "I can adjust the strike to your preference. If you want something more portable, we have the pocket models, but the face is smaller." He lined them up on the counter, one by one: the first, a battered steel cube, function over form, with a bell that could double as an alarm for the entire block; the second, a lacquered wood with a velvet-lined case, the alarm sweet but not terribly insistent; and third, his own invention—a folding brass plate with a toothy row of bells that could be dialed to any volume from "distant memory" to "court summons."

The woman pounced on the first clock, tested the hinge, and ran her thumb over the pitted case. "Too heavy. I need to keep my luggage under twelve pounds. How about the last one?"

Finnian handed it over. "That one's a prototype, but the mechanism is solid. You can set the alarm with this wheel. The ring is quite sharp at full tilt, but I can tune it down."

She examined the mechanism, fingers moving with the quick certainty of someone who'd wound more than a few clocks in her life. "How much drift?"

"Half a minute a sennight, at worst. I'll guarantee it for a year, if you promise not to drop it into any swamps or volcanoes."

The woman smiled, barely. "No promises." She set the brass model on the bench and pressed the test lever. The bell array shrieked—sharp, clear, and so sudden that Finnian nearly flinched. "Perfect," she said, a note of pleasure in her tone. "Can you engrave the dial? I want the hours marked in blue, and a line at every three-hour interval."

He nodded. "Give me a quarter-hour and it's yours."

She paid in coin, with a tip so generous it could only be guilt money. Then she leaned back, waiting, eyes following every move as Finnian worked at his bench. He drew the dial, inlaid the marks, even painted the numbers with a fine brush. Every few minutes, the customer interjected a suggestion or an observation. "The hands are a little thin, don't you think?" or "That case looks like it could use a stiffer spring." She was not trying to be helpful, but neither was she mocking. It was the dialogue of equals, or at least of two people who recognized in each other a tendency to tinker.

It was in the middle of aligning the main gear that Finnian felt the air in the shop change. He'd gotten sensitive to it—first a slow thickening, like humidity before a summer storm, and then a pinprick tension, as though all the clocks had leaned in and held their breath. It was the same feeling that had haunted him since yesterday, the same whisper of a possibility waiting to ignite.

He glanced at the far corner of the shop. The Grandfather Clock stood, silent as ever. Its face reflected nothing but the lamps behind the counter. But Finnian's scalp prickled.

He tried to focus on the engraving. His hand shook—not much, but enough to make the brush miss the mark. The customer watched him with an expression of polite curiosity.

"Is something wrong with the air in here?" she asked. "Feels like a thunderstorm."

Finnian didn't trust himself to answer. He kept his head down, but the air grew thicker, electric. He could almost hear a ticking that wasn't from any clock he'd made.

The woman followed his gaze to the Grandfather Clock. "That one for sale?" she asked, casually.

Finnian found his voice. "Not at the moment. It's a bit... sensitive."

She tilted her head, squinting as if she could see something in the dark between the glass and the wood. "Reminds me of the one my uncle had, out on the edge of Lake Wain. Swallowed a rat once—never worked right after that." She gave Finnian a sidelong look. "This one ever swallow anything?"

He frowned.

The tension mounted, a pressure in the bones. Finnian felt the hairs on his arm stand up. He set down the brush, wiped his hands, and prepared to offer the finished clock. But the customer was no longer watching him—her eyes were glued to the Grandfather Clock, which, in the span of a single heartbeat, had begun to shimmer.

It was subtle at first, a distortion of the numbers on the face. Then the glass fogged over, and the brass numerals began to melt, just as they had before. The minute hand spun counterclockwise, faster and faster, until the air behind the glass darkened and parted—a perfect oval, rimmed in indigo and gold.

The woman stood, unhurried, and approached the clock.

Finnian's mind raced. He remembered Jen's warning, and Leota's advice: don't interfere with the town's gifts, don't try to wrench the wheel against its own momentum. But he also remembered his own horror at the idea of sending someone through a portal unprepared. He took a breath, then another, and asked, softly, "Do you see it?"

The woman smiled, the first real smile she'd shown. "I do."

"Are you sure you want to—" Finnian began, but she raised a hand.

"I've been waiting for this," she said. She looked back, as if memorizing the shop's every detail. "Thank you for the clock, Finnian. You keep good time."

She stepped forward, pressed a palm to the shimmering glass, and was gone—vanished, as surely as if she'd never been.

The portal snapped closed with a soft, wet pop. The Grandfather Clock returned to itself, gleaming and inert, the hands pointing to the correct hour, the face as unblemished as ever.

The air in the shop relaxed. Finnian sagged, running both hands over his face.

He finished the engraving, boxed the clock, and placed it under the counter. Maybe, he thought, the woman would wake on the other side of wherever she'd gone, and her alarm would ring out, bold and beautiful, on a schedule the universe itself couldn't break.

For a long while after the woman's departure, Finnian simply stood behind the counter, hands braced on the wood, letting the soft babble of clocks fill the silence. The portal's afterimage shimmered in his mind, less a memory than a pressure behind his eyes—a twinge, a presence, a suggestion that the shop had just eaten something and was now quietly digesting it.

He considered seeking out Leota, or even Jen, to report what had happened. But the urge faded, replaced by something heavier, and more certain: this was simply how it would be. North Pointe's magic didn't run on warning bells or town meetings. Its currents were deep, slow, and, above all, inevitable.

The thought should have been a comfort. Instead, Finnian felt the unease settle in his chest, as if he'd left a spring uncoiled or a lever not quite flush. He tried to name the feeling, but came up short.

So he did what he always did. He worked.

He pulled the fresh batch of brass from the shelf, unrolled the blueprints for the Variable-Timing Timekeeper, and set about translating vision into matter. The design wasn't as simple as he'd first imagined; every time he solved for one wobble, a new resonance appeared elsewhere. The sidereal drive needed a weightless escapement, but the ratios warped with the day's warmth and humidity. The star-gazer cam he'd designed as a joke turned out to be the only way to keep the pendulum's arc consistent from night to night.

For the next three hours, Finnian drifted. He made note of every misstep, logged every scrap of inspiration, and let the motion of his hands outpace the static in his mind. The bench, which that morning had seemed too neat, was now a riot of files, springs, and shavings. The clocks on the wall kept their rhythm, ticking off seconds in gentle rebuke.

He tested and tuned. He measured, then measured again. He ruined a tiny screw with too much torque, cursed softly, and cut a better one from scratch. Each pass smoothed the mechanism; each tick of progress—however slight—brought him a little closer to true.

As dusk slid through the shop's front window, Finnian looked up, surprised to find his eyes blurry and his hands aching. He stared at the work: a half-complete clock, its guts arrayed on the bench like a dissection, and next to it, a notebook full of furious handwriting and impossible ratios.

He sat back, wiped his brow, and for the first time in hours, let himself listen to the world.

The room was quiet. The unease remained, but it was no longer an enemy—it was, instead, a familiar companion, a tick to be tuned or a drift to be offset. Finnian closed the notebook, covered the clock's exposed works with a cloth, and moved to the window. The green was empty. The sky, a deep blue, promised a clear, cold night.

He debated heading for the inn, for company and supper. But the shop felt right, now, and he didn't want to break the spell. Instead, he made tea, set a crust of bread on the sideboard, and read through Leota's note again, this time seeing not a challenge but a conversation —a dialogue, in gears and stars, with the world's deeper workings.

The hours drifted. Finnian watched the shadows move across the clock faces. He made a few more notes, then, at last, let himself rest.

He slept that night with the windows cracked, letting in the hush of the town and the slow, patient ticking of his own invention. Somewhere in the dark, the Grandfather Clock kept its secrets. But Finnian dreamed only of clocks, and of the gentle, endless ways a man might keep time for a world that refused to stand still.

ten
...

THE NEXT DAY dawned with a clarity that Finnian privately suspected he didn't deserve, the air cold and bright and clinging to the glass in trembling beads. The clocks had started up their usual, comforting riot, and the main street outside was already threaded with the business of morning—Makota's kits making deliveries, Cole and Warren shifting crates, and the occasional distant laughter from the lakeshore where the geese had settled in for the season. Finnian, never one to waste a productive mood, started the kettle as soon as his eyes were open. By the time he'd finished his first cup of coffee, he'd already refined the sidereal ratio for Leota's commission and sketched a compact, devilishly clever escapement to go with it.

What he hadn't done, at any point, was allow the uncertainty of the previous days to gnaw at him. If the clocks wanted to open gateways for travelers and the occasional errant soul, so be it. Finnian would keep building them. It was not his place to doubt the work. He left that sort of thinking to the witches and gods.

On the counter, neatly aligned along the oilcloth, waited the heart of the morning: the Variable-Timing Timekeeper. It was a gorgeous mess of parts and promise, all perfectly proportioned but still lacking the animating principle of a finished device. Finnian always started a build with the largest, most unwieldy components, lining them up at the leftmost edge of the workbench, and then tapering the sequence down to the smallest screws and jewels at the rightmost, like a gradient of mechanical possibility. He'd learned early that this prevented the accident of over-tightening a spring or losing a screw to the floor, though the ritual had become more comforting than necessary over the years.

He laid out the brass plates first, brushing off the tiniest motes of dust with a soft badger-hair brush. The plates gleamed in the sunlight, their bevelled edges catching and splitting the morning into golden shards. He set them down with the same reverence some men reserved for heirloom blades, then reached for the packet of jewelled pivots, each glinting red or blue depending on the angle. Next, the wheels: small, larger, then largest, teeth all counted and tested. The main spring, coiled like a sleeping serpent, sat in a tiny nest of felt, ready to snap the moment its time arrived.

Finnian, like most men of a certain age, talked to himself. He offered a running commentary on every step, addressing the parts as though they were unruly children with great, latent promise. "Not today, you don't," he told a capricious screw, chasing it with the magnet-tipped driver. "Steady, now. No wobble. That's it."

He started by mounting the main bridge, making sure the posts lined up with the pre-drilled sockets. The tactile feel of the driver in his fingers was as familiar as the shape of his own hand, the slight resistance of the screw biting into brass a quiet affirmation that the world was still intelligible and could, in fact, be managed. He dropped the center wheel into place, gave it a tentative spin, and watched the shadow it threw onto the bench. It was a good omen; the wheel ran true.

He built up from there: escape wheel, idler, the all-important starcam for tracking sidereal drift, each dropped in with a delicate, almost parental care. With each new addition, the mechanism grew more plausible, more inevitable. Finnian paused every few steps to check the clearances, holding the assembly up to the lamp and peering through it as though reading a secret text written in the gaps between the gears. Each time, he found a minor flaw—one jewel slightly proud, a trace of burr on the cam, a spindle that didn't quite seat flush—and addressed it with the patience of a gardener plucking out weeds by hand.

It was slow, and it was beautiful. The hours ran past unnoticed.

At the two-hour mark, Finnian realized his stomach was growling, but he worked through it. At four, he felt the tingle in his fingers that meant he was overdue for a break, but he pressed on. The bench lamp had tracked halfway across the workspace by the time he was ready for the most delicate part: setting the double-spring governor that would allow Leota's clock to "wobble" in tune with the proper sidereal rhythm.

He sat back, wiped his brow, and found his hands trembling—not with fatigue, but with the anticipation that comes from being on the verge of completion. He checked the town clock through the window; noon was close, and the light was just starting to flatten, giving every shadow a blueish fringe.

Then, with a gentleness usually reserved for infant kittens or priceless eggs, Finnian placed the governor into its housing. The springs flexed but did not shift. He tightened the screw, then gave the winding stem a half-turn. Instantly, the mechanism came alive, wheels turning in a lazy, sidereal pulse: slow, then faster, then slow again, as the governor modulated the force. The escapement ticked with a tiny, syncopated rhythm that made Finnian's heart flutter in his chest.

He was so absorbed in this small miracle that the town bell caught him completely unprepared.

It was a monstrous, deep-throated bellow that set every timepiece in the shop to vibrating in sympathetic terror. A split-second later, the shop's own clocks joined in—a wild, tumbling chorus of bells and chimes and clacking hands, a dozen different models ringing their own version of the mark. The effect was a wave of noise so thick it drove thought clean out of Finnian's head.

He dropped the governor. The piece bounced, once, on the padded mat, and landed safely in a shallow tray, but the shock left Finnian breathless. For a second, he just sat there, staring at the array of clocks as they screamed out their presence. It was a glorious, terrible, and oddly uplifting sound.

When the last of the echoes had died, Finnian realized two things: the first was that the Variable-Timing Timekeeper had survived its trial run; the second was that he was, quite possibly, starving to death.

He reset the bench, made a last, careful adjustment to the timekeeper, and set it under a bell jar to keep it safe from dust and accidents. Then he dusted off his hands, straightened his vest, and grabbed his coat. The town's clock had shocked him into a new awareness, and suddenly he wanted nothing more than bread and cheese and a pint of whatever was on cask at the Broken Claw.

Finnian locked up the shop and let the bell ring twice as he stepped out—because sometimes, you had to acknowledge the world's insistence that you pay attention. The air outside was sharper than before, the light tinged with that peculiar clarity that only came when you'd spent too long in your own company.

He walked toward the pub, every step measured and precise. And, if his heart ticked a little off the mark, he told himself it was only the side effect of a very good morning's work.

The Broken Claw was in full afternoon song, the air rich with malt and roast and the slow, animal warmth of a stove gone too long untended. Finnian's entrance was lost in the shuffle: the barmaid, short and unyielding as ever, slapping down tankards on the sticky trestle; the traveling merchant and his tired-eyed clerk huddled over plates of cheese and sausage; even Dardrad, lurking at his usual end of the counter, seemed unusually preoccupied. What did not escape Finnian's notice was the undercurrent of anticipation that had settled in the room. Heads turned every time the door opened. The talk was bright and full of echoes.

He found an empty spot at the last communal table and waited. Within two ticks, Dalossalda—her hands floury, her demeanor the very soul of gentle exasperation—brought over a basket of hard rolls and a bowl of soup so dark it could only have been made from the smoked bones of a dozen animals.

"I hope you're eating light, Finnian," she said, setting the bowl with a clunk. "We're all out of the good stuff. Been a day of news."

He thanked her and tore off a chunk of bread, savoring the tang of rye. "What news?"

She eyed him for a beat, as if weighing the danger of letting him know. "Alred's back. Apparently walked out of the lake fog just after dawn, looking for all the world like a man who'd just finished his chores and not, as some would have it, gone missing for, what, two seasons? Three?"

Finnian paused, spoon in midair. "Oh."

"More than that," Dalossalda added. "He's..." She hesitated, groping for a word. "Different."

She left him to his soup and moved down the bar. Finnian watched her go, then scanned the room. He did not have to look far. At the corner table, flanked by Cole Coleson and his wife and a few regulars, sat Alred Grasswalker, wrapped in a plain wool cloak and, if anything, more solidly himself than Finnian remembered. The man radiated a sort of unbothered certainty, a stillness that seemed immune to even the rowdiest of the pub's atmosphere.

Cole was, as always, in the midst of an anecdote, something about a stubborn melon and the hazards of late-summer blight. The others laughed, but Alred only smiled, not so much polite as contented. When his turn came, he took the floor with a slow, unhurried ease.

"I spent some time out," Alred said. His voice was the same, broad and warm and never hurried. "The south road, mostly. Got as far as the old Elven stones. Sat there for a day or two, then circled back through the headland. Took it easy." He shrugged. "It was good."

No one pressed for details, though Finnian sensed a dozen silent questions rolling around the table. After the briefest pause, Alred continued, "Sometimes you just need to see how the season's changed, before you can trust your sense of time."

Cole raised his mug. "To Alred, and to knowing when it's time to be back!"

"To Alred," echoed the table, and then everyone, including Finnian, drank.

Dalossalda returned, her gaze sharp as a sewing needle. "You going to speak to him?" she murmured, half into Finnian's ear.

"I don't want to intrude," Finnian replied, quietly.

She snorted. "That's never stopped you before."

But she moved down the bench, leaving Finnian a gap. He took the cue, gathered his bowl, and, with the diffidence of someone testing a slippery floorboard, seated himself at the edge of Alred's gathering.

He waited for a break in the conversation, then said, "Alred. Good to have you back."

Alred turned, met Finnian's gaze, and offered a handshake—a heavy, deliberate motion that anchored both of them. "Thank you, Finnian. It's good to see you."

"Word is, you were looking for the Sea Elves?"

Alred smiled, but it was a thin smile, as if the answer was too large for the room. "Mmm. I went to the marshes, but never found a trace. Instead, I found…" He paused, then said, "Sometimes the search is the only part that matters. I needed to get the feel for the world again."

A ripple of assent ran down the table. Even Cole, who'd never met a digression he liked, seemed to understand.

Finnian, compelled by the echo of Alred's absence, pressed further. "Was it dangerous?"

Alred shook his head. "There's always danger, but not in the way people think. Sometimes you go out looking for a story and end up in a silence so deep it changes you." He flexed his fingers, as if testing their strength. "This was good. I arrived at the right answer."

"What's the answer?" Cole asked, his tone playful but his eyes sharp.

Alred considered, then said, "There's a pattern to it. Every season has a ratio, a balance. If you chase too hard, you miss the pulse." He let it hang, unadorned.

The table lapsed into a comfortable quiet. Even in the din of the pub, the silence felt intentional, a shared appreciation for the space left between words. Finnian found himself relaxing, just a little, the day's worries eroded by Alred's calm.

It was Dardrad, of all people, who broke the spell. The dwarf stood, tankard in hand, and addressed Alred directly: "You know what everyone wants to know, don't you?"

Alred grinned, the lines around his eyes deepening. "Of course. But knowing isn't always the same as telling."

Dardrad hoisted his mug. "You always were a stubborn one."

"I was a shopkeeper," Alred replied. "It's in the job description."

There was laughter, but Finnian caught the deeper note: relief, gratitude, and something like awe at Alred's self-possession. He wondered if he himself would ever return from a journey with such a clear, simple center.

The talk drifted after that, stories and jokes and the familiar rhythm of friends eating together. Finnian ate his soup, picked at the crust of bread, and watched Alred. There was a difference in him, a gentling, but also a clarity—a sense that, whatever he had gone looking for, he'd found it, and then brought it home to share in whatever way he could.

After the meal, Cole pressed Alred one last time. "You going to re-open the shop?"

Alred looked up, his gaze level and utterly free of evasion. "Maybe not for a while," he said. "There's work to do, but not in the way you think. I was always a bucket, Cole—useful when standing still. But lately I've found a reason to move." He looked out the window, watching the late sun drag itself across the roofs of North Pointe. "I'll be back when I know what to pour."

It was the kind of answer that only made sense if you didn't try to make sense of it. Cole nodded, a little abashed, and the rest of the table let the words settle in.

Finnian left the pub before the sun finished setting. The air was cold on his skin, but the warmth lingered in his chest, and in the steady, regular way his footsteps matched the beat of his own heart. He did not know if he'd ever be as peaceful as Alred Grasswalker, but he suspected it would take more than a lifetime of clocks to find out.

He liked that thought, and let it carry him home.

The light failed early that evening, a trick of lake effect and thickening mist. The green outside the Broken Claw was all puddles and reflected lamps, and Finnian, unable to muster the will for home and its cold hearth, found himself adrift in the low, amber half-light of the bar. The usual suspects had thinned out, replaced by a layer of travelers: wool-clad traders with their satchels, a family of four from the southern marches, and two or three sharp-faced women who never seemed to talk above a whisper. The bread was still fresh, the cheese sharper, and, for once, the noise level sat at a soothing hum instead of a howl.

It was only after his second mug and the arrival of a thick slice of berry tart that Finnian noticed the shift in the room's temperature. Not the literal heat—though the fire crackled hot and dry—but the quickening of attention, the subtle, animal awareness that comes when a person of consequence enters a space. He looked up and saw Elspeth Riverpine, Enchantress of the Mountain, framed in the doorway like the answer to a riddle no one realized they'd been asked. Her hair was loose, caught up in a cloud of static from the cold, her face marked by the deep laugh-lines of someone who never trusted a frown to do the work of a smile.

Elspeth swept in, trailed by a tangle of pine scent and the hush of expectation. She nodded to the bar, accepted a glass of the house's very worst wine, and then, after a slow perusal of the room, took a seat not far from Finnian. She set her elbows on the table, clasped her hands, and stared into her glass as though watching the history of the world play out in the dregs. No one greeted her, but everyone watched, and Finnian wondered if this was what it meant to have the mountain's favor: to command attention not with noise, but with the certainty that every whisper would be carried to the peaks and back.

He watched, as did everyone else, as Elspeth lifted the glass and downed half of it in a single swallow. She made a face, not displeased but rather amused, then set the glass down and caught Finnian's gaze. She smiled, quick and conspiratorial, and Finnian, not sure what the etiquette was for being noticed by a woman of legend, offered a polite nod.

The moment held until the door opened again, this time to admit Leota Harbinger, draped in her usual funereal black, her hair a darker shadow against the coming night. Leota paused just inside, searching for Elspeth, and then, spotting her, crossed the room with a directness that made all the other tables lean back ever so slightly.

They greeted each other with a clasp of hands, nothing dramatic, but the effect was that of two stones dropped into a pond—every surface rippled. Leota slid into the chair beside Elspeth and the two began talking, low and intense, their words lost to the general din but their expressions sharp and animated.

Finnian tried not to eavesdrop. He failed. There were only so many distractions available: the clock on the wall, which ran a full minute slow; the man at the next table, who was quietly taking apart his own pocket watch; and the third mug of ale, which, if anything, made Finnian's mind more attuned to the movements of Leota and Elspeth.

At first, there were just the two of them, heads together, voices pitched for secrecy. But now and then, one or the other would shoot a glance his way, and Finnian felt a distinct flutter in his gut that was half anticipation, half dread. It was not unlike the feeling he'd had in the moments before the Grandfather Clock had opened its first portal.

After a time, Leota rose, excused herself with a word to Elspeth, and glided over to Finnian's table. She sat without invitation, her fingers curled around the mug she'd brought from the bar. For a minute, she just looked at him, and Finnian tried to muster a defense. He failed at that, too.

"So," she said, "how's that big clock?"

He didn't bother asking which one. "It's alive," Finnian replied. "And more stable than I thought possible."

Leota nodded, as if this was the answer she expected. "Good. You'll want to keep it close. At least for the next week."

Finnian's stomach dropped. "Should I be worried?"

Leota considered. "No. But Elspeth is."

He followed her gaze. The mountain witch had her eyes fixed on them now, elbows still on the table but posture subtly more alert.

Leota lowered her voice. "You've opened gateways in the last few days, Finnian. That's... more than most. Elspeth says the boundary is thinning."

He braced himself. "Is that a problem?"

Leota's smile was quick and edged. "Only if you want it to be. Elspeth believes the god of the mountain is curious about you, and that's not always a blessing. But it's not a curse, either."

The room's noise seemed to fade. "What should I do?"

She shrugged. "If it happens again, let it happen. Don't fight it. And, for what it's worth—" here her gaze softened, almost fond "—

most people who walk through a door come back better for it. Or they don't come back, and we trust it's for the best."

Finnian digested this, then laughed, unable to help himself. "So my job is to do nothing?"

"For once, yes." Leota's amusement was genuine. "Or, if you prefer, make more clocks."

He felt the pressure in his chest ease. For the first time since the first portal opened, the idea of doing nothing seemed not just possible, but preferable.

Elspeth joined them, carrying her glass and a fresh pitcher of something that shimmered with iridescent blue at the rim. She poured, offered a toast—"To doors, and those brave enough to keep them open"—and drank. The three of them sat together, the evening spinning out in stories of things lost and found, of magic gone awry and mundane repairs that changed lives in ways no one expected.

At some point, Elspeth caught Finnian staring at the clock over the bar and said, "You know, the lake keeps its own time. Nothing in this world can hold it steady. That's why we don't try."

Finnian smiled, feeling a warm kinship for the first time in days. "Maybe that's the trick, then."

They lingered until closing, the last trio in the room. Dalossalda swept around them, collecting empties and humming a tune that had no rhythm at all. When the fire was down to coals and the windows all steamed, Leota rose, wrapped herself in her black shawl, and offered Finnian a hand up.

"Walk us home?" she said. He took the hand, and Elspeth looped her arm through his other. Together, they walked out into the wet, cold dark, the three of them a strange, perfect clockwork—each a separate wheel, each making the others go.

The green was empty, the world pared back to just them, their breath and footfalls pacing out the short trip to Leota's house. At her door, Leota stopped, turned, and fixed Finnian with that clever, knowing look. "If you dream of doors tonight, remember to open them."

He nodded. "I will."

Elspeth grinned. "And if you can't, let them open you."

He watched them vanish into their houses, then stood in the street for a while, looking up at the low, roiling clouds and the dark edge of the mountain.

He thought of all the clocks in his shop, and all the ways they marked time. Then he turned for home, feeling—for the first time in a very long time—not like a man out of step, but a man exactly where he was supposed to be.

eleven
...

THE NEXT MORNING, Finnian opened the shop early. He liked to give the gears a head start on the day, winding each by hand, feeling for any stutter in the mainspring or whisper of friction along the bearings. There was a sweet moment of almost-silence, the clocks not yet working themselves into their layered chorus, the only sounds the brush of his sleeve and the occasional hollow clink from the back shelf. The sun hadn't quite cleared the roofs along the lane, but the window glass was bright with its promise.

The bell over the door let out a three-chime salute—Finnian had tuned it that way, for fun—heralding his first customer well before the hour.

Bartram Lastmaker flowed in with his usual kinetic cheer, scarf trailing, arms already reaching as if to hug the room itself. "Springdale! I knew you'd beat the sun to your own threshold."

Finnian grinned, dusting his hands and greeting the cobbler with a half-bow. "You're nearly as early as the clocks."

Bartram laughed, round and loud, and let the door shut behind him with a faint click. "You know what they say: 'First up, best shod.'" He set a bulging cloth bag on the counter. "And, I hope, best supplied."

The two men exchanged the universal look of small-town tradesfolk: a quick, all-encompassing inventory of each other's mood and health, followed by a glance at the weather through the window, and then straight to business.

Bartram wasted no time. "I've a commission for you," he said, fingers drumming on the counter with excitement. "A clock! Not just any, though. I need one that chimes not only on the mark, but also at every half—" He paused, searching for the term, then snapped his fingers. "Half-candle mark. I mean, hour. Every half hour. Can you do it?"

Finnian pretended to think, but the answer was already springing up behind his eyes. "Certainly. Most table clocks do so, but it's an easy matter to adjust the hammer for the extra chime. Any particular reason for the urgency?"

Bartram tugged his earlobe, sheepish now. "My hands, Springdale. When I get into a run, they don't stop. I'll lose a whole morning to a single stubborn pair of boots if I let myself." He pulled a shoe from the bag and flexed it in his palms. "You see, the new lasts I'm using—they're too inviting. And then suddenly it's past midday and I've forgotten to eat, or to let the glue set, or, on more than one occasion, to tend to the next poor customer."

Finnian took the shoe, inspected the supple leather. "It's beautiful work," he admitted. "You've got a real eye for the join here." He pressed the toe gently, admiring the cobbler's precision.

Bartram glowed under the praise. "Thank you, friend. But I need something to interrupt me before I stitch myself into a grave."

Finnian nodded, understanding completely. "A clock that doesn't let you get lost in your own best intentions." He set the shoe aside and led Bartram to the wall of timepieces, shelves lined with every variety of clock: pendulums, twin-bells, spring-winds, a few specialty pieces with decorative touches Finnian had added for his own amusement.

Bartram went straight to the largest, an oak-cased regulator with an imposing face. "This one," he said, tapping the glass. "It looks like a judge."

Finnian's smile broadened. "It is. I tuned the chime to be authoritative but not punitive. May I show you?"

He set the clock to ten minutes before the hour and wound the bell mechanism. The minute hand crept forward, and at the mark, the clock gave out a deep, sonorous note—once for the hour, then, with a patient pause, another softer chime for the half. Finnian caught Bartram's look of delight and let the clock run on, demonstrating its precise, steady chime at the bottom of the hour.

"I'd set it in the workshop," Bartram said, already plotting the space in his mind. "Let it rule over the chaos."

Finnian reset the hands. "You want a simple chime, or something… friendlier?"

Bartram laughed. "Friendlier, but with backbone. I'll ignore it otherwise." He looked Finnian square in the eye, the way men do when confessing to greater faults. "The trouble with time, you see, is that if you don't mark it, it marks you."

"Then let's make the marking memorable," Finnian replied.

Bartram beamed, thrilled by the notion. "That's what I love about you, Springdale. Every solution is also an improvement."

Finnian made a quick mental inventory of the springs and hammers he'd need to swap out. "Give me two days to adjust the mechanism. I'll even carve your name on the inner plate, so if you ever forget yourself completely, the clock can remind you who you are."

Bartram's laughter boomed again, and he thumped Finnian's shoulder in gratitude. "I'll bring bread from Makota's as payment," he said. "And a story or three."

"Bring both," Finnian said, "and I'll make sure the clock never lets you lose a moment."

Bartram lingered a moment, running his hands over the shop's shelves, pausing to inspect a particularly elegant pocket watch. "You ever think of making one for yourself?" he asked. "A clock that interrupts your own labor?"

Finnian considered. "I prefer the quiet, but sometimes I think a chime every now and then would do me good."

Bartram nodded, then, more softly: "Don't let the hours slip, friend."

He left in a swirl of coat and good feeling, the bell over the door singing its three-note refrain after him.

Alone again, Finnian took the regulator off the wall, laid it carefully on his bench, and opened the back. He felt the satisfaction of solving a puzzle and the comfort of providing a tangible kindness. As he inspected the hammer and measured the spacing for the extra chime, he imagined Bartram's workshop filling with the steady, gentle reminders: eat, breathe, pause. Live.

There were harder jobs, Finnian knew. There were clocks meant to change the world, or at least to chart the strange workings of its undercurrents. But this one, he thought, was the most honest kind—an invention meant to keep the very best of a person from slipping away.

He oiled the gears, reassembled the movement, and made a note to tune the chime to a particular warmth—a sound to pull a craftsman gently out of his work, rather than jolt him out of it. He smiled to himself, already anticipating Bartram's next story, and the one after that.

By the time the sun finished its slow crawl past the rooftops, Finnian had the new chime installed, the clock ticking with pleasing certainty, and the faintest aroma of fresh bread already drifting up from the bakery down the lane.

He let the shop fill with the sound, and then he wound every clock again, just because he could. He was still admiring the measured clamor of his newly tuned clocks when the bell sang again, this time with a sharper, more insistent note—a clear sign that someone had entered with a purpose.

Wilem Cartwright didn't so much walk as stride, his steps quick and loud on the wooden floor. He wore the apron and heavy boots of a man for whom accidents were a daily currency, and there was a permanent line of sawdust at the hem of his trousers. Wilem's hair was peppered with silver, his hands nicked and patched with old scars, but his eyes were as bright and cunning as a magpie's.

He wasted little time with pleasantries. "Springdale," he called, by way of greeting, "need your help with something."

Finnian recognized the tone; this was not a shopping visit, but a puzzle to solve.

He set aside his tools and gave the cartwright his full attention. "You want a clock for your workshop, or for the house?"

"Neither," Wilem said, grinning. "Something different. You ever made a timer for speed?"

Finnian blinked. "You mean a stopwatch?"

Wilem nodded, hands already miming the shape of a wheel in the air. "Got a job—two jobs, really. First, I want to know how fast my carts can run. Second, if I build a better one, I want proof." He set his hands down on the counter, flat. "I've been timing with a candle, but it's not precise enough. Soot blows out, or the draft messes with the burn."

Finnian's mind started to race. "You want to measure elapsed time. Not the hour, but the span of a race, or a run from here to the lakeshore."

"Exactly!" Wilem's voice was eager now, like a child's. "I've got Cole's oldest pushing the carts, but I swear, half the time he's sandbagging just to see if I'll notice."

Finnian laughed. "Let me see." He fetched a small, battered timer from the shelf—a holdover from his first experiments, a thing meant for tea but equally at home in a workshop. "This will count out a minute and ring a bell. But if you want more than that, I'll have to build you something special."

Wilem inspected the timer, squinting at the dial. "Needs to start on the instant. None of that slow wind-up. Maybe a lever. And if you can, make it so I can read it while I run alongside the cart. My eyes aren't what they used to be."

Finnian nodded, already imagining the improvements. "What if I mounted it to the cart? Or, better—what if I built a ratchet that would let you track the wheel's turns, then translate that into distance covered? You could have a second mechanism, triggered by a lever, to start and stop the clock on a coin."

Wilem's face lit up. "Now you're talking. Like one of those distance clocks on the big ships. The more the wheel turns, the more it ticks."

Finnian grabbed a pencil and sketched on a scrap of paper. "Here—see this? If I fix a small arm to the wheel, every time it spins, it nudges this lever. The lever advances a gear, which moves the hand on a dial. At the same time, a spring-driven mechanism keeps a separate hand moving to count the time. You'd get both measures at once: distance and time."

Wilem watched the lines unfold, jaw slightly open. "You could even use it for racing. Line two carts up, see who wins by more than just a nose."

"Or," Finnian added, "tune the wheel so precisely that you know how much drag the new design has over the old. Even the smallest change in weight or axle will show up."

Wilem let out a low whistle. "This is going to be better than I hoped." He jabbed a thumb at the drawing. "Can you make it by week's end? I'll pay double." He grinned. "Double Highelk steaks from Dardrad's, that is."

Finnian waved him off. "Let me tinker a bit first. I'll have a prototype by tomorrow evening, and if it works, I'll build the final one before the moon turns."

Wilem grunted, but it was the sound of a man who trusted the craftsman before him. "You're a genius, Springdale. If this works, I'll tell every wagoner from here to the capital."

"Just bring me the test cart, and I'll mount it myself," Finnian said, already lost in the planning.

Wilem nodded, then, after a moment, added: "Say, do you ever sleep? You always seem to be working when I pass by."

Finnian chuckled. "Sleep is for those with fewer gears turning in their heads."

Wilem barked a laugh, then glanced at the wall clock. "Well, I won't keep you. I know a man in the grip of inspiration when I see one."

He clapped Finnian on the shoulder, hard enough to jar the shelves, and left with the same decisive stride that brought him in.

As the bell over the door died down, Finnian rolled up his sleeves, spread out the sketches, and began the design in earnest. There was nothing like the challenge of a new mechanism, nothing so satisfying as the promise of a device that had never existed before. He lost track of the hours, tracing gear trains, plotting the interplay of levers and escapements, and making lists of every brass rod and jewel bearing he'd need to make it all work.

At dusk, when he finally looked up, the shop was a mess of diagrams and prototype parts, the air heavy with the scent of metal filings and the tang of oil. Finnian looked at what he'd drawn, and for a moment, let himself bask in the simple delight of invention.

Not for the first time, he wondered if this was what the god in the mountain had intended for him—not the careful keeping of time, but the bold, reckless joy of making it work in new ways.

He stashed the sketches in the front drawer, wiped his hands, and stepped outside for a breath of evening air, already hungry for the next challenge.

From the shop's front stoop, Finnian could see nearly the whole length of the green. The sky was indigo now, and the candles under the bakery's sign glowed warm and inviting against the deepening cold. Finnian, content from a day's honest labor, watched the slow migration of townsfolk along the lane, and then he saw something odd enough to catch his eye: at the rear entrance to the town's mysterious restaurant, Alred Grasswalker and Llewel Magcaryn stood, heads close in quiet conversation.

It was not a scene of drama—just two men, one broad and earthbound, the other all poise and mountain air, their words so private they barely broke the hush of twilight. Finnian watched as Llewel pressed a hand to Alred's forearm, a gesture more of benediction than farewell, then nodded with grave formality and stepped back, closing the door to the restaurant behind him. For a long moment, Alred remained, gazing at the closed door, fingers idly tracing the seam of the canvas bag at his side.

Curiosity pricked, Finnian made his way across the green. Alred was already turning toward the path that wound around the lake, his back set in the determined line of a man about to walk until he ran out of world.

"Alred," Finnian called, more loudly than he intended.

The former dry-goods merchant paused and turned, the familiar slow smile spreading across his face. "Evening, Finnian. You're working late, or is this your version of a holiday?"

Finnian smiled back, but didn't waste time. "I saw you with Llewel," he said, "and thought you'd left the town behind for good."

Alred shrugged, the gesture as easy as breathing. "I almost did. But the mountain never really lets you go, does it?"

Finnian didn't know if he agreed, but he nodded just the same. "If you're leaving again, I'd like to know why."

Alred regarded him with a sudden, unusual seriousness. "I owe you an explanation. Or at least a story. You've always had a knack for stories, Finnian, even if you're too modest to say."

He set the bag down and took a seat on the low stone wall by the path. Finnian followed suit. The air was thick with pine smoke from the nearer hearths, and in the distance the lake was a dull, black mirror, collecting starlight by the handful.

"You ever hear of the Memory Keepers?" Alred asked.

Finnian shook his head. "Not by that name. We had archivists in the city, but—"

Alred grinned. "Not the same. The Elves—Llewel's kind, specifically—once kept all the old stories, the rules, the histories. It was a sacred job. You could say they kept time, in their own way." He looked down at his hands. "But over the centuries, memory got muddled. Truths lost, fables mistaken for fact. The Keepers faded away, one by one."

Finnian pictured Llewel, all deliberate movement and subtlety, and felt the truth of it. "But he's here now."

"He is," Alred said. "And he's the best I've seen. He makes order out of chaos—just by being himself, I think."

Finnian considered this. "I thought you were after the Sea Elves. Some old answer, or—"

Alred shook his head. "I was. But the more I searched, the more I realized I was just running from my own story." He offered a thin smile. "Llewel showed me there's no sense in chasing down every lost thing. Sometimes you have to start from where you are."

They sat in silence, watching the faint wind chase leaves across the green.

Finnian ventured, "Does this mean you're staying, after all?"

Alred picked up the bag, but didn't stand. "No. I think I'll wander a bit. But not to find lost elves, or to chase after rumors. I just want to see what else is out there." He looked Finnian in the eye, more direct than usual. "You ever feel like the clocks are just a way to pretend time is simple?"

Finnian laughed. "It's never simple. But it helps to keep it regular."

"Maybe so," Alred said, then reached into his bag. He pulled out a small stone, round as an egg and polished to a glassy smoothness by years in a river. He held it up. "This is for you."

Finnian took the stone, surprised by its weight. "What is it?"

"A keepsake," Alred said. "To remind you that time isn't always straight lines and tidy ticks. Sometimes it's a current, sometimes a circle, sometimes a loop you run until you find your own start."

Finnian turned the stone in his hand. It was, he supposed, unremarkable—just a smoothed, slightly blue pebble. But the more he looked, the more he saw the subtle bands of color, the places where the river had carved its own rules.

"I don't know what to do with it," Finnian confessed.

"Just hold onto it," Alred said. "If you ever figure it out, you'll know."

They sat a while longer, neither in a hurry to break the spell. At last, Alred shouldered his bag and rose, dusting his trousers. "I should go, before the cold sets in. But Finnian?"

"Mm?"

"Don't let the clocks run you. You're better than that."

Finnian smiled, warmed more by the words than by the brisk evening air. "You take care of yourself, Alred. And if you ever want to tell a story, you know where to find me."

Alred grinned, then turned for the lakeshore, his silhouette shrinking into the twilight.

Finnian sat with the stone for a while, turning it over and over, searching for a meaning that might never be there. At length, he stood and walked back to the shop, letting the weight of the stone anchor his thoughts as much as his pocket.

Inside, with the familiar ticking around him, Finnian set the stone on his workbench. It didn't belong to any clock, didn't fit any pattern, but he liked it all the more for that.

He looked around at the hundreds of clocks, each marking time in its own way, and for the first time, wondered if he might someday invent one that ran not in lines, but in loops and spirals, or even in the erratic, beautiful chaos of memory.

He fell asleep that night with the stone in his hand, dreaming not of seconds and marks, but of currents and eddies, of time worn soft and shapeless by the river's patient will.

Finnian woke early, the river stone still clutched in his hand. The clocks of his shop—every one of them—had kept perfect time through the night, yet he felt out of sync, a quarter-mark slow to rise and a full candle behind in spirit. His dreams had been a patchwork of old memories, some real, some invented: afternoons spent by the city canals, arguments with his father about the meaning of tradition, moments of fierce, irrational laughter with friends whose names he'd nearly forgotten. Through it all ran a single, impossible thread: Alred, walking through every landscape like a ghost with a destination only he could see.

He dressed without thinking, hands automatically smoothing out every wrinkle and fussing every button into place, then crossed to the shop window and peered out. The green was shrouded in morning mist, lake air pooling in every hollow. A lone set of footprints tracked across the dew, leading straight out of town and vanishing into the bracken. Finnian knew, with a certainty that needed no proof, that Alred had left before dawn, never once looking back.

He went through the motions of opening the shop—unlatching the door, wiping the glass, setting the first batch of clocks to their daily pace—but the old rhythms felt empty. There was a gap in the world, a brief flicker where the pulse of things should be. He let the clocks ring out their hour, but even their overlapping notes sounded faint, like a memory of music rather than the thing itself.

For a while he simply stood behind the counter, staring at nothing, the river stone cool and stubborn in his palm. He waited for the urge to work, but it never came. Eventually, he hung a placard in the window: "Closed for Maintenance." Then he walked out and circled the green, the way Alred had always done.

The sun broke through at last, and with it came a sense of movement—a ripple in the town's routine. Finnian saw children chasing a stick down to the water, Dalossalda's oldest daughter sweeping the stoop at the bakery, even Jen, the constable, strolling the edge of the green with a practiced air of unconcern. But nowhere, not at the lakeshore or the inn or the little path behind the bakery, could Finnian find any trace of Alred's particular brand of calm.

He ended up at the benches by the market fountain, river stone still in hand, elbows braced against his knees. For a long while, he just sat, listening to the faint chorus of clocks carried on the lake breeze. The silence was gentle, but stubborn.

After a time, he heard the familiar, measured steps of Leota, her black dress trailing slightly through the puddles. She didn't ask permission to sit; she simply did, eyes fixed on the fountain.

"You're closed," she said, not quite a question.

"Just for today," Finnian answered.

She nodded. "I saw Alred leave this morning. Or rather, I saw the space where he'd been, and knew he was gone."

They were quiet together. Leota broke it, her voice softer than usual. "Did he say why?"

Finnian shrugged. "He left a story. And a stone."

Leota glanced sidelong at his hand. "A lesson in disguise."

He let the stone roll between his fingers. "Maybe I'm not clever enough to get it."

Leota's lips twitched, but not into a smile. "You're clever enough. That's the problem."

They sat a while longer. Finnian realized he felt better, simply for not being alone with the silence.

"I have your project," he said, to change the subject. "The sidereal clock."

She looked at him, one eyebrow arched.

He hesitated. "I know how to make it, but I don't know what it's for."

Leota reached into her sleeve and produced a slip of folded paper. She placed it on his knee. "That's the spell it's meant to anchor. I can't explain it, not in the way it deserves. But you'll understand, I think, once it's ticking."

He took the paper, but didn't open it.

"You should build it," Leota said. "Not because it's your job, but because you're the only one who'd care to do it right." She rose, adjusting her shawl. "And if you ever figure out what to do with the stone, let me know."

He watched her walk away, a dark line against the morning. The stone felt heavier now, as if it had soaked up every word they'd spoken.

When Finnian returned to the shop, he did not wind the clocks, nor did he sort the shelves, or even sweep the dust. He unlocked the cabinet under his bench and withdrew the variable escapement gears he'd milled months ago for a commission that never came through. He laid out the brass plates, the sapphire pivots, the main spring, and all the other parts of the mechanism, but he didn't assemble them. Instead, he spent hours simply arranging them, trying to see the pattern that wanted to emerge.

He opened the slip of paper from Leota and read the notations. The script was precise but the math behind it made no sense. There were ratios that flexed, a cadence that refused to repeat, and a set of instructions that didn't so much guide as dare him to improvise. At first it made him angry—the way Alred's stone had—but the more he puzzled, the more it drew him in.

After a long afternoon, he began to build the prototype. Every time he tried to force the gearing into a regular rhythm, the mechanism seized or stuttered. But if he allowed the tiniest bit of slack, or let the ratios slip ever so slightly, the whole thing came alive—ticking not like a regular clock, but in a living, unpredictable way, almost as if it was breathing. The minute hand would race, then dawdle, then leap ahead again, always returning to the hour, but never by the same route twice.

He tried not to hate it, but it defied everything he'd ever learned.

Still, he couldn't put it down. By evening, he had three prototypes, each slightly different, none of them obedient to a standard measure.

He set them side by side, wound them, and waited.

The shop filled with the strangest sound he'd ever heard: a conversation of clocks, a symphony of uneven, wild tics and tocks. He realized then that it wasn't chaos, not really. It was something more—an order he couldn't yet see, but which, he sensed, was right for the purpose.

He sat at the bench, river stone in his palm, and listened until long past midnight.

In the dim lamplight, the new clockwork spun and drifted and settled itself, never once matching the steady pulse of its neighbors. Finnian imagined Alred, wherever he'd gone, feeling the odd current in the world and knowing it was time to pause, or to run, or maybe just to laugh at the very idea of time itself.

Finnian was tired, and he didn't know if what he'd made was a triumph or a disaster, but he was certain it was honest, and that it belonged in the world.

He placed the river stone on the workbench, directly next to the ticking, wayward clocks.

And in that quiet, unpredictable rhythm, Finnian heard the old friend's farewell, and the future's reply.

twelve
...

SEVERAL DAYS' worth of morning had come and gone in North Pointe, each one passing a little easier and a little quieter, as if the wild potentials of the prior week had exhausted themselves and fallen into step with the rest of the world. Finnian, for his part, was content to let the air go still. All the clocks in his shop were wound and ticking, every last one of his custom commissions—Galhani's timer, Makota's personal timer, Jen's "Emergency Detention Bell"—delivered and already stirring up minor revolutions in their respective corners of the town. Even the odd request from the bakery had been resolved. Makota, as it turned out, preferred her morning alarm to sound like a particularly aggressive crow, and so it did.

The exception was Leota's sidereal clock. The mechanism and variability was still giving Finnian problems—although if he was being honest with himself, they were delightful, intriguing problems he'd obsess over for a few hours each day.

With the day's orders boxed and stacked by the door, Finnian allowed himself the rare luxury of tinkering for pleasure. He had returned, as if by gravity, to his most ridiculous project: the Toast-Buttering Machine. It occupied nearly a third of his workbench, a gleaming snarl of cogs, levers, and silvered trays, half-dismantled from the previous week's overzealous butter explosion. The morning sun licked through the front window and found every flaw and fingerprint on its bright, mechanical surface.

Finnian sat, sleeves rolled, and worked the crank with a gentle, almost parental touch. The first prototype of the Jam Dispensing Unit was finally ready—at least, ready to test. A brass hopper, hand-filled with last autumn's apple-berry jam, fed a glass tube which terminated in a delicate, spoon-shaped nozzle. With a careful turn of the dial, Finnian could control the thickness of the spread. In theory.

He set a single, innocent slice of bread onto the receiving tray and aimed the Jam Spoon accordingly.

"Moment of truth," he muttered, and gave the crank a slow, steady turn.

The machine responded with a fussy whirr, a twitch of the loading arm, and a gratifying plop of jam squarely in the middle of the bread. Finnian grinned. He eased the crank back, then forward, letting the spreader arm glide over the surface. The jam laid itself in a tidy, even stripe.

It was, to his way of thinking, a miracle.

He was so engrossed in adjusting the spreader's return angle that he almost missed the sound of the shop bell—three brisk chimes, as precise as a command.

The man who entered was not a regular. Finnian could usually place a face within a second, but this one gave him nothing: he wore the nondescript brown of a traveling tradesman, clean but patched, with a hat set low and a gait that was practiced at being overlooked. He hovered just inside the door, squinting at the arrangement of clocks and the bright commotion of the machine.

After a few ticks, the man found his words. "I heard you were the one for odd inventions."

Finnian, caught in the act of dabbing a fingerful of jam for quality control, nodded. "If it can be made to work, I can make it work. Can I help you?"

The man approached the counter, gaze locked on the Toast-Buttering Machine. "Is that what it looks like?"

"It's exactly what it looks like," Finnian replied, unable to hide the pride. "Automatic, multi-stage, precise to a single crumb. The jam is new; the butter is still a challenge, especially in colder weather."

The man's face brightened—he looked, briefly, like a child seeing a conjuring trick. "You could save whole minutes every breakfast. And for a shop? Even more."

"Hours a year," Finnian said, deadpan. "Generations, if you eat enough toast."

The man laughed, a little too hard. "Incredible. Truly incredible." He leaned in, eyes darting over the mechanism. "Does it actually—?"

Finnian pushed the prototype forward. "See for yourself. The crank is manual for now, but I've got a mainspring in the works. The steam-powered version… Well. I'll get there."

The man barely hesitated. He set his hand to the crank and turned. The machine sprang to life, more graceful than ever. The jam spoon loaded, glided, returned; the bread moved along its tiny rail; the spread was even and generous. At the end of the cycle, the bread advanced to a small, built-in guillotine, which neatly sliced the crust with a satisfying snick.

The man's mouth dropped open. "By the gods, it works."

Finnian tried not to beam, but failed. "With some margin for error. The final model will have settings for different types of bread, a rotary jam selector, and a built-in cleaning function. I'm still refining the butter mechanism—temperature's a problem."

The man, still cranking, was visibly enthralled. "If you could automate the butter, too, you'd never need a kitchen hand for breakfast again."

Finnian could have sworn the air in the shop brightened a shade. "That's the dream."

They watched together as the machine completed another cycle, this time with a thicker spread and a less fortunate bread slice, which tore slightly under the jam spoon. The man made a tutting noise and adjusted the dial, as if it were his own invention.

At last he let go of the crank, fingers jam-stained. "You are an artist," he said, almost reverently. "I wish more people understood what machines can do for the world."

Finnian shrugged, but the compliment landed. "Most people just want the result, not the labor behind it."

The man nodded, eyes distant. "Not me." He wiped his fingers on a handkerchief. "Speaking of which—I do have a commission, if you're not already full up."

Finnian gestured to the empty shop. "Plenty of time. What do you need?"

The man reached into his coat, withdrew a battered notebook, and opened to a page thick with equations, columns of numbers, and a crude sketch of a sun, moon, and—Finnian's heart did a little leap—a star chart.

"I'm an alchemist," the man said, lowering his voice, as if the clocks might eavesdrop. "I need a timekeeping device of uncommon precision, set not to town hours, but to a particular alignment—sunrise, and then a secondary event at the precise moment of the moon's rising, three days hence." He tapped the notebook. "I've tried water clocks, sand, even chemical timers. None are reliable enough."

Finnian, utterly at home now, nodded. "What's the margin of error?"

"None," the man said, so fiercely it startled Finnian. "If I miss the conjunction by more than a breath, it's wasted. I need a clock that will sound a bell at the exact moment—no drift, no lag."

Finnian pondered this, fingers absently smoothing a smudge of jam on the bench. "I have a design for a regulator that can be set to any event, so long as you provide the reference. But the bell..." He looked at his wall of clocks. "I can tune the bell to be heard through three feet of stone, if needed."

The man smiled, full and open. "Do it," he said.

Finnian wiped his hands and set to work. He had, in his private drawer, a hand-sized regulator movement with a double escapement—a model he'd built for himself, once, but abandoned in favor of the workshop's big clocks. He opened the case and set the mechanism on the counter.

The man watched, almost vibrating. "Can you program it for the three days, and then... is it safe to carry?"

"It's safer than anything you'd get from the capital," Finnian replied, already winding the movement. "Set it for the conjunction, and it'll chime a minute before, then again at the mark." He handed it over, careful to demonstrate the setting levers. "If you want to be doubly sure, I can make a second. Set them both, compare the ring. If they disagree, you'll know something's off."

The man grinned. "Perfect. Yes. Two, if you can. I'll pay whatever you ask."

Finnian said, "Just bring me more of that jam. The rest is on the house."

They shared a genuine laugh. It was only then, as the man cradled the regulator, that Finnian noticed something odd: a prickle along his arms, the faintest taste of lemon and steel in the air. He looked at the clock, then at the man, and was about to ask if he'd felt it, too, when the world seemed to tilt.

The man's eyes went wide. "Do you—?"

Finnian only nodded.

In the next instant, the air around them thickened; the humming of the shop's clocks all aligned, their ticks coming into a single, dreadful synchronization. Finnian felt a chill, not of cold but of inevitability.

The vision hit with a force that left them both gasping: Finnian saw the customer, older, hunched over a crucible in a windowless room, rays of sunlight streaming through a giant lens. A clock—Finnian's clock—sat on the table. At the chime, the man lifted a vial and poured its contents into the crucible; the mixture flared with blue-green light, and then the vision twisted, spiraling out into darkness.

The shop returned, loud with the overlaid echoes of a hundred clocks. The Grandfather Clock in the corner, long since unwound, stood at attention, its face gleaming.

Then, with no warning, the Grandfather Clock chimed. Once. Twice. A third, impossibly loud peal.

The resonance tore through the shop, making the glass in the windows buzz. The air before the clock shimmered, bent, and, in a silent burst, a gateway formed: a perfect, oval portal rimmed with indigo and gold.

The customer dropped the regulator, and Finnian, acting on instinct, caught it before it struck the bench. He looked up and saw the man frozen, gaze locked on the vortex. The man took a breath, eyes wild, and then, without another word, stepped through.

The portal closed with a whoosh of displaced air. The Grandfather Clock's face returned to normal, hands at rest. The other clocks in the shop staggered, then resumed their irregular chorus.

Finnian stared at the space where the man had stood. His heart pounded. He realized he was still holding the regulator.

He set it down, carefully, as if it might detonate. Then he sat, hands braced on the workbench, and listened to the clocks for a very long time.

After the better part of an hour, he looked at the Toast-Buttering Machine. A small glob of jam had oozed out and formed a red, glassy bead on the counter. Finnian picked it up, chewed thoughtfully, and found it sweet, if a touch sharp.

He wiped his hands, rolled his shoulders, and went to fetch a broom.

After sweeping up the little beads of jam and the oddities left by the morning's adventure, Finnian slumped into his chair and let his gaze drift to the small, squat regulator clock resting on the edge of the workbench. The clock seemed innocent, even bashful, as though it wanted nothing more than to keep time in peace and be ignored by supernatural portals.

Finnian stared at it for a while. His hands rested palm-down on the bench, the wood still sticky with the ghost of jam. He felt hollowed out, as if some essential part had been drawn through the gateway along with his vanished customer. The shop's noises were back to their usual, comfortable unevenness, but Finnian could sense a faint, residual resonance in the air—something left behind, coiling around the mainsprings and bell gongs of his clocks.

He reached for the regulator. The case was warm from the man's grip. Finnian wound it once, gently, then set it ticking in the shallow silence. He watched the balance wheel swing, back and forth, back and forth, until his own breathing fell in line with its rhythm.

Slowly, as if not to startle himself, Finnian set the clock on the shelf. He straightened the other clocks, refilled the oil in the front counter lamp, and swept up the fragments of crust and dried glue from beneath the Toast-Buttering Machine. The ritual of tidying, however minor, steadied him. His hands moved with more confidence; his breath, deeper.

Finally, he returned to the bench. The Toast-Buttering Machine sat patient, waiting for its maker to regain his nerve. Finnian gripped the hand crank, feeling the familiar resistance. He loaded another slice of bread, filled the jam hopper, and began to cycle the machine, one slow revolution after another.

The spreader arm dipped, smeared, retracted. The jam spoon loaded and cleared. The slicing blade, true to form, stuck at the midpoint and required a tap on the guide rail to finish its stroke. Each step, Finnian marked in his mind. There—a hitch in the cam. There—a pause as the spring hesitated, and there, a moment when the butter spindle shivered against the bread, tearing rather than spreading.

He repeated the cycle, twice, then ten times, then twenty. He ran the machine with an obsessive slowness, adjusting the tiniest screws, loosening the guide rods, penciling notes along the margin of his schematic every time he caught a skip or a tremble in the mechanism. For every flaw he found, a solution presented itself: a secondary stop here, a counterweight there, a ratchet so fine it could split a second into ten thousand increments.

After an hour of this, his breath had settled. The world felt less slippery. He realized, with faint amusement, that he'd found himself in the same place as before—making the imperfect perfect, but one small piece at a time.

He let the last slice of bread pass through the machine and watched it emerge, only a little lopsided, with a thin, shining layer of jam spread edge-to-edge. Finnian took a bite. It was good.

He wiped his hands, and, just for a moment, allowed himself to feel whole again.

The clocks kept their time. The world ticked on.

By the time the next sennight rolled around, it was clear that Finnian's little experiment in precision was having unintended side effects. North Pointe, once notorious for its meandering mornings and the cheerful chaos of townsfolk on their own schedules, had grown abruptly punctual. Makota's kits now delivered to the mark; the market's opening bell no longer sounded into a void, but called forth a line of eager buyers waiting for the exact moment the doors were unlocked. Even the pub, for generations a refuge for those who preferred the soft edge of time, found itself with a half-dozen regulars who arrived and departed according to a strict, clock-driven regimen.

Finnian noticed the difference first in the conversations at his counter. Where once people had asked for clocks to match the sun, now they demanded clocks that matched each other, with no tolerance for even the smallest slip. He'd fielded three complaints about a timer running slow, and once, spectacularly, two neighbors had shown up simultaneously to argue about which of their wall clocks was truer—a debate that ended with both standing in silence, watching the seconds tick past, until the least precise blinked and retreated.

It was into this tightly-wound atmosphere that Jen arrived, boots loud and deliberate, eyes sharp and just a touch annoyed.

"You've got to stop," she said, not bothering to knock the snow from her coat. "You're driving the town mad."

Finnian, bent over the Toast-Buttering Machine's innards, looked up in surprise. "What did I do?"

Jen shrugged off her coat, revealing her constable's sash and the flat, sardonic line of her mouth. "You know what you did. I've had complaints from three people this morning—all before second bell, mind you—that their clocks are 'too perfect' and now their lives are chaos."

He grinned. "That doesn't sound like chaos to me."

Jen snorted. "You try telling Minnie that. She actually made an appointment with me, Finnian. An appointment. Said she'd be 'precisely at the stroke of the bell.'" She shook her head, as if to clear it. "And you know what Bertram's done? The fool's started counting his stitches by the mark. He's got a timer in the shop, rings it every time he changes thread, and he's begun rushing, just to hear the next bell. I thought the man was going to burst an artery."

Finnian wiped his hands and came around the bench, trying not to laugh. "I was just making what people asked for."

Jen raised an eyebrow. "I'm not saying it's wrong. But maybe—just maybe—it's not right, either."

He motioned to the Toast-Buttering Machine, which gleamed under the lamp, newly polished and only slightly stained with jam. "If it's any consolation, I've made no progress at all on this. It still tears half the bread and jams at random. No pun intended."

Jen eyed the contraption. "That's what I came to see. I figured if anything could survive a brush with order, it'd be your breakfast machine."

He gestured for her to try it. "Go on. See if you can get a slice through in one piece."

Jen took up the crank with the solemnity of a woman about to confront a longstanding enemy. She turned it, slow and steady. The hopper dropped a slice, the spreader arm deployed, the jam spooned and spread with remarkable evenness. The slicing blade, true to form, stuck just before the end, forcing Jen to give the guide rail a gentle kick. The bread made it through, a little mangled but mostly whole.

Jen broke the silence with a low whistle. "Not bad. Still fights back, though."

Finnian nodded, accepting the verdict. "I keep trying to tune it out, but every time I fix a hitch, it crops up somewhere else. I could spend the rest of my life smoothing the sequence, and never get it quite right."

She selected the mangled bread, spread some butter (by hand, for now), and took a bite. "That's the problem with chasing perfection. Sometimes, the error is the point."

He considered this, but the engineer in him resisted. "But if you know where the error is, you can fix it."

Jen grinned, jam on her teeth. "Maybe. Or maybe you just move it around, like a lump under a rug."

They stood together in companionable quiet, broken only by the soft ticking of the shop's clocks and the faint, wet chew of Jen finishing the toast.

She finished the slice and dusted her hands. "Look, I get it. I know some things have to be precise. If you're fixing a bridge, or defusing a bomb—yes, please, be on time. But if you're running a bakery, or a bar, or..." she waved a hand at the array of timepieces, "life in general, you've got to leave some space for the world to just... breathe."

Finnian, sensing the edge of a lesson, tried to keep the mood light. "If I made a clock that ran deliberately a little slow, do you think anyone would buy it?"

Jen's laugh was deep and honest. "If you did, I'd buy one for myself and two for every regular at the Broken Claw." She sobered. "But seriously, Finnian. Sometimes less precise is smoother for the spirit. Even the God of the Mountain is rumored to nap through most of the year."

He let the silence stretch, then said, "But what if you need both? Precision and... whatever the opposite of precision is."

Jen considered. "I think that's the point. Balance, right? Have the exact timer for your explosive, but let the jam machine run wild. There's a time for being on the mark, and a time for missing it entirely."

Finnian reached for the phrase. "A rigidly defined area of doubt and uncertainty?"

She lit up, proud. "That's exactly it."

He smiled. "I'll work on it."

Jen clapped him on the shoulder, nearly knocking him into the Toast-Buttering Machine. "That's all anyone can ask. Keep an eye out for trouble, will you? If the clocks start opening portals again, I'd rather not lose half the town."

"Of course," Finnian said. "Though at the rate things are going, we'll just synchronize our disappearances."

She grinned and shrugged on her coat. "Don't tempt me." At the door, she paused, turned, and gave him a rare, genuine look. "You're doing good work, Finnian. Just remember: sometimes the best fix is letting things wobble."

He nodded. "I'll do my best."

When she was gone, Finnian lingered at the bench, gazing at the Toast-Buttering Machine. He watched its gears and cams, all the places they refused to behave, and considered Jen's words.

For a minute, he simply listened—to the clocks, to the faint murmur of the street outside, to the uneven pulse of his own heart.

Then, with a wry smile, Finnian fetched his notebook and began sketching: not a new gear, but a new kind of escapement, one that let the bread advance a little off the line each time, a deliberate randomness. He wrote: "Make it wobble."

He spent the rest of the morning designing a mechanism that would, every so often, shift the timing just enough to make the outcome unpredictable. Not much, just enough to keep a man guessing.

By noon, he had a model. By dusk, he'd tested it a dozen times, delighting in the fact that the bread sometimes landed perfectly, sometimes folded in half, and sometimes—marvelously—landed jam side down on the plate, in the manner of all toast since the dawn of time.

Finnian laughed, the sound muffled by the late afternoon quiet, and realized he'd never felt more at home in his own skin.

He wound the clocks. He wound the Toast-Buttering Machine. He let the world run, sometimes to the mark, sometimes not, and found he liked it better that way.

And, for the first time since the clocks had started their secret games, Finnian looked at the Grandfather Clock and thought, Maybe it knows what it's doing, after all.

The next morning, and every morning after, North Pointe's clocks kept a little less perfect time. But the jam was sweeter, and the bread softer, and the world's ticking, though never quite true, was all the more honest for it.

thirteen
. . .

THERE WERE, by Finnian's own admission, more efficient ways to make a cup of tea. Even the most conservative tally of his shop's timepieces and errata showed at least eleven clocks within sight of the back workbench—every one tuned, in some small way, to the shifting needs of a town that had long ago abandoned any hope of running on a single, common schedule. Yet here he was, before sunrise and with the heating yet to take the edge off the morning, hunched over a workbench littered with the elements of what he had privately dubbed the Automated Tea Brewer Mark II.

The first Mark I model had been a resounding, if sticky, disaster. It was meant to combine the gentlest percolation of lake water with a careful steeping of Makota's second-harvest chamomile, finished by a clockwork arm that stirred the cup with a perfect, spiral precision. In reality, the device had scalded the shopcat, ruined three mugs, and coated every horizontal surface with a viscous, herbal slick that Finnian was still finding in places a week later.

He was determined that Mark II would be different.

He swept aside a brace of half-dismantled watches and made room for the new assembly. The core was a gleaming copper kettle, polished to a shine that doubled as a mirror. He had grafted to its underside a set of miniature steam pistons—castoffs from a toy locomotive commission gone off the rails, so to speak—and piped them together with the thinnest lengths of lead tubing he could beg from the smithy. The kettle perched on a cradle of heat-tempered glass, above a single brass spirit burner, just large enough to boil a teacup's worth of water without risk of explosion.

To the side of this arrangement, Finnian positioned the masterpiece of his current invention: a tiny water wheel, its blades hand-carved from hard maple, with each spoke fitted with a sliver of river-polished agate. The wheel's job was simple in theory: as the steam pressure built in the kettle, it forced a valve open at the precise moment the water reached temperature, which diverted the hot stream into the water wheel's reservoir. The wheel, in turn, rotated at a measured pace, timed by a hair-thin chain looped over an escapement fashioned from an old tower clock. As the wheel made its revolution, it actuated a lever that raised a counterweight, which eventually tripped the tea-infuser arm.

That arm—an elaborate, jointed affair of steel and bone—waited in the up position, its tiny mesh basket loaded with exactly two grams of dried chamomile blossom. At the proper moment, the lever tripped, and the arm would dip the basket into the boiling cup. Finnian had fitted a small sand timer to the mechanism so that, after an interval of three minutes, the basket would lift clear, drip once, and come to rest on a waiting porcelain drip tray. All this, for a single cup of tea.

The tools arrayed around the operation were as varied as the machine itself: calipers for measuring the bore of the piston, a jeweler's screwdriver for the escapement, a battered awl for adjusting the chain tension, and three sizes of file for chasing burrs off the more fragile parts. Finnian worked in a rhythm that was half habit, half compulsion, his fingers as nimble as any spider's and twice as stubborn. Every now and then he would mutter under his breath, words barely intelligible but full of intent. "No. Tighter there. A hair less tension—" or "That's it, darling, steady on." He paused, wiped a smudge of machine oil from his spectacles, and leaned in to inspect the weld between two lengths of tubing, his nose mere inches from the gleaming surface.

He loved this part—the minute adjustments, the trial and error. There was a joy in the small failures: a valve that sputtered instead of hissing, a gear that seized for want of a sliver more clearance, a counterweight that misjudged its moment of glory and sent the infuser flying with a wet, floral splat. All these he took in stride, making a note in his ledger with each improvement or setback. He had long ago discovered that if he simply let the design run wild, it would eventually reveal its own logic.

By the time the sun crested the bakery roof, Finnian had coaxed the Automated Tea Brewer Mark II into a state he dared call "precariously stable." He loaded the burner with a capful of spirits, set the kettle atop its cradle, and double-checked every connection. The water, sourced fresh from the lakeshore that morning, sloshed eagerly inside the kettle's belly. The basket's mechanism, now wound and waiting, quivered in anticipation.

He stepped back, wiped his brow, and surveyed the tableau. It was absurd, even by his own generous standards. The entire apparatus occupied nearly the whole of his largest work tray, and the weight of all its parts surely exceeded the weight of the tea it was built to brew by a factor of a hundred. But it was, he thought, beautiful. The lines of brass and bone, the gleaming surfaces, the way each curve resolved into a purpose.

Finnian rolled up his sleeves, squared his shoulders, and struck a match. The flame caught with a soft pop, and the burner's blue tongue licked at the bottom of the kettle. He watched, breath held, as the first beads of condensation appeared on the copper, then as the pressure in the pistons began its silent, invisible work. The anticipation was exquisite.

At precisely the four-minute mark, a single, clear note sounded— the release valve had hit its target. The hot water whooshed through the pipe and filled the waiting cup, spinning the water wheel with a delicate, measured whirr. Finnian grinned, unable to help himself. The wheel moved with perfect grace, its agate blades catching the light and throwing flecks of rainbow across the cluttered workbench.

As the wheel completed its revolution, the infuser arm sprang to life, dipping the basket into the steaming water with all the dignity of a courtier at a ball. Finnian's eyes shone. The sand timer, inverted as the arm went down, trickled its load with a slow, hypnotic pulse. The smell of chamomile filled the workshop, blending with the familiar scents of oil, brass, and old paper.

Three minutes later, exactly as planned, the infuser arm lifted, paused, and deposited the basket on its porcelain tray with a polite little clink. The wheel slowed, the levers reset, and all was silent except for the faint ticking of the shop clocks and the gentle gurgle of the cooling kettle.

Finnian regarded the cup. He waited for the sense of letdown that always followed the completion of a project, but it didn't come. Instead, he felt a small, sharp pride. The tea, when he finally tasted it, was perfect.

He let the cup warm his hands, standing in the quiet for a long minute. Then he began making notes for the Mark III.

The day he decided to test the limits of his patience and his invention, Finnian ate breakfast with unusual deliberation. The crust of rye, the hard cheese, the single, shivering coddled egg—each was consumed with the focus of a man about to face an ordeal of uncertain duration and certain complexity. He drank his tea—hand-brewed, for now—then spent a full candlemark winding every clock in the shop, including the recalcitrant ones that only kept time for the sake of argument.

When the main room was as orderly as it was ever going to be, he retreated to the workshop and took one last inventory of the Automated Tea Brewer Mark II. Every part gleamed in the cold morning sun, as if the device itself anticipated the coming trial.

Finnian made a few last-minute tweaks, adjusting the tension on the basket arm and resetting the sand timer. Then, with an almost ritualistic flourish, he filled the kettle, packed the infuser basket, and primed the spirit burner. The tea was Makota's best, a rare lot of golden chamomile she'd hoarded through the winter. The water was from the lake, filtered and boiled twice for purity. There was nothing left to do but begin.

He struck a match, set the burner alight, and started the clock.

The first hour was all latent energy and slow accumulation. The burner's blue flame licked steadily at the bottom of the kettle, but the air in the workshop remained cool, shot through with the sharp tang of ethanol and the fainter, promising scent of dry flowers. Finnian settled onto his tall stool and watched the device as it warmed. He resisted the urge to tinker, letting the slow parade of pressure and expansion have its way.

He watched the copper sides of the kettle for the telltale fog of condensation. He watched the pistons, waiting for the first microtwitch that would signal motion. The wheel, the counterweights, the lever arms—each seemed frozen in anticipation. The only movement was the slow drift of sunlight across the workbench, a golden line that inched from the tool caddy to the elbow of his soldering iron.

It was during the second hour that the real action started. The pistons flexed, just perceptibly, and with a faint, satisfyingly mechanical click, one nudged open the pre-valve. A thin hiss, like a snake making up its mind, whispered through the pipes. The water was close to boiling.

Finnian leaned in, eyes bright. He rested his chin on his folded arms, watching every minute twitch, every tremor in the mechanism. He could see the pressure gauge—repurposed from a failed egg timer —climb, slowly, steadily, into the red. He loved this stage. The build-up. The implied promise.

At the two-hour mark, a bead of sweat had formed at Finnian's temple. The room was warm now, the burner's heat augmented by the reflected sun and the cumulative tick-tick of a dozen clocks. He unbuttoned his collar, dabbed at the sweat, and allowed himself a private smile. Most people would have thrown up their hands by now. Most people would have said, "Just pour the hot water and be done with it." But Finnian wasn't most people.

The kettle whistled, a faint, almost coquettish sound. At the precise moment the pressure peaked, the piston released, slamming open the valve with a wet, eager shush. Hot water whooshed down the pipe, catching the water wheel dead-on. The wheel spun, its maple spokes blurring, the agate inlays sparking rainbow halos against the shop wall. As it spun, it wound the next stage—a gear train that would, over the course of thirty minutes, slowly raise the brass counterweight until it reached a hair-trigger at the top of its arc.

Finnian checked the time. Perfect. He scribbled a note: "Gear train, minimal drift. Water wheel rate = 0.992:1 predicted. Counterweight friction negligible." He underlined negligible three times.

He stood, stretched, and walked a lap of the shop. From the workshop window, he could see the green outside, now bright with late morning. The bakery's windows were open, the air perfumed with baking bread and a hint of vanilla. Finnian inhaled, let the scent mingle with the warm, oily metallic of his own workspace, then returned to the stool to witness the next stage.

Over the next candlemark, the counterweight inched higher, the slow build of potential energy its own private epic. At the exact moment the clock struck noon, the counterweight reached its apogee and tripped the lever with a delicate, trembling click.

The lever—elegant, over-engineered, wholly unnecessary—rocked back and forth with stately deliberation, transmitting its motion through a series of rods, cogs, and pulleys. The chain of causality snaked across the workbench, bending, twisting, magnifying and dampening in turn, until, at last, it reached the tea basket arm.

With a soft, almost reverent sigh, the basket arm descended, dipping the mesh into the steaming cup. The sand timer flipped as it did, its load of fine glass grains marking the last stage of the process.

Finnian sat back, and for a few heartbeats, just breathed.

The workshop was quiet but for the hissing of the cooling kettle, the faint tick of the sand, and the intermittent click of the slowest clock in the room—a barn clock that Finnian had never managed to synchronize, but kept anyway out of respect for its obstinate refusal to be on time.

He felt the satisfaction bloom in his chest, a physical sensation that curled around his ribs and squeezed. The machine worked. It was absurd, and excessive, and glorious.

He closed his eyes, letting the moment hang.

Then, with no warning, the sand timer finished. The basket arm lifted, the mesh dripping gold into the cup below. The entire machine reset itself—gears slipping, weights dropping, pistons exhaling a final hiss. And there, in the perfect center of the work tray, waited a single, flawless cup of tea.

Finnian was about to lift the cup—he'd already composed a congratulatory toast in his head—when he noticed something odd at the edge of his vision.

A shimmer, like heat rising off stone, curled up from the leftmost corner of the workbench. Finnian frowned, set the cup back, and leaned in.

The air wobbled, then bent. In the space beside the machine, a small, round shadow appeared, growing quickly from the size of a coin to that of a dinner plate. The shadow thickened, darkened, and then, with a sound not unlike the uncorking of a bottle, a perfect oval portal opened into the world.

It glowed, not the eldritch blue of prior incidents, but a deep, burnt orange, the color of sun through a glass of aged brandy. And with it came a smell—distinct, sharp, layered: the dust of old books, the sweat of leather, and something else, deeper, almost chemical.

Finnian froze. His hands, halfway to the cup, hovered in the air. He felt his heart pounding in his chest.

He set the cup down, watched as the portal stabilized, and listened to the low, humming vibration that seemed to pulse out from the center of the machine.

He let his tools clatter from his hands, unheeded, as he leaned forward, unable to look away.

For a full minute, nothing happened.

Then, the workshop's clocks all rang in unison—a sound Finnian had never heard before, not in all his years in North Pointe. The portal seemed to pulse in time with the chimes, the orange deepening, the shadow inside sharpening.

Finnian swallowed, hard.

He'd wanted a perfectly brewed cup of tea. What he'd gotten was something else entirely. His first thought, as the portal's outline steadied and its color deepened, was that he had miscalculated the gearing somewhere. The whole affair had the unmistakable aroma of failure: the burnt scent of an overdriven coil, the chemical twang of spent spirits, the ozone snap of an arc misfiring in the dark. The edges of the oval shimmered and vibrated, a juddering oscillation that set his teeth on edge and sent a faint, metallic taste into his mouth.

He took an involuntary step backward, bracing himself against the edge of the workbench. The world on the other side of the portal was, at first, nothing but swirling color—muted browns, grays, and a sickly institutional green, all blurred together like a half-forgotten nightmare. It wasn't until his eyes adjusted to the strange frequency of the light that he made out the shapes: a room, small and suffocating, packed to the ceiling with ledgers and reams of yellowed paper. Every surface overflowed with stacks of documents, bound and cross-referenced, each tagged in neat rows with illegible but somehow oppressive script.

Behind the largest desk—really more of a barricade—sat a man, hunched and hollow-eyed, with a familiar patch of white hair above his ears and a pair of battered spectacles perched on the bridge of his nose. He wore a drab, dun-colored shirt and a vest that had lost its buttons, sleeves rolled up to the elbow to reveal arms that had seen neither sun nor exercise in many, many years.

Finnian stared, paralyzed. The man in the portal stared back.

It was himself. Or a version of himself, aged and ground down to a nub by years of pointless, ceaseless calculation. The twin's hands moved with nervous energy, shuffling papers, making notes, cross-checking figures, then moving back to the start and repeating, never finishing a single task. The alternate Finnian's mouth was set in a thin, rigid line; the cheeks sagged under the weight of effort spent on nothing at all. The only break in the rhythm was the occasional, desperate glance up at the wall clock—then a shake of the head, the sinking of shoulders, and a grim return to the cycle.

It was the eyes, though, that finished the job. Even through the warping shimmer of the portal, Finnian could see that they were the same shade, the same sharp, analytical blue. But the light behind them was gone, as if the core of what made him himself had been siphoned off, drop by drop, through decades of bureaucratic misery.

The two Finnian Springdales regarded each other in silence for a span that might have been seconds or years.

Then, with a sudden, jerking motion, the man behind the desk shoved aside a pile of ledgers, scattering dust and scraps of paper into the air. He stood, revealing a body that had forgotten how to stand straight, and leaned in, palms flat on the desktop. He stared through the portal—not just at Finnian, but into him. His lips twitched, as if to speak, but no sound came.

Instead, the alternate Finnian shook his head, once, twice, with a finality that needed no translation.

He sat back down, hunched deeper than before, and resumed his endless tallying, the movements of his pen growing sloppier and more desperate with each line.

Finnian stumbled backward, knocking over a tray of screws. The sound—a scatter of metal on tile—broke whatever spell held the room. He gasped, clutching at the workbench for support, and felt his own heart hammering in his chest. His hands shook, so badly that he had to press them flat to the table to keep from dropping the next tool he touched.

He glanced back at the portal. The alternate world was still there, but now the color seemed even flatter, the light more jaundiced, the weight of the ledgers more suffocating. The Finnian in that world had not noticed the spill, nor the noise, nor even the portal itself. He was lost again in the grind, devoured by the very system he'd so meticulously built.

The automated tea machine, center stage for this madness, clicked and whirred. It had reset itself, ready to begin the cycle anew. The solitary cup of tea sat cooling on the drip tray, the surface swirling with a faint skin of chamomile oil. Finnian stared at it, unsure if he wanted to smash the machine to bits or drink the entire cup in one gulp.

Instead, he did neither. He stood in the sudden stillness, breathing hard, and tried to make sense of what he'd seen.

It wasn't the vision of horror that haunted him, not exactly. He'd long known that his need for precision, for order, could run out of hand—he'd seen it in his father, in his master, in a dozen other men who'd let the world's chaos crush them. But to see the endpoint so clearly, so literally... That was a cruelty he had not prepared for.

Finnian looked around his workshop, at the thousand tiny projects, the bits and bobs, the stacks of notebooks filled with sketches and ratios and plans for machines he would never build. Was it really so different from the ledgers and files in that other world?

He wiped a hand over his mouth, trying to banish the taste of dust and fear. He wanted to laugh. He wanted to scream. He wanted to take the infernal tea machine and hurl it into the lake.

The portal shimmered, then began to shrink. Its edges wavered, the color faded, and the warping of the air grew less severe. In the final moments before it vanished, the alternate Finnian looked up once more. Their eyes met.

This time, there was something new in the gaze. Not a plea for help, not even a warning—but a kind of exhausted resignation, a knowledge that the cycle would never break, not by any action within that room. And with that last, hollow look, the portal collapsed in on itself, leaving only a faint ripple in the air and the echo of a hundred clocks, all ticking in uneasy unison.

Finnian let the silence settle. He listened to the clocks, to the faint drip of condensed water from the kettle, to his own slow, ragged breathing.

He looked at the tea machine again, but now it seemed less an invention and more a warning—an omen, carved in brass and bone and maple.

He reached for the cup, lifted it in trembling hands, and drank.

It was perfect.

And he hated it.

fourteen
. . .

IT WAS the kind of morning that demanded atonement—a gray, penitent chill in the air, the clocks stuttering as if each minute carried a faint undertone of regret. Finnian had risen early, but not out of excitement. There was work to be done, always, but his hands found the tools with less certainty, less conviction than he'd once prided himself on.

He kept the shop's lamps low and let the dullness of the outside world seep through the glass. He cleaned, not out of need, but because it kept the mind numb: each bristle of the broom, each cloth across the counter, was a way to silence the echo of what had happened yesterday. The cup of tea he'd made went half-cold in its place, the taste of it flat and faintly bitter, as if the leaves themselves knew better than to promise comfort.

The bell over the door rang, a flat two-chime greeting, and Finnian braced himself. His first thought was that it might be Jen, here to chide him for what she called "cranking up the tension on the town's mainspring," or perhaps Leota, on the prowl for her sidereal project. But it was neither.

The man who entered wore the starched black of a certain kind of priest: high collar, traveling cloak, and a clean-shaven face that looked both wind-burned and recently scoured. He carried nothing but a book in one hand and a heavy walking stick in the other, and moved with the faint urgency of a man who resented even the seconds it took for a door to swing closed.

"Good morning," Finnian said, voice still hoarse. "How can I help?"

The priest's eyes swept the shop, cataloging every clock, every unfinished project, as if searching for a threat or a challenge. He kept his hands on the book, a finger marking a page, and replied, "We are a party of six, pilgrims from St. Andarin, heading east by the trade road. The next town is four days at the best pace, and we must arrive precisely at dawn on the Festival of the Twinned Lanterns. Not before, and not late." He paused, as if waiting for Finnian to contradict him.

Instead, Finnian only nodded. "A timekeeper for the road. Durable, easy to read. Do you prefer a bell, or—?"

"Neither," the priest cut in. "The less noise, the better. But it must be accurate, down to the mark. We have a strict schedule. The others are not..." He hesitated, searching for a polite word. "They are not disciplined. I need a device to impose that discipline."

Finnian considered the request. He had, on the shelf behind him, a run of four carriage clocks, each hand-tuned within a second of the town bell. There was also the possibility of a pocket watch—he had one half-finished, just awaiting the final jewel in its escapement. Normally he would have offered a rundown of options, shown off the mechanisms, perhaps even made a joke about the hazards of trusting too much in clocks when the world itself bent time for its own amusement.

But today, he simply reached for the nearest carriage clock, checked its wind, and set it down in front of the priest. "This will serve. You'll need to wind it every morning, but it won't drift more than a few ticks in a week, as long as you keep it upright."

The priest picked it up, hefted it, and then held it to his ear as if testing for signs of heresy. "Acceptable," he said. "But what about pace? Can you provide a means of regulating our walking?"

"Distance?" Finnian asked, eyebrows rising for the first time that day.

"Yes. I want to know exactly how far we've traveled each day. And how quickly. I do not wish to be at the mercy of the sun and the road."

Finnian nodded. "I have a pedometer. It's not the latest design, but it's true enough if you calibrate it to the stride of the user." He pulled a small wooden device from under the counter—a box with a dial on its face and a leather strap for the waist. "This will count steps and translate them into distance. You can match your pace to the clock. If you keep to a thousand paces an hour, the math is easy."

The priest took it, turned it over, and then finally looked at Finnian, as if seeing him for the first time. "You have a reputation," he said, "for more than accuracy. They say you can make devices... special. Is this one of those?"

Finnian felt the memory of the day before tighten in his throat. He almost told the man about the dangers of making things too precise, about the perils of certainty, about the vision of a life so perfectly measured that every possibility vanished. But the words stuck. He only shrugged. "It will keep time. And so will you."

The priest tucked the clock into his cloak, and the pedometer into a side pouch. He slid a coin across the counter, a denomination a little too large for the purchase. "I will pay extra if you swear to its accuracy."

Finnian touched the clock, then the pedometer. "It will be as accurate as your own will."

The priest's hand hovered over the devices. For a moment, Finnian thought he might ask about the other clocks, or perhaps the odd tensions in the shop, or the way the clocks seemed to lean in whenever a customer told the truth. But the man only took his things and said, "We leave at dawn. If there are flaws, I will return."

Finnian managed a smile. "Safe journey. And may you arrive exactly when you intend."

The priest nodded and turned for the door. But as he reached for the latch, his eyes darted to the Grandfather Clock in the corner. Finnian followed the gaze.

The Grandfather Clock, silent for days, now ticked with an audible thump. The priest's fingers clenched on the door, knuckles white.

Then, as if they'd both agreed to it, Finnian and the priest turned back to the counter, where the devices waited.

The room went cold. The ticking faded.

And there it was—a vision, as clear and unambiguous as a bell ringing at midnight.

He saw the priest and his party, marching in perfect step along the trade road. They ignored the sun, ignored the birds, ignored even the other travelers who called out for help. At every hour, the priest consulted the clock. At every mile, he checked the pedometer. His party fell behind, sickened by the pace, but he did not stop. The goal—dawn at the festival—was everything.

At the last night before the town, the party made camp. The priest alone kept watch, pacing in perfect circles, eyes fixed on the horizon and the ticking of the clock. He did not see the travelers left behind, or the girl who lost her way in the marsh, or the farmer with the broken cart.

The vision ended.

Finnian blinked, his breath ragged. The priest stood very still, then touched the clock as if to ground himself.

"There is a cost," the priest said, voice different now, softer and less certain.

"There always is," Finnian replied.

The Grandfather Clock boomed, twice, the sound so sharp it rattled the glass in the lamps. The air rippled, and in the space between the priest and the door, the portal opened—this time rimmed in gold and blue, the oval taller than a man and flickering at its edges like a torch held in a high wind.

The priest did not hesitate. He tucked the clock under his arm, cinched the pedometer at his waist, and stepped through.

The portal snapped closed, the air in the shop snapping back like a stretched wire. The only trace of what had happened was a faint scent of candle smoke and the imprint of a leather shoe on the mat.

Finnian sat, and let the silence seep into his bones. He stared at his own hands, the trembling gone, but with it something else: the sense of fun, of possibility, of being able to make things right by making them better.

He sat for a very long time, and when he stood, it was to wind every clock in the shop—not to synchronize them, but to set each one just a little off, a second fast or slow, a tiny slip to let the world breathe.

And for the first time in his life, he did not check to see if they were right.

He let the next hour pass without meaning to, lost in the hollow rhythm of the shop. It was only when the baker's bell tolled that he remembered the outside world at all. He cleaned up, washed his hands twice, and, almost against his own will, locked the shop behind him and set out for the trade road.

The morning cold had not lifted. A fine, half-melted slush sucked at his boots and turned the lane to a surface slick enough that each step was a meditation on the value of friction. He passed a few neighbors, their greetings quieter than usual, their eyes quick to return to the work of the day. It suited Finnian. He wasn't sure he could have managed a smile, even for Makota's youngest, who was parked on a barrel and blowing perfect rings of steam into the air.

The trade road ran east from the town's edge, flanked for the first half mile by spindly, leafless poplars and the occasional, surprisingly stubborn patch of autumn color. It was a straight, unadorned line—no distractions, no deviations, just a route for goods and travelers. Finnian could see the group from a hundred yards: the pair of handcarts, the heap of canvas-wrapped baggage, and the party of pilgrims standing in a loose ring, watching a repair underway.

Wilem Cartwright knelt beside one of the handcarts, sleeves rolled high, fingers already ink-stained with axle grease. He worked the way a master did, not rushing, but never stopping, every move purposeful and final. Warren stood at the cart's far end, both enormous green arms bracing the frame so it wouldn't shift under Wilem's adjustments. Even at rest, the ogre looked like he could have hoisted the whole cart one-handed.

Of the pilgrims, three sat on a roll of bedding, heads bowed in a silent conversation, while a fourth paced slow, deliberate circles, hands pressed together as if in prayer. The fifth—a small, nervous man—hovered at Wilem's elbow, eyes flicking from the cart to the horizon and back, as if expecting the missing priest to return at any moment.

Jen was there, boots planted wide, coat unbuttoned, the blue-and-white sash of her office draped with the studied carelessness of someone who needed everyone to know who was in charge but who hated the idea of anyone thinking she cared. She leaned against a milestone marker, talking in low tones with one of the sitting pilgrims.

Finnian felt himself shrinking as he approached. He wiped his hands on his coat, tried to find a neutral expression, and waited at the edge of the group until Jen saw him.

She waved him in with a two-fingered beckon. "Springdale! Good timing. We're just about to see if Wilem's magic can get these folks rolling again."

Wilem looked up, grinned through a patch of stubble, and said, "Don't let her fool you, Finn. The only magic here is your shop's timer. The last time I fixed a cart this fast, it was because my wife was yelling in the next room."

Warren snorted, a sound like distant thunder. "You want to race? I could pop the other wheel off and set it back before you finish this one."

"Don't tempt me," Wilem shot back, but his eyes were on the axle. "There's still time for it to break again."

Finnian tried to smile, failed, and cleared his throat. "Jen, could I speak with you? Privately?"

She read his face, and her own amusement flickered out. "Sure. Over here." She led him out of the circle, past the milestone and a little ways down the road, just far enough that the breeze muffled their words.

Jen waited. When Finnian said nothing, she offered, "Is it about the clocks?"

He shook his head. "It's the priest. He—he's gone."

Jen's eyes narrowed. "Gone where?"

"Through a portal," Finnian said, voice low. "Just like the others. The clock and the step-counter, too. It happened as soon as he touched them both."

Jen exhaled, slow and careful. "Did you see where?"

Finnian hesitated. "Somewhere on the road. Marching alone. The rest of the party… they were behind. He never looked back."

Jen nodded, not surprised. "I figured as much. You know, Springdale, it's a wonder anyone in this world ever gets where they're going. So much noise about the destination, but no one ever asks why they wanted to be there in the first place."

She took a step off the road, stomped the mud off her boots, and looked back at the group. "I should tell them. They'll want to know what happened."

"Do you think they'll be angry?" Finnian asked.

Jen shrugged. "Maybe. But grief and anger, they're just different faces of the same coin. Sometimes, when you flip it enough times, you get bored of the game and move on."

She rejoined the pilgrims, Finnian in tow. The small, nervous man —who now looked more lost than nervous—stood as they approached.

Jen addressed them all at once, voice loud enough for the workers and the ogre to hear. "There's news about your priest. Finnian saw him take a shortcut, you could say. He's already on the path ahead. Might even be waiting for you at the next town."

The pacing pilgrim frowned. "He left without us?"

Jen shook her head. "I think he just got too wrapped up in the schedule. Sometimes, when you focus too hard on the next step, you miss what's beside you."

Wilem, finished with the cart, brushed his hands off and said, "Happens in my shop, too. If I watch the clock, I get worse, not better."

The sitting pilgrims said nothing, but one—the oldest, a woman with sun-scarred cheeks—raised her chin and said, "He always was like that. Even at home. If we fell behind, he'd keep going. He thought that was virtue."

"Maybe it is, for some," Warren rumbled. "But for others, it's just a lonely walk."

The words hung in the cold air, heavy but not unkind.

The small pilgrim looked at the ground, then up at Finnian. "Do you think we should still go?"

Finnian, caught off guard, realized he had no answer. But Jen did.

"Go, or don't," she said. "But maybe don't worry so much about the clock. The Festival of the Twinned Lanterns won't mind if you're a day early or a day late."

The group sat with that a moment. Then the old woman said, "We'll go. But slower, I think."

Jen nodded, and the small man said, "Thank you," not sure who he was thanking.

The pilgrims began gathering their things. Wilem and Warren reassembled the handcart, talking quietly about axle grease and the virtues of overbuilding. Jen stood beside Finnian, her arms crossed against the chill.

He waited, expecting a lecture or a wry joke. Instead, Jen said, "You did what you could. Sometimes the world wants what it wants."

Finnian looked at the road, then at the cart, then at his own hands. "It feels like a cheat. Like I'm a cog in someone else's clock, and I never even see the face."

Jen smiled, but it was the kind that made you want to fix the thing that caused it. "If it helps, no one ever sees the face. We're all gears, even the ones that think they're the mainspring."

She gave him a pat on the arm, solid and not at all condescending. "Come by the pub tonight. Sam has something she wants to show you."

He nodded, not trusting himself to speak.

As he watched the pilgrims set off, slower now, he wondered if the world would ever run smooth—or if, perhaps, that was the point.

———

The Broken Claw was almost empty when Finnian arrived, which would have surprised him in any other mood. The pub was a constant—the hearth always stoked, the bar always lined with bread and beer, a handful of regulars always present to fill the air with a low, pleasant hum. But tonight the benches were bare except for Jen at the bar, Sam behind it, and a single, ancient man dozing in the corner with a chessboard for company.

Sam smiled as Finnian entered, but didn't call out. Jen lifted her mug and gestured for him to join her.

He sat, blinking against the firelight. The first thing he noticed was that all the clocks were gone. Every wall, every shelf that used to hold a ticking thing, now bore nothing but the faint shadow of where it had once hung.

Sam caught his glance. "Moved 'em all to the back. Jen's idea." She poured a pint with practiced ease. "Some people just don't know when to quit."

Jen grinned, unrepentant. "If you can't control time, at least control the clocks."

Finnian tried to match their good humor, but found himself slipping back into his own thoughts. "Does it bother you? Not knowing the exact hour?"

"Not in the least," Sam said. "You know, back when I was soldiering, you could tell the officers from the grunts because the officers always asked what time it was. The grunts just waited until they were hungry, then found a reason to eat."

Jen sipped her beer. "And in my experience, the more people needed to know the hour, the less they got done. All that energy spent worrying about being late."

"Maybe," Finnian said, "but if you don't keep track, you could waste half your life before you realize it's gone."

Jen raised an eyebrow. "Or you could spend your whole life worried about wasting it, and never get around to living."

Finnian laughed, more out of habit than amusement. "If you're here to give me a lecture, I'd rather you just throw me out."

Sam poured him a pint anyway. "No lectures. We just wanted to see how you were holding up."

He accepted the mug, let the cool foam touch his upper lip before daring a sip. "You know the strange part? I don't feel any different. Even after..." He let the words trail off.

Jen picked up the thread. "After you watched a man walk out of his own story?"

Finnian nodded. "Or maybe I just want to pretend I had nothing to do with it."

Sam set her elbows on the bar, hands folded. "You're a clockmaker,

Finn. You're used to seeing all the parts. But sometimes, things just go, and there's nothing for it."

He turned to Jen. "You said you wanted to show me something."

She finished her beer and set the mug down. "Right. Come with me."

Sam gave a little wave. "Don't let her get you lost."

Jen led Finnian out into the night. The cold had sharpened; every surface glittered with ice. The town square was lit by the low, orange glow from the bakery window and the wavering lamp at the far end of the lane.

Jen stopped in the center of the green and turned a slow circle. "What do you see?" she asked.

Finnian took in the view. "Nothing. It's empty."

"Exactly." Jen grinned, but there was a hint of sadness behind it. "Do you remember what it was like before the clocks? Before everyone started living by the minute?"

He tried, but the memories were jumbled. He remembered games in the green, arguments at the market, the impromptu concerts put on by Makota's kits and the traveling minstrels. There had been noise, and mess, and laughter that ran late into the night.

Now, the green was silent. The paths were swept. The benches were aligned, and even the lamp's glow felt like it was keeping time.

"They're all home," Finnian said.

Jen nodded. "They're all home, because now everyone knows exactly how many minutes they have before it's too late to finish the bread, or too late to get the kids in bed, or too late to wake up on time. They're efficient." She spat the word like a curse. "Even the town meetings—they're over before I've finished writing my notes. No more shouting matches, no more drawn-out stories. Just 'all in favor' and 'motion passed' and out the door."

Finnian looked down at his boots. "I thought I was helping."

Jen's voice softened. "You were, Finn. You are. But maybe not in the way you hoped."

He stared at the empty green. "If I stopped fixing the clocks…"

Jen shook her head. "You couldn't, and you wouldn't. But maybe you could make a different kind of clock. One that lets people lose time, instead of always chasing it."

He thought about that. He thought about the odd, misaligned clocks in his shop. The way the bread sometimes landed jam-side down, and the way the lake never kept to any schedule but its own. He thought about Alred, and the pilgrims, and the way people drifted in and out of each other's lives.

Jen nudged him. "Don't take it so hard. The world's just a big clock, and sometimes it needs a little chaos to keep it running."

Finnian smiled, truly this time. "If I made a clock that ran backwards, would anyone buy it?"

"Only if it made a good sound when it struck," Jen said. "People like that."

They stood in the cold a little longer, watching the town stay still.

After a while, Finnian said, "Maybe tomorrow I'll bring back the clocks. But only the broken ones."

Jen grinned. "That's the spirit."

He walked home slow, letting the night decide the pace. For the first time in a long while, he didn't care if he arrived early, or late, or at all.

fifteen

. . .

THE FOLLOWING AFTERNOON, the clocks in Finnian's shop kept their usual conversational chatter, but the mood was changed, as if even the gears themselves were trying to decide whether precision or looseness made for better company. Finnian, for his part, had set aside the Toast-Buttering Machine and once again cleared the bench for his most interesting commission: Leota's Variable-Timing Timer.

He'd started the morning full of intent to be simple, to take Jen's words about "letting things wobble" to heart and make a clock that erred on the side of randomness. And yet, as was his nature, Finnian had quickly become enthralled by the idea of precise imprecision. It was one thing to let a clock drift; it was another entirely to design a clock that drifted by design, a mechanical whimsy with mathematical bones.

Now, with sleeves rolled high, he surveyed the mess he'd made in the name of progress. The workbench was a battlefield of incomplete assemblies: half a dozen brass gear trains, a row of mismatched escapements, a scatter of weights that rolled away at the least provocation. Finnian had made three separate attempts at a randomizing governor, each one more elaborate and less functional than the last.

He stood, hands on hips, and addressed the parts as though they'd let him down personally. "Well, there you have it," he muttered. "You try for a little creative disorder, and it goes straight to riot."

He plucked the largest gear off the tray and balanced it on his finger, watching the way the light winked from its teeth. He'd fashioned this one from an old city-tower repeater, filed the teeth to just the right mix of sharpness and imperfection. If he got the balance right, the escapement would "randomly" advance at different intervals—a kind of controlled chaos, only predictable in its refusal to be so.

On the bench, the other parts glimmered in their own way. He'd set out three types of jewel bearings—ruby, sapphire, and the rare but stubbornly beautiful moonstone, which had a way of shifting color depending on the light. He couldn't help but admire the effect: even at rest, the bits and bobs seemed to conspire toward some undiscovered logic.

He picked up the sketchbook he'd been using for notes. The page was a riot of arrows, circles, and ratios. He'd tried to articulate the effect he wanted: a timer that kept uneven hours, or perhaps one that would, every so often, jump a beat or skip ahead, enough to unsettle but never to lose its way entirely.

He ran a finger down a column of numbers, each annotated with a single word—slip, race, pause, stutter, glide. He'd always liked the notion that time itself had moods. Today, it was as if the entire shop was stuck on "pause," waiting for him to declare a winner among the wreckage of failed attempts.

With a gentle touch, he began slotting together the latest candidate. The moonstone bearings first—they fit the arbor with a satisfying click. Then the primary gear, which seated into place like a coin in a vending box. Next came the heart of the mechanism: a tiny, uneven flywheel, lashed to the gear by a pair of lopsided pins. This was where the magic, or at least the mischief, would happen.

He checked the mesh. There was just enough slack to allow for a stutter, but not enough to seize. He grinned. "That's the spirit," he said, and fed in the escapement, which was designed to slip every third beat, or maybe every fourth, depending on the ambient temperature and the phase of the moon.

He wound the spring, just a hair. The assembly shuddered, then ticked: once, twice, a staccato triple, then a long pause before it started again, as if catching its breath.

Finnian let out a low whistle. "You lovely, unreliable thing," he said, giving the gear a little flick. The timer responded with a new rhythm: tick-tock-pause, tick-tock-tock, pause, then a rush of ticks before the whole thing wobbled to a standstill.

He let it rest and turned back to the other half-assembled bits. He spent the next hour building up a second model, this time with the sapphire bearings, and a slightly heavier flywheel. The effect was different—less prone to sudden stutters, more likely to build up speed and then slam into a dead stop.

He watched both models, side by side, as they did their odd little dance. He tried to keep track, to predict which would "win," but every time he thought he had the pattern, it changed.

Finnian felt a surge of pride, mixed with a thrum of irritation. He'd wanted to let go of control, to build a thing that delighted in unpredictability. But now, faced with the evidence of his own handiwork, he desperately wanted to chart, graph, and domesticate the randomness—put a ratio to the chaos, a metric to the madness.

He scribbled a new note in the margin of the page: "Perhaps it's not about random, but about choice."

He couldn't help but laugh at himself. "Letting go, but never letting it be," he said, the words feeling both true and faintly mocking.

For the next half hour, he cycled between the two models, swapping in different combinations of weights, gears, and pinions, trying to see what effect each had. Sometimes the timer would race, sometimes it would hesitate for long stretches, like a child refusing to go to bed. At one point, it even ran backwards for a full three ticks before correcting itself, a feat that made Finnian snort out loud.

He set both timers running and sat back, arms folded, watching as the patterns merged and diverged. It was, he realized, exactly what Leota had asked for—a variable-timing device that didn't just mark time, but argued with it.

The air in the shop was now thick with the sounds of dueling clocks, the uneven beats clashing and harmonizing in unpredictable ways. Finnian felt the tension, the odd joy of not knowing what would happen next.

He leaned forward, chin on his hands, and regarded his creation. There was a wildness in it, a spirit that defied order, but there was also a stubborn, mechanical beauty—a kind of truce between control and abandon.

Finnian reached for his tea, which had grown cold. He didn't mind. He sipped, and watched the timers run.

He thought of Jen, and her words about letting the world breathe. He thought of Leota, and her desire to anchor a spell to the irregular heartbeat of the universe. He thought, not for the first time, that he was perhaps overqualified for building things that didn't want to behave.

He picked up a pencil, twirled it between his fingers, and made another note.

"Maybe the real trick," he wrote, "is knowing when to let the error stand."

The timers clicked and clattered, refusing to be tamed.

He was in the process of swapping out a moonstone bearing for a sapphire one—his fingers slick with the residue of oil and tea—when he heard the faint click of the shop door.

He didn't look up right away. It was the sort of click that usually signaled a customer who was afraid of making demands, or perhaps a neighbor coming to borrow a bit of time and nothing else. In any case, he'd grown used to letting the shop greet its visitors for him: the clocks, especially the wall-mounted regulator, always tolled out a soft, welcoming note whenever someone entered. This time, the regulator's bell made only a single, shy chime.

Finnian wiped his hands on a cloth and straightened. The man who stood just inside the threshold could have been mistaken for a retired monk, or maybe a half-blind oracle—white hair to the shoulders, beard as wild as an uprooted bush, clothing patched and dusted with flour from a hundred years of handling sacks and ledgers. He moved with a deliberate, economical slowness, as though each footstep had to be measured before the floor would agree to hold it.

For a moment, Finnian couldn't place the face. Then it came to him:

Knodalon, the keeper of the lakeside storehouse. Or, as some in town said, the ghost who haunted the bench outside it, never leaving, never sleeping, simply observing all that came and went. In all his years in North Pointe, Finnian had never seen Knodalon this far inside the walls, let alone in a shop. For all he knew, the man might not even know how commerce worked.

Finnian managed a greeting. "Ah—Knodalon. Good afternoon."

Knodalon did not respond, but let the door settle quietly behind him. He advanced into the room, gaze flicking across the shelves not with curiosity, but with the cool, slow appraisal of a surveyor checking a boundary line. He passed by the wall of timers, the pendulums, the row of old-fashioned pocket models, and paused at the bench where Finnian had been working.

Finnian suddenly felt the urge to hide the prototype timer—was it too ugly, or perhaps too naked, for this visitor? He kept his hands steady and waited.

Knodalon's eyes lingered on the moonstone timer for a full count of three, then drifted onward. He circled the room, bypassing Finnian as though he were a piece of furniture, and stopped at the glass cabinet where the more ornate pieces were displayed. Here he spent the most time, peering through the glass at the careful arrangement inside.

It was a cabinet Finnian was proud of, a little vanity project in itself. The upper shelf held his showpieces: a table clock shaped like a lion, its mane made from interlocking brass slivers; a perpetual calendar that reset itself every morning at sunrise, no matter the season; and, at the far right, the so-called "Celestial Orchid," a tiny desk clock carved in the likeness of a flower, each petal a delicate, gear-driven marvel.

Knodalon opened the cabinet with the same soft, measured touch he'd used on the door. His hand hovered over the choices, then—without a single tremor—he picked up the Celestial Orchid and turned it over in his palm. He held it close to his face, eyes almost closed, as if listening for a secret. Then he wound the key, set the clock on the counter, and watched the petals open, one by one, on a schedule that only the clock understood.

Finnian, uncertain whether to intervene, just waited. He could feel the tension rise in the air, as if the shop itself was holding its breath.

Knodalon let the Orchid run for a while, then, with the same care, returned it to the counter. He considered the other two, but after a moment, set both hands on the glass and leaned in close to look at the lion clock.

He did not touch it, only watched the slow rise and fall of the mane as the gears cycled. Finnian found himself doing the same, both men staring as the shadows crawled over the brass. At the strike of the hour—by Finnian's count, it was the mark just after two—the lion gave a single, decorous roar, a sound designed to be more charming than loud.

Knodalon did not flinch or smile. He looked at Finnian then, a direct gaze that seemed to cut through every layer of air between them.

Finnian braced himself for a question. But Knodalon only nodded, as if to say "This will do," and, with a silent efficiency, lifted the clock from its shelf and cradled it against his chest.

The room went very quiet.

Finnian coughed. "Would you like me to—ah—wrap it, or adjust it, or—?"

Knodalon shook his head once.

The door bells chimed.

The woman who entered was a compact bundle of nerves and purpose. She wore a jacket that looked as if it had been patched by three different species—leather, waxed canvas, and some kind of iridescent beetle carapace Finnian couldn't name. Her eyes darted about, taking in every surface, every artifact, every scrap of brass. She had the look of someone who'd spent years in places where "indoors" was just a theory.

"Finnian Springdale?" she said, barely waiting for a nod before pressing on. "I need a clock. Not a fancy one. A field piece. Something you can bash against a rock and it'll keep ticking. Can you do that?"

Finnian, still off-balance from the day's prior visit, nodded. "That's most of what I do."

"Good. It's for work. Mistral Mountains, high passes—sunrise and sunset are hard to judge, and I need to mark the light cycles. The animals are... sensitive." She paused to catch her breath, then said, "Name's Skerry. I'm a naturalist, or as much as anyone gets to be these days. I'm supposed to catalogue the dawnrunners, the spiral-tailed jinkers, and at least three types of whistlepup that only come out at very specific intervals."

She produced, from inside her jacket, a notebook the size of her fist, bristling with pressed leaves and a shed whistlepup tooth as a bookmark. "If I don't record the precise moment the dawnrunners break cover, the data's worthless. Same for the jinkers; if I'm even a half-candlemark off, they'll have moulted their crests and I'll miss the entire cycle."

Finnian smiled, despite himself. "You'll want a movement with a luminous dial, then. Maybe a bell to sound the mark, in case you're watching and not watching."

Skerry's eyes went wide, hopeful. "Do you have one?"

"I have three," Finnian said, and went to the display case. "And if none suit, I'll make a fourth."

He set them out on the counter. The first was a pocket watch in a battered steel case, face painted with a faded orange that almost glowed in the dusk. The second, a rugged carriage clock, its handle reinforced with a strip of what Finnian suspected was orcish sinew. The third—a favorite of his—was a wrist model, originally a vanity commission for a miner who wanted to show off at the bar, but never came to collect. It had oversized hands and a tiny, cheerful bell that rang at the hour and at any interval set by the dial on the side.

Skerry took to the wrist model immediately. "This one," she said, already strapping it to her wrist and testing the range of movement. "Can you reset the chime? I need it to mark every thirty-eight minutes, not every sixty. That's the jinker's foraging period."

Finnian grinned, glad for the clarity of a real, tangible problem. "Give me fifteen minutes and it's yours."

She fidgeted, but stayed close, poking through the rest of the clocks and timers. She spoke as she worked. "You probably get a lot of odd requests," she said, not really a question.

Finnian shrugged, adjusting the regulator on the wrist clock. "I once made a timepiece that only ran in the dark, for a mole-keeper who lived underground and wanted to wake at the proper dusk. That one was a puzzle."

Skerry brightened. "Did it work?"

"Not perfectly," Finnian said, smiling ruefully. "But he said the errors made it more authentic. It only woke him up at true night about half the time, and the rest of the time he got extra sleep. He seemed happy."

Skerry laughed, a sharp, short sound. "Maybe I should learn from that."

She walked the length of the counter, eyes scanning every surface. "What about that one?" She pointed to the Celestial Orchid, still winding down from its last cycle. "It's beautiful, but it looks like it would shatter if you glared at it."

Finnian chuckled. "That one is for someone with more patience than sense. The petals only open at the proper hour if you set it perfectly. Most people don't have the time to wait for it." He glanced at the blue ticket still tucked under its base, a curious ache blooming in his chest.

Skerry nodded, then returned to the wrist clock. "Will this keep in snow? I'll be above the treeline for at least a week."

"I'll seal the back," Finnian said. "If you hear the bell go muffled, you'll know it's iced over."

He made the adjustment, quick and sure, and set the chime to Skerry's interval. When he slid the watch across the counter, she caught it with both hands, as if catching a living creature.

She held it to her ear, eyes closing for a moment, just to listen.

"I'll need to pay you in coin, or trade. I have some rare mosses, or a pair of—" She rummaged, produced a waxed-paper envelope. "Dragonfly larvae, if that's a thing you like?"

Finnian waved it off. "Consider it a gift, if you bring back a story. Or at least a sketch."

Skerry's grin was infectious. "Deal." She slid the notebook across the counter. "You can have a look now, if you want. I keep the best ones in the middle."

Finnian flipped the notebook open, careful not to lose the whistlepup tooth. The sketches inside were shockingly good: quick, confident lines, every animal caught in a pose of movement or surprise. There were notes, too, running alongside: "Jinker, morning of first frost, coat at half shed"; "Whistlepup pack—yips matched to each other, synchronized at sunrise." He admired the work, then closed the book, smiling.

"Do you ever wonder what they see in you?" he asked.

Skerry blinked. "What?"

He gestured at the drawings. "The animals. You observe them, they observe you. I sometimes think the only reason clocks keep time at all is that they know someone's watching. Otherwise, they'd just do as they pleased."

Skerry thought about it. "I think they're annoyed by me, mostly. But I like to think the world's better when it's being watched." She tucked the notebook away, snapped the watch onto her wrist, and said, "Thank you, Finnian."

"Be careful," he replied. "Some places up there don't keep the same time as the valley. The light can trick you."

"Noted," Skerry said, and headed for the door, already rolling her sleeve to keep the watch visible.

Finnian felt a prickle along the back of his neck.

From the back of the shop, the Grandfather Clock gave a double chime—a sound that was neither loud nor soft, but exactly the right size to fill the world.

The front of the shop shimmered. Finnian blinked. There, in the place where the door had been, was a perfect oval of air, rimmed in gold and blue, swirling with a light that looked at once like sky and water and fire.

Through it, Finnian saw the wildest place he'd ever imagined: a slope of broken stone, peppered with blue and red lichen, and bounding across it, a pack of spiral-tailed jinkers, their coats flashing in the sun. Above, on a blackened snag, a whistlepup howled, its voice so clear that Finnian could feel it in his teeth.

Skerry stared, mouth open, at the scene, then back at Finnian.

Knodalon raised one shaggy eyebrow.

He didn't know what to say. He nodded, once, and Skerry nodded back. She stepped through.

The world rushed in to fill the gap, the portal collapsing like a curtain drawn at the end of a play.

Knodalon stood perfectly still, watching the place where Skerry had vanished. He waited a while, then, with a single, deliberate motion, walked out, clock in hand.

Inside, the shop's clocks sputtered back to life, as if waking from a long, agreeable nap.

Finnian watched them, wondering if they'd ever tell the right time again.

sixteen
...

THE NEXT MORNING, Finnian Springdale found himself staring at the ceiling above his bed, searching for a logical reason to get up. For all his years of routine, he'd never needed to invent one before—the shape of the day had always formed itself in the whirr and click of gears, in the anticipation of a mechanism to perfect, or at least the faint, perverse joy of correcting a flaw in someone else's handiwork. But now, every possible outcome felt hazardous. His clocks had begun opening doors to fate—sometimes literally—and even the ones that didn't seemed to infect the town with a fever for punctuality and efficiency. He'd built his reputation on making things work better than they ought, but lately, "better" had started to taste a lot like "worse," and the aftertaste lingered.

He lay still, listening. In the silence between the breathing of the house and the muted tick of his own bedside regulator, he could hear the town's rhythm, even from here: the bakery's morning bell, the carts in the lane, the heavy tread of Warren the Smith passing on his daily circuit to the forge. There was something new in the cadence, something that made the hairs on Finnian's neck prickle, though he couldn't put a name to it.

He got up, dressed with unconscious economy, and stood for a moment in the center of his bedroom. He looked at the workbench by the window, then at the tidy row of tools arranged on the wall. They looked back at him, ready and waiting, as if nothing had changed. But Finnian hesitated. He feared that the very act of choosing what to do next might trigger another burst of fate, some new, unintended acceleration in the world outside.

He forced himself to the kitchen, made a cup of tea with the Mark II Brewer (which, despite its past, had lately worked without incident), and then just stood, sipping, as the light grew in the window. Even the tea tasted too sharp, as if the leaves themselves were eager to get the day over with.

He watched his shop from behind the glass, half-expecting to see something dramatic—a rift, a portal, a crowd of townsfolk marching in lockstep past the door. But nothing remarkable happened, at least not at first. The market square beyond was filled with its usual traffic: bakers and butchers, the blacksmith's apprentice on an early errand, even the children ferrying bread and cheese to and from the houses around the green.

And yet, it was all off. Finnian realized, with a jolt, that he hadn't seen a single person pause to chat. Not even Makota, who was known to spend entire mornings gossiping with customers, nor Bertram the cobbler, whose habit of leaning in doorways and pontificating on leather was nearly as reliable as the town bell. Today, everyone walked with speed and direction. People acknowledged each other with a nod or a brief smile, but no one lingered, no one stopped. Even the children seemed to treat their errands like a timed race, darting along the paths with single-minded focus.

It wasn't just the townsfolk. The traveling merchants, usually prone to lingering by the fountain or haggling for the pleasure of it, marched through the square in a straight line, barely glancing at the wares or the architecture. The green itself, typically a tapestry of lounging, laughing, and loitering, was now a corridor—a straight shot from one end to the other, efficiency incarnate.

Finnian felt a wave of cold dread slosh in his belly. He'd lived here most of his life, but he'd never seen the town move like this. It was as if everyone had synchronized themselves to the same hidden metronome, and the music left no room for adagio or cadenza.

He stepped out into the street, letting the door close behind him with a precise, well-oiled click. The air had the clean chill of a day set to break sunny and cold, and Finnian hugged his jacket closer. He wandered toward the market without conscious intent, his feet tracing the old familiar lines but finding them subtly altered.

At the bakery, Makota's kits darted in and out, each one loaded with a neat stack of loaves. Finnian watched as Makota herself met a customer at the threshold, exchanged a brisk greeting, handed off the bread, and then shooed the next in line forward. There were smiles, even laughter, but it all seemed to slide off the surface—nothing stuck. The flow was constant, brisk, and relentless.

Finnian approached the counter. Makota didn't even blink at his arrival, just reached for a fresh roll and pushed it into his hand. "Morning, Finnian!" she called, already pivoting to the next customer. "We've got a rush today. No dawdling!"

He managed a thank you, but she was already gone. He tried to linger, to make a comment about the weather or the latest clock commission, but it was like trying to interrupt a waterfall.

He moved on, more uneasy than before. At the edge of the green, he caught sight of Cole Coleson, who, in previous times, would have waved him over for a chat or at least a brief exchange about the state of the town's crops. Today, Cole was marching from the grocer's to the stables, two sacks in hand, not even breaking stride as he crossed Finnian's path.

"Good day to you, Finnian!" Cole called, never slowing. "Hope the clocks are treating you well!"

"Ah, yes, thank you," Finnian replied, but the words were wasted on the air. Cole was already gone.

He wandered toward the trade road, head full of static. Maybe, he thought, it was just market day pressure, a rare confluence of urgency. Maybe the recent influx of travelers had set everyone on edge. Maybe, maybe, maybe. But the more he watched, the more it felt intentional, orchestrated—like the town itself had become a mechanism, and someone had tightened the spring just a little too much.

The old, dry joke about North Pointe was that nothing here ever ran on time, but Finnian had loved that about the place. He'd always thought it gave the town a personality—unpredictable, rough around the edges, alive in the way only a slightly unbalanced clock can be. Now it ticked, with a precision that felt less like order and more like fate closing in.

He looked for a reason to laugh it off, and found none.

Out on the trade road, the traffic was heavier than usual—carts and riders, pilgrims in matching robes, and a pair of high-shouldered traders driving a wagon loaded with barrels. They all moved with purpose, eyes fixed on the horizon, voices low and businesslike. No shouting, no haggling, no songs. Even the hawkers were subdued, their calls trimmed to the minimum. Finnian had seen funeral processions with more verve.

He leaned on the low stone fence by the road, chewing his roll and scanning the distance. That was when he saw Knodalon, perched on his customary bench, just beyond the town gate.

The old man had always been a fixture—so still and patient that people joked he was part of the landscape. But today, Knodalon was not watching the world pass by. He was staring at the clock Finnian had sold him yesterday, the lion clock, cradled on his knees.

Finnian watched as Knodalon held the clock up, turning it to catch the light, then set it down and stared at its face. His lips moved in time with the pendulum's swing; his head, usually so motionless, gave a slow, steady nod at each tick. There was an intensity to the focus, a hunger that made Finnian's chest tighten.

After a few minutes, Finnian realized that Knodalon was not just observing the clock. He was matching it, tuning himself to its rhythm. With every sweep of the lion's tail, Knodalon's head dipped a fraction, like a metronome of flesh and bone and memory.

Finnian watched, transfixed. In all the years he'd known Knodalon, he'd never seen the old man so invested in anything. He wanted to approach, to ask what was happening, to break the spell. But he stayed back, a sense of dread rooting him to the spot.

Then, without warning, Knodalon lurched to his feet. He clutched the lion clock to his chest, glared once at the sun, then strode toward the storehouse with a speed that bordered on panic. His movements were abrupt, alien. He ignored the passing carts and nearly collided with a pair of travelers, never slowing, never speaking.

Finnian tracked the motion, jaw slack. He glanced around, half expecting someone else to notice, to react, to comment. But the townsfolk kept their paths, heads down, eyes set on their own destinations. Only Finnian seemed to register the change in Knodalon, or the subtle, grinding wrongness in the world.

He stared after the old man until the storehouse door banged shut behind him. For a long moment, Finnian just stood there, clutching the unfinished roll. He felt the urge to drop it, to throw it, to break something—a gear, a clock, the entire morning.

Instead, he walked back toward the shop, slow and deliberate, feeling every tick of the invisible metronome pressing against the inside of his skull.

He thought of all the clocks he'd made, the way each one ticked with a little piece of himself. He wondered, not for the first time, if he was the one being wound.

He didn't like the answer that came.

The street was empty as he made his way home. The green was silent, every window in the houses showing only brief flickers of movement. The market had already cleared, stalls emptied, swept, and shut tight. Even the air seemed to hush, as if waiting for a cue that was about to sound.

He reached his front stoop, hesitated, then turned to look back at the town. Nothing moved. The sun hung in the sky, bright and pitiless.

He wondered if the whole world had started to run on a clock, and if so, whose hand had set the time.

He thought about Knodalon and the lion clock, about the way the old man's head had nodded in time, about the desperate run to the storehouse. Finnian had lived in North Pointe long enough to know what was normal and what wasn't, and this—this was the very opposite of normal.

He opened the door, stepped inside, and let the silence settle around him. The click of the latch sounded like the tick of a clock, a reminder that time kept marching, whether you wanted it to or not.

Finnian stood in the entryway, staring at his own wall of clocks, each one ticking away in the measured chaos he'd always loved. He thought of all the ways they could go wrong, and all the ways he'd tried to fix them. He wondered what would happen if he simply let them run, flaws and all.

Today, the wall of clocks sounded not like a random chorus, but a single, synchronized choir.

He stood in the middle of the shop, frozen. He listened. There was no layering, no discord, not even the usual lazy overlap of a few seconds' drift from clock to clock. The ancient, inherited shelf clocks matched the fastidious city regulators; even the experimental, deliberately unruly models, designed to wander from true, now tocked and ticked in perfect, ruthless harmony.

Finnian's scalp prickled. He closed his eyes, and for the first time since childhood, he counted seconds aloud, matching the rhythm to the sound. He made it past sixty without a single misstep.

He moved to the wall, running his hand beneath the regulators, the cheap carriage clocks, the delicate, custom-tuned pieces he'd built for friends and never sold. Each tick landed like a tap to the chest, not just heard but felt, a little electric jolt—sixty-two, sixty-three, sixty-four— on and on, flawless and inescapable.

The feeling was wrong, all wrong. His entire philosophy as a craftsman had been that true perfection was a myth, that every clock needed a little margin for error or it would rebel in a fit of breakdown or stutter. But here, in this moment, his entire shop had staged a mutiny. They had unionized, and now they kept a time that was not his own.

He wandered behind the counter, opened the repair drawer, and picked up a half-dismantled movement. Even in pieces, the escapement lever trembled at the exact mark of the second, as if yearning to be reassembled and join the massed choir. Finnian set it down, uneasy.

The pressure of the hour approached, and he could feel it in the soles of his feet, a thumping in the floorboards that kept time with his pulse. He looked up at the massive, old Grandfather Clock at the back of the shop. Its hands crept toward the hour. There was nothing to be done but wait for the inevitable.

And then it struck. Every clock in the shop gave out a note—bells, gongs, chimes, and the subtle ping of metal on metal—all at the same instant. The sound was not loud, but it was so dense and complete that Finnian's breath stopped in his chest. He felt the pressure in his teeth, vibrating, as the sound poured over him in a wave.

He staggered, nearly knocked off balance by the force of it, and caught himself on the edge of the workbench. The chime faded, replaced by the steady, inhuman perfection of the synchronized tick.

Finnian's mind raced, searching for an explanation. There was none, except the obvious: something in the world had snapped to a new order, and his clocks—his beloved, stubborn, idiosyncratic clocks—had been pressed into service.

He looked out the window, desperate for distraction, and saw the lane outside as a time-lapse painting: every person moved with purpose, their footsteps and gestures landing at regular intervals, as if the whole town had agreed on a new, inviolable schedule.

But then, a hiccup: one of Cole Coleson's children, the older boy, lingered in the middle of the path. He had stopped to watch a small bird on the fence, its plumage a blot of brilliant yellow against the gray morning. The boy leaned in, tilted his head, and reached out, as if to coax the bird closer.

At that instant, Finnian's clocks began to hum.

It was not a sound made by any individual piece, but an emergent, collective whine, just at the edge of hearing. It grew, a soft, agitated thrum, vibrating the glass of the shop window. Finnian watched as the boy, oblivious to the pressure building, continued to watch the bird, smiling in quiet wonder.

The hum grew sharper, then, all at once, snapped back to silence as the boy—perhaps called by his father, or simply remembering his errand—turned and ran off. The bird darted skyward, vanishing, and the town's clockwork order resumed without a hitch.

Finnian stepped away from the window, feeling light-headed.

He could not help but imagine the town as a single, massive clock, each person a gear or lever or balance wheel, all pressed into alignment, all forced to keep the same, relentless time. The vision was beautiful, in a way, but it was also terrifying. It left no room for error, no space for breath.

He turned, and looked at his own shop, now a part of this greater machine. The clocks kept ticking. The walls, the shelves, the very boards underfoot vibrated with the new order.

Finnian remembered what Jen had said, about letting the world breathe. He tried to believe it was possible, that someone, somewhere, could break the pattern. But in that moment, it seemed that the world had no intention of allowing even a single, accidental pause.

He sat at his workbench, hands folded, and tried to think of what to do next.

But the only thing he heard was the ticking, and the only thing he felt was the growing certainty that even the smallest error would be hunted down and eliminated, as soon as it dared show itself.

He closed his eyes, and waited for the next hour to strike.

He lasted only a quarter hour at the workbench. The pressure of the ticking grew unbearable, a cold sweat prickling under his shirt as the clocks counted out every mistake he'd ever made. He tried, for a few minutes, to lose himself in the mechanics—to tinker, to invent, to distract himself with the familiar comfort of brass and oil—but the effort was hollow. Each time he reached for a tool, his hand landed exactly at the next second, as if some invisible conductor guided his every move.

He thought, for a moment, about smashing a clock. Just one. Just to see if it would break the spell. But the idea filled him with the kind of dread he'd reserved, in younger days, for the breaking of a living thing. There was no rebellion in him, only a creeping sense of guilt, as though he'd personally set this entire machinery in motion.

He stood, restless, and let the shop door drift open behind him. The street outside was as before: efficient, relentless, every person and animal playing their part. Even the birds seemed to fly in pre-arranged patterns, flocking and scattering with mathematical grace.

It was too much. Finnian turned for the only place he could think of—the Broken Claw. If there was any remaining comfort to be had, any trace of the old world, it would be found at the bar, among the people who had always held time in contempt.

He crossed the green, boots crunching the frost in a regular, unvarying pattern. He barely noticed the cold. At the pub, the windows glowed with lamplight, and inside he could see the shapes of people at their usual places. He took a breath, steadied himself, and went in.

The Claw was packed, but perfectly orderly. Every seat was filled, but no one shouted or jostled or sang off-key. The regulars sat in lines, each with a mug in hand, all facing the bar like students in a classroom. There was a pleasant murmur of conversation, but it was modulated—no voice rose above the others, and each pause landed exactly on a multiple of some invisible rhythm.

Sam ran the bar as always, but with a new, almost martial precision. Her long white hair was tied back in a sharp braid, and her hands moved with the efficiency of a trained swordswoman. She poured, wiped, refilled, and set down every drink with the same graceful economy, never breaking stride, never lingering for banter.

Finnian slid onto a vacant stool at the end of the bar. Sam gave him a quick, knowing smile, but didn't greet him aloud. She was too busy with the task at hand: pouring three mugs of ale, each one filled to the identical mark, each topped with a foam head that might as well have been sculpted.

At the far end, one of the miners—Finnian thought his name was Hadden—held a stopwatch in his hand. It was not one of Finnian's, but the mechanism was familiar; he'd seen the type in the capital, used for timing horse races and, less honestly, for outwitting the city guard. Hadden watched Sam's hands, thumb poised on the button. Each time Sam started a pour, Hadden clicked the stopwatch, eyes glued to the dial. His grin grew wider with every round.

Sam noticed. She arched an eyebrow. "Timing me, Hadden?"

The miner didn't even try to deny it. "You're running perfect," he said, voice full of awe. "Never seen anything like it. Three and a half tics every time."

Sam's smile sharpened. "It's all in the wrist." But she watched the stopwatch now, matching her pours even more exactly.

The other patrons picked up on the game. Soon a chorus of bets flew back and forth—how long for a full round, how long for a refill, whether Sam could draw three pints in under ten seconds. No one raised their voice or cut in line, but the mood was bright, contented, and, above all, utterly synchronized.

Finnian stared at the stopwatch, and felt the bottom drop out of his stomach. There was something unnatural in the way it pulsed—a faint, metallic resonance in the air, as if the device was not just recording the time, but conducting it. When Sam poured at a slightly different pace—just a hair slower, just enough to break the pattern—the stopwatch vibrated, displeased. Hadden clicked his tongue and muttered, "Off by a tenth," as if he'd witnessed a personal failure.

Finnian tried to speak, to ask Sam for a drink or to joke about the new sport, but his words caught in his throat. He watched, instead, as Sam reset her movements, correcting the error. The next pour was dead-on, and the stopwatch sang its approval in a low, contented purr.

He looked around the room. Every person was caught in the rhythm—conversations, drinks, laughter, all landing at precise, pre-ordained intervals. No one seemed to notice, or care, that the old, sprawling mess of the Claw had been replaced by something much more efficient.

Sam slid a mug to Finnian, foam trembling at the perfect rim. "You all right?" she asked, keeping her voice low.

He nodded, but didn't trust himself to speak. He sipped, and tasted nothing but the cold, clean snap of the beer. Even the flavor seemed… regular.

Sam leaned in, voice pitched just for him. "If you're wondering, it's not just the bar. It's the whole town. Even the drunks keep their stagger on beat."

Finnian managed a weak laugh. "I noticed."

She poured another set, pausing just long enough to let the noise of the room surge, then fade. "You think it's you?" she asked.

He nodded again.

She shrugged, but her eyes were gentle. "If it is, it's not a bad thing. People get more done. Fewer fights. Even the kids are easier to wrangle." She wiped down the counter, watching his face. "But if you don't like it, maybe you can fix it."

"Or break it," Finnian said, surprising himself with the sharpness of his own voice.

Sam grinned. "Sometimes that's the same thing."

Hadden called for another round, stopwatch at the ready. Sam obliged, this time pouring with such precision that the miner actually applauded. The room hummed with approval, the sound of a job well and perfectly done.

Finnian left the mug half-full. He slid off the stool and threaded through the room, out the door, and into the night.

The street was empty. Even the shadows fell at measured intervals, each lamp pooling light at exactly the same distance from its neighbor. Finnian took a deep breath, let the air fill his lungs, then strode across the green, boots landing in perfect time with the clocks that ruled his shop, his house, the world.

He could not say what drove him, but he found himself running now, cutting across the square and back to his shop, desperate for something he could not name.

Inside, the clocks were waiting.

seventeen
. . .

FINNIAN REACHED the exact center of the green with a nervous energy he hadn't known since the week the shop roof nearly caved in from an unseasonable hailstorm. It was a perfect, cloudless day—cold, but with a sharp clarity that made the lake shimmer and the distant mountains seem near enough to touch. He'd always loved this view; now, it felt like a painting that had been straightened so fiercely that the whole wall might collapse.

There was a distinct sensation of time tightening around him. The world itself seemed to draw breath and hold it, a single moment stretched thin and trembling. Finnian's boots landed on the frosted grass at precisely the same interval—tick, tock, tick, tock—as every clock in his shop and, he suspected, every clock in North Pointe.

A soundless pressure built in his ears. He pushed forward, gaze fixed on the squat silhouette of his shop beyond the green, its gables bright with the morning sun. If he hurried, if he just reached the shop, he could—he didn't know what he could do, not really, but movement felt better than standing still.

Halfway across the green, Finnian heard the town bell wind up for the hour. There was a moment of blessed, familiar hesitation—a drag, a delay, a lazy draw of breath as the old iron gears considered whether it was worth the effort.

Then, suddenly, it bellowed the hour. A single, ringing note, too early by at least seven minutes, by Finnian's internal count. The strike was not only premature but sharp, urgent, as if the bell itself had grown impatient with the situation.

He stopped dead. The shock of the sound hit him in the chest. The next instant, a ripple passed through the green—a visible, physical shudder that bent the grass blades and sent a burst of birds skyward from the edge of the square.

Around him, every window in every building seemed to rattle at once. The bakery's sign swung on its chain, smacking the wall. The glass in the herbalist's window vibrated so hard that the bottles inside danced off their shelves, shattering in a series of bright, chiming crashes. Finnian saw, out of the corner of his eye, the neat row of clocks in Prudence Simonsdotter's tailor shop leap forward as one, hands spinning to match the bell.

The next strike of the bell came even harder—now the clocks across the green all chimed in furious synchrony, a choir of gongs and pings and delicate hammers, all racing to catch up with the new order. Finnian felt it in his teeth, in the fine bones of his sinuses, a pressure that built with each echo.

And still the bell was not done. Another, another—each one a fraction faster, a fraction louder, a fraction more insistent than the last. The world was winding up, and nothing could stop it.

Finnian staggered the last few paces to the shop, flung open the door, and nearly fell inside.

His clocks—his beautiful, well-meaning, slightly off-kilter clocks—were in revolt. The regulators on the north wall spun so fast their hands blurred. The cheap shelf clocks on the east side hopped in place on their pegs, vibrating with an audible whine. Every glass face fogged and cleared, fogged and cleared, as the difference between bell time and clock time collapsed in a violent, city-wide synchronization.

At the back of the shop, the Grandfather Clock stood at rigid attention. Its brass pendulum swung with a heavy, deliberate force, carving the air in broad, defiant sweeps. Finnian felt its tick in his chest, in his bones, and in the tips of his fingers. He moved toward it, more on instinct than intent.

The shop windows gave a long, warbling groan. Behind Finnian, several of the smaller clocks began to slide off their shelves, landing with a series of soft, fatal thumps on the floor. The tiny tourist timer Makota had given him last solstice—a cheap tin thing with a rooster on its face—exploded outright, gears scattering like shot. Finnian barely ducked in time to avoid a flying minute hand.

He made it to the Grandfather Clock, which towered over him, its casing thrumming with an energy he'd never seen in the old beast. He reached for the weight chain, hoping to slow the pendulum, to introduce just a little error—anything to disrupt the tidal pull of time.

But as he laid his hand on the chain, the pendulum stilled. For a half-second, the clock was silent. All the others in the room seemed to gasp in anticipation.

The Grandfather Clock began to tick backward.

It was not a gentle thing. The pendulum reversed with a violence that sent a crack shooting up the length of the case, splitting the polished wood along an old, invisible fault line. The hands, instead of drifting back with dignity, spun counterclockwise in a dizzying spiral, minute and hour racing each other to midnight.

Finnian recoiled, clutching his fingers. The clock groaned, a deep, pained noise that vibrated in the pit of his stomach. The glass in its face bulged, then cracked, letting out a brief, icy rain of fragments.

Finnian, heart hammering, staggered back into the middle of the shop. The whole room was a blur of motion—gears slipping, wheels unwinding, escapements snapping open and shut in desperate, uneven bursts. The clocks no longer just ticked; they shouted, howled, each one warring against its own limitations.

Then the Grandfather Clock let out a final, massive chime—a toll so low and resonant it seemed to come from the earth itself. The casing buckled around the pendulum's anchor, splintering at the base. For a moment, it looked as though the entire thing might fall, but then the clock simply… stopped. Dead silence.

In the aftershock, Finnian could hear every heartbeat in his body. The air was filled with dust and the faint, sweet tang of ozone.

A single second passed.

Then, with the precision of a military order, every other clock in the shop snapped to the exact same time. Even the shattered ones, their hands twisted and broken, seemed to point, somehow, to the same invisible hour.

Finnian sank to his knees. His hands shook so badly he had to brace them on the floor.

The Grandfather Clock, defeated, ticked once—soft, almost apologetic—then slumped against the wall, its cracked face staring blankly at the ruins of its former self.

Finnian looked at the damage, the wreckage, and the evidence of a world that had finally slipped its gears.

Somewhere, outside, the town bell rang the hour again. This time, it was exactly on time.

Finnian choked out a laugh, then pressed a hand to his mouth, unsure if he was laughing or weeping.

The clocks were still. The air in the shop buzzed with the memory of what had just happened.

For the first time, Finnian realized that the trouble he'd brought into the world wasn't going to be fixed with a file and a little oil.

He crawled to the Grandfather Clock, hands trembling, and pressed his palm to the cracked wood. The old clock was warm, as if it had a fever.

He didn't know what to do. He only knew that something vital had broken, and the world would be waiting for him to fix it.

He sat with his hand pressed to the Grandfather Clock until the faint warmth faded from the wood. He wanted to pretend that time, for once, had stopped. But all around him, the other clocks still hummed with a cold, metallic authority, as if daring him to challenge their supremacy. Even the ruined ones seemed to vibrate with purpose, their broken hands twitching toward the next mark.

He hauled himself to his feet, head spinning. The world beyond the shop window glared with winter light. For a moment, Finnian debated locking the door, hiding under his workbench, and letting the whole mess run its course. But that wasn't his way, and it never had been.

He took a deep breath, straightened his spectacles, and stepped outside.

The air had changed—thinner, somehow, as if the town now exhaled in perfect, measured intervals. The square, once a jumble of voices and motion, stood utterly still. Finnian scanned the green, expecting to see chaos, but instead, he found the opposite.

Children, who moments before had been chasing a battered ball across the grass, now sat in a precise ring on the ground, legs crossed, hands folded in their laps. They stared at each other, waiting. Not fidgeting, not whispering, just waiting. Finnian counted the heads—eight, not a one out of place.

A clock in the bakery chimed the quarter-hour. Instantly, the children stood, walked to the edge of the green, and vanished down their respective lanes, not a word exchanged. The abandoned ball rolled to Finnian's feet and stopped, as if awaiting permission.

He left it where it was, unsettled.

He turned, searching for signs of grown-ups. The bakery's door stood wide, but Makota and her kits were nowhere in sight. Even the ever-present aroma of baking bread had vanished, replaced by a faint, antiseptic tang. Finnian glanced at the tailor's across the square—normally a wellspring of color and chatter—but its windows were dark. The only movement was the flick of a curtain as someone peered out, then withdrew with military precision.

Finnian's feet carried him toward the main lane without conscious thought. Each step landed on the frost at exactly the same interval—he tried, once, to break stride, but found his body resisted, as though something in the air demanded conformity.

A dog crossed his path, its gait stiff and regular, tail held at a mathematically perfect angle. It stopped, regarded Finnian with something like apology, then turned and continued its patrol, neither sniffing nor barking nor acknowledging the world in any way. Even the pigeons—usually a raucous cloud above the bakery roof—now perched in evenly spaced ranks along the eaves, each one preening with identical, clockwork gestures.

He passed the grocer's next. Cole Coleson, big as a barn and twice as loud on a normal day, stood behind his counter, arms folded, gazing blankly at the scales in front of him. At the stroke of the next minute, Cole filled a sack with apples, tied it off, and set it on a shelf with three other sacks, each identical in weight and fullness. He wiped his hands on a towel, counted to four, and repeated the process.

Finnian rapped on the window, hoping to catch Cole's eye. For a moment, he thought Cole hadn't seen him. Then, with a forced, jerky motion, Cole turned, raised his hand in a salute, and gave a tight, artificial smile. It looked like a man rehearsing the memory of friendliness. Finnian felt a cold spike of fear.

A door slammed to his left, sharp as a starter's pistol. He turned just in time to see Prudence Simonsdotter step onto the stoop of her shop, baby on her hip, a bolt of brilliant blue fabric under her arm. Prudence's usual posture was graceful and reserved, but now she stood ramrod straight, chin high, her free hand gripping the doorknob as if to anchor herself to the world.

She scanned the green with a quick, precise motion, saw Finnian, and called his name—not as a greeting, but as a question.

"Finnian!" She blinked, as if surprised to hear her own voice. "What is this?"

He started toward her, but his steps felt sticky, as if the ground conspired to slow him.

Before he could answer, Cole emerged from his shop. The big man wiped his hands again, then strode to the stoop, moving in perfect time with Finnian's own pace. He stopped three feet from Prudence, nodded once, then stood with hands at his sides, waiting.

Prudence tried to step forward, but her feet skidded against the stoop, unable to clear the invisible line. She reached for Cole, and for a moment, Finnian saw real emotion—worry, maybe even panic—flicker across her face. But then, as the shop clock inside struck the minute, she jerked back, almost yanked by her own muscles, and the door behind her slammed shut. The blue fabric unspooled from her arm, fluttered to the ground, and settled in a perfectly symmetrical puddle.

Cole, left alone, looked confused. He stared at the empty air, then, as the clocks ticked, turned precisely on his heel and marched back inside. The door closed behind him with a soft, final click.

Finnian, frozen mid-step, realized that every person in town was being sorted and slotted, their every movement paced and controlled. Even the air seemed to wait for the next chime before daring to move.

He called out—"Prudence!"—but the sound was swallowed, as if the world itself abhorred even that small discord. He tried again, louder, but now his own voice sounded tinny and insubstantial, a sound effect played for an audience of none.

The baby's cry echoed from behind the door, then abruptly cut off.

Finnian's mind whirled. He tried to trace the cause, to plot a way out. It wasn't just the clocks anymore—it was the town itself, or the magic that undergirded it, all gone rigid with the new order. North Pointe had never been a place of rules; now, it had become a machine, and every soul in it was a cog, forced to turn or be ground away.

He backed away from the tailor's, heart pounding. He tried to break his own pattern—slowed his walk, then sped it up, then stopped entirely—but every instinct, every muscle, screamed to stay with the beat. He clenched his hands, forced himself to stand utterly still, and focused on the air in his lungs.

For a split second, nothing happened. Finnian dared to hope.

Then the town bell rang again.

This time, the sound was so pure, so inhumanly exact, that Finnian felt it in the marrow of his bones. The shop windows shivered. The children on the green reappeared, lined up in new, evenly spaced ranks. Even the crows above the grocer's cawed once, together, then fell silent.

Prudence's door opened, just a crack. She peered out, eyes wild, then quickly retreated.

Finnian thought of the Grandfather Clock, of the way its pendulum had reversed and shattered the case. He thought of Jen, and her words about balance and error and the need for a little chaos.

He looked at the world around him—a town that had once been alive and lopsided, now perfect to the point of madness.

For the first time, Finnian knew he had to act. Not to fix the clocks, but to break them, to shatter the precision before it consumed everything he loved.

He squared his shoulders and, for the first time in his life, stepped deliberately out of rhythm, one foot forward, one held stubbornly still.

The world protested. The air pressed back. But Finnian gritted his teeth and forced the error to stand.

Somewhere behind him, a window cracked—not with the clean snap of a clock, but the jagged, unpredictable fracture of a world fighting for its freedom.

Finnian smiled.

It was a start.

He didn't pause to savor his small rebellion. The air still pressed on him like a hand against his chest, and every sound—the creak of a window, the shuffle of a shoe on flagstones—throbbed with the undercurrent of a world about to break. He looked down at his own shoes, then back at the empty green, and made a decision.

He took the path toward the trade road, every step a conscious fight against the regular beat that wanted to run his legs for him. He zigzagged, let his stride drag on the left, then stuttered twice on the right, just to spite whatever force had taken hold. The path seemed to resist, but Finnian pushed harder, teeth clenched. He rounded the bakery—Makota's windows dark, the usual parade of loaves and buns absent—and stepped out onto the road.

It was worse here. Travelers and locals alike moved as though yoked together, all at the same distance, all at the same pace. Every wagon wheel turned in precise counterpoint to the others; even the horses' hooves landed with the regularity of a metronome, their breaths fogging the air in matched bursts.

Two carts, one laden with wool and the other with vegetables, rolled side by side, their drivers not even bothering to glance at each other. Normally there'd be banter, haggling, a bit of rivalry or a slow-motion race. Today, there was nothing but the silence of effort expended without joy.

A pair of children—Finnian recognized the youngest Coleson and one of the baker's brood—walked down the center of the lane, each carrying a bundle of mail. Their feet made no sound, but Finnian could see the slight flinch each time a clock in a nearby house chimed, as if the sound was a tether snapping them into their next appointed step.

At the threshold of the Broken Claw, Jen stood in the open doorway, her blue sash draped perfectly, her boots planted like she was anchoring the building to the world. Her face, usually a mask of ironclad calm or dry amusement, now radiated an unease Finnian hadn't seen since the river nearly burst its banks two springs ago.

He raised a hand. "Jen!"

She lifted her head, eyes sharp but unfocused. "You see it too, then."

Finnian reached her in three haphazard steps, the last one nearly a stumble. "What's happening?"

She answered without her usual drawl. "Everyone's running on rails. People, animals, even the fires in the pub hearth—they flare on the hour and die down just as quick. I've tried to break it, but..." She lifted her hand, fingers trembling, then clenched it into a fist.

From behind, a sharp caw rang out, then another, then another—three crows, perched on the gutter above the pub, each calling once, in perfect sequence. Jen glanced at them, then looked back at Finnian.

"I don't like this," she said, soft, as if the world itself might overhear and punish her for dissent.

A door creaked across the lane. Leota stood on the stoop of her little house, the hem of her black dress swaying like a shadow caught in a wind that didn't exist. She held a hand to her forehead, eyes squeezed tight, as if fighting off a headache or a bad memory.

"Finnian!" she called, voice shaky. "Come here, please—quickly!"

He darted across the lane, ignoring the rhythm that tried to herd him like a sheep. Jen followed, boots loud in the hush.

Leota looked worse than usual: skin pale and almost translucent, hair loose around her shoulders, hands fluttering like anxious birds. She barely waited for Finnian to reach the bottom step before launching into her tirade.

"The town is—wrong," she spat. "All the gifts, all the little magics, they're not working as they should. I can't get a feel for the home's heart at all. It's like it's still here, but behind a wall of glass. I've never felt anything like this." Her eyes met Finnian's. "It's in the clocks, Finnian. It's in you."

He flinched. Jen stepped in, voice even. "What do we do?"

Leota looked at the ground, then back at the town. "Break the cycle.

Make a mess. Anything to loosen it, or..." She trailed off, pressing her palm to her temple. "If it stays like this, the town's defenses will fail. The next bad weather, the next trader with a temper—"

As if summoned, a commotion erupted farther up the road. Two merchants—one a burly wool seller, the other a spindly man in a patched blue coat—stood nose to nose, fists clenched. Their wagons blocked half the lane. In normal times, they would have argued, then bought each other a beer and laughed it off by noon. But now their voices were flat, words landing in the exact same cadence, never overlapping, never pausing for breath.

"You're blocking the lane," the wool seller intoned.

"You should have arrived on the quarter hour," replied the blue coat.

Both men stepped forward at the exact moment, shoulders colliding. Finnian could feel the fight building, as predictable as a wind-up toy.

Jen's jaw tightened. "I'll stop them," she said, but her feet stayed rooted to the spot.

Finnian grabbed her sleeve. "No, wait—"

The two merchants raised their fists, but before a punch could be thrown, both jerked as if yanked by strings. Their arms snapped to their sides, their faces went blank, and they turned, in perfect synchronization, and marched their carts in opposite directions. The crowd that had begun to gather did not speak, did not move, but stood in even ranks along the fence, eyes tracking the scene with eerie detachment.

Finnian shivered. Even the conflicts were regulated now.

Leota exhaled, breath clouding in the cold. "See? Even the chaos is predictable. The town's peace gift is gone, Jen. Yours is too, I think. No one's dissuaded from violence, just... put off until the correct interval."

Jen swallowed. "If someone wanted to hurt this place, now would be the time."

Finnian's mind spun. "Can you do anything? Magic, or—?"

Leota shook her head. "It's like casting a spell with both hands tied behind my back. I can try, but..." She looked at the sky, eyes black and bottomless. "If you can break the rhythm, even for a second, maybe I can get in. Otherwise—"

She didn't finish. She didn't need to.

Finnian squared his shoulders. "Then I'll do it. I'll—" He hesitated, looking for inspiration. "I'll break every clock in town if I have to."

Jen, for the first time all morning, grinned. It was a pale imitation of her usual smirk, but it was there. "That's the spirit."

Leota's hand closed around Finnian's. "Please, hurry. I can feel the town slipping."

Finnian nodded, and without another word, ran for his shop. Every window along the lane shuddered as he passed. The world screamed at him to fall back into line, to let the minutes and hours march on, but Finnian pushed harder, desperate to find the flaw, the error, the one place where the mechanism failed.

He barreled through his front door and into the chaos of his ruined shop.

The clocks were waiting, but so was Finnian, and he was ready to make them wobble.

eighteen
. . .

HE DIDN'T GET a chance to touch a clock before there was a knock at the door.

It wasn't a normal knock. It was a brisk, fussy little staccato, three taps at precisely the same interval, repeated twice, then a pause, then three more. Finnian's mind, even now, couldn't help but parse it as clock time: 3:3, pause, 3:3. He wiped his hands on his apron and opened the door.

On the stoop, in a perfect tableau of bureaucratic disaster, stood two Púca.

The first was barely knee-high, with bristle-bright white hair and a red vest festooned with more buttons than Finnian had ever seen on a being not employed by the train commission. A spiral-bound notebook hung from a strap around its neck; it clutched a blue pencil in one hand, and a battered clipboard in the other. The creature's ears stuck straight out, flattened by the pressure of its own industry. It greeted Finnian with a sharp little bow.

"Project Manager Púca, at your disposal. You have a situation," it declared, the words so fast and clipped that they nearly tripped over each other.

Behind it, the second Púca was much the same, except it wore a green accountant's shade and carried a ledger so heavy it required both hands. Its entire demeanor was that of someone who wished, more than anything, to be somewhere else. Even its beard seemed to droop in anticipation of paperwork.

Finnian had never seen either of these Púca before. He stared, dumbfounded, and the Project Manager Púca gave him a look that said, in perfect silence, "We do not have time for this."

"We're here to perform a site inspection," said Project Manager Púca. "Clockwise walkaround. Standard. But you—" it jabbed the pencil at Finnian's chest—"are the root cause. The bread crumb in the mainspring. The loose screw, if you will."

"Is that a technical term?" Finnian managed.

"It is now," said the Púca, already pushing past him into the shop. "Excuse the intrusion, but you'll agree it's warranted. Adjuster Púca, with me."

The Adjuster Púca gave a martyred sigh and trudged after its superior, leaving a faint trail of graphite shavings and auditorial gloom.

Finnian closed the door, then opened it again, just to make sure he wasn't hallucinating. The green outside looked exactly as before—except now, for the first time in hours, a single crow had broken ranks and was pecking at the blue ribbon of fabric in front of the tailor's shop. Finnian watched it, clinging to the normalcy, but behind him, Project Manager Púca was already narrating the disaster.

"Time drift exceeds regional tolerance," it called out. "Environmental crosslink at seventy percent. Incipient metaphysical meltdown."

Adjuster Púca looked up from its ledger. "Should I mark 'crisis imminent' or 'crisis already in progress'?"

"Both," snapped Project Manager Púca. "Be thorough."

They made a circuit of the shop, inspecting the shelves, poking at the battered wall clocks, occasionally jotting a note or, in the Adjuster's case, groaning quietly to itself. Finnian trailed behind, hands half-raised, torn between trying to explain himself and simply hiding under the counter.

The two Púca reached the Grandfather Clock, which had ceased its violent ticking and now glowered in the corner like an invalid plotting revenge. Project Manager Púca circled it, muttering, "So this is the locus. The breach."

Adjuster Púca peered at the split in the case, then at the pendulum, which had come to rest mid-swing, defying both gravity and reason. "We're going to take a bath on this, aren't we."

"If we're lucky," said the other, "we'll drown before they ask us for a root-cause analysis."

They both turned to Finnian.

"Explain," said Project Manager Púca.

Finnian straightened his spectacles and tried to marshal his thoughts. "The clocks—well, all of them, really—started syncing up. I tried to reintroduce error, but the system rejected it. When I touched the Grandfather Clock, it reversed, then—"

"You broke the time cycle," said Project Manager Púca, scribbling rapidly. "A classic over-tune. Someone must have told you to 'make it better.'" It glared at Finnian over the rim of its clipboard.

"That's… what I do?" Finnian offered, weakly.

"Aha!" crowed the Púca, spinning the pencil in triumph. "Hubris. Classic."

Adjuster Púca muttered, "I hope you have liability insurance."

"We're not insured?" said Project Manager Púca, scandalized. "Not even the town? Do you have any idea the kind of claims we're facing?"

Adjuster Púca visibly wilted. "I'll have to fill out the Red Ledger."

"Fill out two. This is a double event."

Finnian, who had only been following about half of this, tried again. "Can you fix it?"

The Project Manager Púca made a sound that was somewhere between a sneeze and a chortle. "Sir, fixing things is for other departments. We're here to log the chaos, catalog it, and—if absolutely necessary—escalate." It grinned, which on a Púca was not a comforting sight.

"But—" Finnian gestured at the shop, the street, the silent world outside. "People are being… erased. Their souls, or—something like that. If we don't break the pattern, it'll be permanent."

Project Manager Púca nodded. "That's usually how these things go, yes." It spun on its heel, surveying the shop, and raised its voice as if addressing a crowd of invisible auditors. "Catastrophic regularization event, phase two," it intoned. "Emotional range collapse, cognitive drift, full system lockdown. Now, let's see—"

It reached up and flicked the pendulum of the Grandfather Clock.

The world inverted.

Finnian fell, or possibly rose, or maybe just twisted in place—the sensation was so total that it left him with only the taste of copper on his tongue and the sense that his insides had been neatly rearranged. For a moment, he saw the shop from a great height, as if looking down on a snow globe, every clock ticking in perfect sympathy, every Púca running in tiny, terrified circles.

The Grandfather Clock shuddered, gave a single, decisive tick, and then—

A circle of blue-gold light irised open in the air.

The Púca Project Manager was drawn into it, clipboard and all, by an invisible force. It didn't scream; it only managed a dignified, "Oh for the love of—" before it was sucked into the vortex. The Adjuster Púca stared in horror, ledger shaking in its hands.

The circle snapped shut, leaving behind only a faint smell of burnt ozone, a scattering of loose blue pencil shavings, and a sensation of profound regret.

Finnian was on his knees, breathing hard, one hand clutching the workbench. His vision cleared in time to see the Adjuster Púca drop the ledger and run for the door, keening, "Not covered, not covered, not covered!" as it vanished into the square.

The shop was silent, except for the clocks. They hadn't stopped. In fact, they sounded stronger, more confident than ever, ticking off the seconds with a brutality that dared anyone to miss their next appointment.

Finnian wiped his forehead, then immediately regretted it; the sweat was cold and gritty with the residue of metaphysical disaster. The Grandfather Clock still stood, but its face had shifted: the hour hand now pointed straight up, but the minute hand had spun into a figure eight, a symbol Finnian didn't recognize but instinctively understood was Very Bad.

He staggered to his feet, heart pounding. For a moment he simply stood in the middle of the ruined shop, hands trembling, trying to decide whether to laugh, cry, or simply retire and take up fishing.

A clatter at the window made him jump.

It was Jen, boots planted wide, her coat half-buttoned, her face an open challenge to the world. Next to her was Leota, looking even paler than usual, one hand clamped around the shoulder of a third Púca, this one in a tiny hard hat and reflective vest.

Jen shouted, "You in one piece, Finnian?"

He fumbled with the door, nearly tore it off its hinges, and shouted back, "Something's gone wrong! The Púca—one of them—was eaten by a portal!"

"Par for the day," said Jen. "Hold tight, we're coming in!"

Leota managed a tight smile, then directed Safety Inspector Púca (so the vest proclaimed) to check the perimeter. It immediately set to work measuring the distance between the doormat and the threshold with a little folding ruler.

Jen barreled through, scanning the shop with an efficiency Finnian envied. She went straight to the Grandfather Clock, eyed the figure eight, and let out a low whistle.

"That's new," she said. "What did you do?"

"I didn't— I mean, I tried to stop it, but—" He looked around for help, realized there was none, and settled on, "It's gone critical."

Leota stepped inside, gaze fixed on the face of the clock. She muttered a few words under her breath, then asked, "Did you see where the Púca went?"

"Into the—" Finnian gestured, helpless. "The portal? I think it's a gateway now. To somewhere else."

Safety Inspector Púca clambered onto the counter and peered at the face of the clock, then at Finnian. "What's your risk mitigation plan?" it asked, voice high and tremulous.

"Smash it," suggested Jen.

Leota shook her head. "If it's linked to the town's magic, breaking the clock could shatter the boundary entirely. We need to decouple it. Or at least dampen the flow."

Finnian felt, for the first time in days, a flicker of hope. "Could you—could you make a counter-spell?"

Leota grimaced. "Maybe. But I'd need something to anchor it to, something with a strong sense of self. The world is running on clockwork now. It wants everything to obey the rules. It hates—" She hesitated. "It hates error."

Finnian nodded, seeing the logic. "So we make it love error again."

Jen grinned, fierce and real. "You always did have a way with lost causes."

He looked around the shop, then at the battered, stubborn timers on his bench. His hands found the moonstone timer—the one that never worked the same way twice—and he wound it, just a bit, and set it next to the Grandfather Clock.

The timer shuddered, ticked, then skipped a beat.

The Grandfather Clock made a pained sound, its case vibrating with the effort. The figure eight on the face wavered, then snapped back to a normal minute hand.

Leota's eyes widened. "It's working. Keep going!"

Finnian rummaged for every misaligned, defective, or "personality-laden" timer he'd ever made and set them all ticking at once. The air in the shop filled with the music of error: stutters, skips, runs, and glorious, chaotic drift.

The Grandfather Clock quivered, then let out a long, low bong—a single note that seemed to shake the dust from the rafters.

Outside, the sun flickered. Shadows danced in the green. Finnian could see, through the window, the children's ring break apart; two of them tumbled into the grass, giggling for no reason at all.

He grinned, wild with relief.

Then the portal opened again.

This time, it was bigger, and it yawned with the hungry certainty of a job half-done.

Finnian didn't hesitate. He grabbed the worst clock he could find—a bent regulator with a hair-trigger and a cracked face—and, without so much as a warning to Jen or Leota, hurled it into the portal.

The world held its breath.

There was a sound—a chorus of clocks, all shattering at once—and then, as suddenly as it had opened, the portal slammed shut.

The Grandfather Clock fell silent, its hands landing on twelve and six, proper as you please.

In the aftermath, the shop was a ruin, but it was a beautiful one. The air was thick with the smell of burnt ozone, and maybe, just maybe, a whiff of fresh bread from the bakery. Outside, the world had gone back to its old, comfortable lopsidedness. The children chased the ball; the crows argued over the ribbon; Cole Coleson, who must have been watching from his window, raised a mug in Finnian's direction.

Inside, Jen clapped Finnian on the back, nearly knocking him down. "You did it," she said.

Leota looked at the battered timers on the bench, then at Finnian, and nodded. "Sometimes the best fix is letting things run wild."

Finnian felt, for the first time in memory, like he'd done exactly the right thing. Even if it broke every rule in the book.

He looked at the battered Grandfather Clock, which now ticked with a lazy, unhurried confidence, and decided to leave it that way forever.

And just for good measure, he set all the other clocks in the shop to different times, so they could argue about it for years to come.

In the aftermath, the Project Manager Púca did not return. The Safety Púca left behind a warning triangle and a note that simply read "Systemic Instability—Monitor Closely."

Adjuster Púca was never seen again, but Finnian sometimes heard, late at night, the faint sound of an adding machine in the distance, followed by a groan.

He slept well that night, the world just as it should be: a little slow, a little fast, and full of the honest chaos of a life well-lived.

In the morning, the town's return to disorder was less dramatic than Finnian expected. He had half-anticipated waking to crows cawing the hour, children fighting in the square, and every wall clock in his shop cheerfully ticking out its own interpretation of time. Instead, the world was soft and gray, the light shifting gently through the window and across the floorboards, and the clocks sounded their marks with the comfortable, unsynchronized rumble of a family reunion.

For the first time in memory, Finnian stayed in bed long enough to hear the first, and then the second, and then the third set of chimes from the kitchen, the workshop, and the bedroom all collide in a chaos of disagreement. He smiled, stretched, and resolved to approach the day at whatever pace suited him.

The smile lasted until he reached the shop.

There was a cluster at the front door. Jen stood, boots muddy and arms folded, next to Leota, who looked like she'd slept not at all. The witch's eyes were shadowed with fatigue, but she wore her usual grim focus as she scanned the street. In front of them, arrayed like a picket line, stood three Púca, each in a different color safety vest.

The one in bright orange announced itself: "Crisis Response Púca, on the scene! Please remain calm and do not operate any unlicensed timepieces without proper training or supervision."

Its partner, in a vest that shimmered between yellow and blue depending on the angle, piped up, "First Responder Púca. Anyone in need of bandages, tea, or emotional counseling, check in here."

The third, smaller than the others and with a pair of binoculars slung around its neck, added, "Finder Púca. If you have misplaced an item, a person, or your sense of humor, I can assist for a nominal fee."

All three wore their panic plainly, shuffling from foot to foot, glancing over their shoulders as if expecting the sky to crack open at any moment.

Finnian opened the door. "Is there a problem?" he asked, instantly regretting the phrasing.

"Finnian," said Jen, pushing into the shop ahead of the Púca, "Leota says you set off another event last night. Something about a portal and a complete system reset?"

He tried to explain, but the Púca took over. Crisis Response Púca held up a pre-filled checklist and began reading aloud:

"Number of portals opened in last twelve hours: one. Number of project managers missing in action: one. Number of clocks running outside of standard deviation: forty-seven. Number of townspeople reporting 'odd sensations': All."

First Responder Púca produced a tray of herbal compresses and offered one to Finnian. "It's for the headache," it said, eyes wide with shared pain.

Finder Púca simply wandered the perimeter, peering behind shelves and under the workbench, muttering, "It's got to be here somewhere."

Leota followed Jen inside, blinking at the clocks. "You undid the alignment," she said, "but now the magical cycle is... fragmented." She pinched the bridge of her nose. "It's not chaos. It's more like... segmented order. Time isn't flowing. It's snapping forward in little bites."

Jen squinted at the Grandfather Clock, which now ticked with a soft, petulant click. "That sounds bad."

"It is," said Leota. "It's not as dangerous as before, but it's not stable, either. The town's magic has lost its sense of rhythm. If we don't restore a smooth flow, every shop's gift will stutter. There could be—"

She was cut off by the sudden, unnerving sensation that the entire world had blinked. Finnian felt it in the root of his teeth: one moment, the sun was barely peeking over the bakery roof, the next it was a good finger higher, shadows sharper, the light a full candlemark ahead. The change wasn't gradual. It was like someone had swapped out the world for an updated version, with none of the transition in between.

"Did you see that?" Jen said. "It just—jumped."

Leota nodded. "That's what I meant. The energy is quantized." She looked at Finnian with the exasperation of a teacher confronted by a particularly stubborn student. "You regulated the divine, Finnian."

He sputtered. "I—no—I only meant to break the pattern! Not—"

Crisis Response Púca, eager for purpose, stepped between them. "Recommend containment! Please designate a safe area for further experimentation."

First Responder Púca nodded. "We can mark the perimeter with traffic cones and kettle whistles."

Finder Púca, who had finally climbed onto the workbench, called out, "I found the source!" and pointed triumphantly at the Grandfather Clock. "It's acting as a governor for the whole town. Until we reset it, you'll have time skips every time the cycle overfills."

Leota looked to Finnian. "Do you know how to reset it?"

He hesitated. "Maybe. If I can reintroduce some randomness, or even better, build a feedback loop—"

Jen clapped him on the shoulder, hard enough to rattle his teeth. "Just do what you do best, Springdale. Make it up as you go."

Crisis Response Púca was already organizing the other clocks into neat rows, prepping a log of potential failure states. First Responder Púca provided tea for everyone (and a mug for the Grandfather Clock, which the clock rejected by knocking it to the floor at the next tick). Finder Púca took up a post by the window, binoculars scanning for any sign of returning portals or missing Púca managers.

Finnian examined the Grandfather Clock. Its case was still cracked, but the hands now moved in careful, ponderous steps—never drifting, never racing, just clicking from mark to mark with inhuman patience.

He tried to slow it, speed it, or even make it skip, but every touch met resistance. The clock's mechanism had become a physical manifestation of all the world's new stubbornness. It wouldn't be tuned, only obeyed.

Frustrated, Finnian looked for something—anything—that might disrupt the stasis. He remembered the moonstone timer, and the way its unpredictable rhythm had, even briefly, thrown off the clock's balance.

He fetched it from the bench and wound it up. The timer clicked and whirred, refusing to tick at any consistent pace, stuttering and lunging with a freedom that felt almost obscene compared to the disciplined clockwork around it.

He held the timer next to the Grandfather Clock, hoping for an effect.

At first, nothing happened. Then the Grandfather Clock ticked, then hesitated, then ticked twice, then stopped for a full second. The minute hand shuddered, unsure.

Outside, a shadow—midmorning, by Finnian's guess—crept

partway across the square, then halted. The light held, the world paused.

Leota's eyes widened. "You're doing it," she whispered. "It's re-learning how to drift."

Crisis Response Púca updated the checklist with, "Positive anomaly detected—proceed with caution."

Jen, ever pragmatic, took a clock off the shelf and threw it hard at the floor.

It bounced, landed upright, and continued ticking without missing a beat.

She stared at it, then looked at Finnian. "It doesn't want to be broken, Finnian. It's gotten stubborn."

He gritted his teeth. "Then I'll have to be more stubborn."

He fetched every oddball timer, regulator, and escapement he'd ever built and lined them up along the base of the Grandfather Clock. Each one ticked at its own pace, out of sync with the others, but all together they built a kind of musical friction, a riot of error and randomness.

The Grandfather Clock shook, its chimes growing louder. The minute hand trembled, then began to drift—just a little, but enough to put it at odds with its own hour.

The world outside snapped forward, but not as far this time. Then it stuttered, almost stopped, then lurched again, the gaps between jumps growing smaller and smaller.

Leota, watching with both hands gripping the counter, said, "It's almost there. Keep going."

"That's all I've got."

Jen leaned out the shop door. "It's not back to normal, yet." She frowned. "Why does Knodalon have a clock?"

"I—" Finnian began.

Leota interrupted. "The town's magic still doesn't feel right, either. We need to do something more."

Finnian considered. "A Universal Synchronizer."

"How will that help?" Jen asked, unconvinced.

"A Universal *De*-Synchronizer, then," Finnian amended. "Something to throw *all* the clocks out of sync."

"Can't you just do that manually?" Jen asked.

Finnian shook his head. He stepped over to a shelf and moved one clock's hands an hour ahead. The clock trembled for a moment, the world *snapped,* and the clock was again telling the correct time. "I need something seriously disruptive."

Leota frowned. "Well, I'd get on it. From the feel of things we haven't got much—"

"Don't," Jen growled.

nineteen

. . .

"DON'T," Jen growled. "We get it."

"—time," Leota finished, the words popping like a fuse in the dry air. "If I'm reading the flow right, the next temporal skip will be larger than the last. And it's about to hit."

Finnian absorbed this, mind already mapping the edges of the problem. He stared at his workbench, the mess of improvised timers and the old, stubborn clocks, and saw, all at once, the grim poetry of the day: every solution led to a bigger, stranger mess. The world had gotten a taste for the clockwork, and it wasn't about to let go.

He ran a finger over the moonstone timer, let it stutter under his touch. It was the only piece in the shop that hadn't been brought back into sync by the Grandfather Clock's iron gravity. The rest were already closing ranks, minute hands snapping into sudden alignment, hour chimes growing thicker and more impatient.

Jen said, "Well, Springdale? Got a plan, or are we just going to let the town catch on fire?"

Finnian shook himself out of the trance. "There's one thing left. But it's the sort of thing you build when you want to make sure it's the last clock you ever build."

Crisis Response Púca, who had already logged three new incident reports, perked up at this. "Is it catastrophic?"

"Probably," Finnian said. He thought of the countless warnings in every apprentice's manual: Never build a synchronizer unless you intend to surrender the entire system. Never build a master clock unless you're prepared to destroy all the slaves. He thought of the footnote at the bottom of the page, in tiny, terrified script: DO NOT ATTEMPT UNLESS ENDGAME IS ACCEPTABLE.

He cleared the bench. The other clocks vibrated, restless, but he ignored them.

Jen, seeing the change, nudged Leota. "He's doing the thing. We should stay clear."

Leota nodded, but didn't retreat. Instead, she drew a line in the dust along the threshold, murmured a word, and watched it glow faint blue. "This will keep the worst of it in, or at least slow it down."

Finnian's hands were already moving. He started with the moonstone timer, stripping out its drift governor and setting it in a cradle of cold-forged brass. The next piece came from the remains of the Celestial Orchid—he plucked the main spring, already half-unwound from its morning's trauma, and spliced it directly to the timer's ratchet wheel. From the parts bin he drew a dozen balance wheels and two escapement arbors, their teeth honed to the kind of precision that bordered on cruelty.

For the core, he hesitated. In the back of the drawer was a jewel that he'd never used: not a ruby, not a sapphire, but a single sliver of raw, uncut diamond, too wild for any clock but perfect for a governor designed to override the world. He cradled it in his palm, feeling its weight, then slotted it into the heart of the new device.

Every step, every motion, was watched. The clocks' faces gleamed in the half-light, hands frozen or twitching in anticipation. The shop grew colder, the shadows thickening into the corners, as if the act of building something this final was drawing the warmth from the air.

Jen asked, low-voiced, "Is it going to work?"

Finnian didn't answer. He couldn't, not without ruining the rhythm. He worked faster, setting the assembled parts into a frame scavenged from an old travel clock—a battered iron housing, ugly as a barn cat but tough as one, too. He locked the works together with a screw and a wire borrowed from his own shirt cuff.

The device, when complete, looked nothing like a clock. It looked like a wound-up animal, tense and predatory, its innards visible through a web of hair-thin gears and trembling springs. It radiated a nervous energy, a sense that at any moment it might lunge for the throat of the next nearest mechanism.

Crisis Response Púca, unable to keep away, inched closer to inspect it. "What do you call it?"

"Universal Synchronizer. Or a Time Bomb, if you're feeling honest."

"You said—"

"A De-Synchronizer won't work. There are too many clocks in town. I can't disrupt them all at once, which means the ones I don't will just push back. This should bring them all into perfect sync—"

"That's the problem."

"—and then shut them down."

"Oh."

The Púca scribbled this down with both hands at once.

Finnian set the Synchronizer in the center of the workbench, then reached for the oldest regulator in the shop—a battered piece, its wood case gone soft with age, its glass face patched with candlewax. He set this next to the new device and, with a pair of tweezers, connected the two via a strand of silver wire. Then he went around the shop, linking every other clock to this central node, each with a wire, a drop of solder, or, in one case, a ribbon of baker's twine doused in graphite paste. It didn't have to be elegant; it just had to be connected.

Each time he made a new link, the clocks hummed louder. The Grandfather Clock began to tick in earnest again, the minute hand carving long, angry sweeps.

Leota muttered, "I can feel the magic shifting. Like a weather front coming in."

Finnian nodded. "It's drawing from the entire system now. When I flip this switch, it'll yank every clock in town under one controller. And then, if I'm lucky, I can kill them all at once."

Jen frowned. "What happens if you're not lucky?"

He grinned, showing more teeth than he meant to. "Then at least it'll be over quick."

He checked the wiring, the connections, the spring tension. He looked at the Synchronizer, which now shuddered on its base, and the Grandfather Clock, which seemed to lean forward in anticipation.

The entire room waited.

Finnian's hand hovered over the switch.

He looked up. "You two might want to—"

"No," Jen said, stubborn. "We're not missing this."

Leota, for once, agreed. "Just do it, Finnian."

He drew a breath, slow and deliberate. The air tasted of copper and cold sweat.

He pressed the switch.

The Synchronizer snapped to life, the mainspring unwinding with a scream so high-pitched it rattled the fillings in his teeth. The diamond governor glowed a furious blue, and every clock in the shop went dead silent for a single, perfect second.

Then, as if responding to a conductor's downbeat, they all ticked at once.

The force of it knocked Finnian back a step. Sparks jumped from the silver wire to the workbench. Every clock in the room reset to midnight, then, with a series of sharp, accelerating ticks, all began to run in reverse.

Leota shouted, "It's working! The pattern's broken!"

Jen, who had braced herself on the counter, looked out the window. "It's not just the shop. Every clock on the green just jumped backwards. Even the bakery's wall clock—look!"

Finnian saw it too: across the square, the clocks in every window reversed, the light in the bakery flickered, and the chime from the bell tower bellowed a deep, confused note. "That's... not right." He reached for the Synchronizer, ready to dampen it if need be, but the device was already winding down. The diamond governor blazed, then faded; the mainspring snapped and clattered to a stop. The universal linkage frayed, wires popping loose and drifting to the floor like strands of gray hair.

The air in the shop was suddenly sweet, the copper taste replaced with the ghost of cinnamon and warm bread.

Jen, after a beat, asked, "Did it work?"

Finnian looked around, waiting for the backlash. When none came, he said, "Maybe. But the shop's still standing, so that's a good sign. Maybe"

Leota crossed to the Grandfather Clock, had gone silent, the case still cracked but no longer radiating doom. She pressed her palm to the wood, and when she pulled away, her smile was real, if tired.

Jen clapped Finnian on the shoulder. "That was brilliant. Or insane. Or both."

Crisis Response Púca, who had fainted at the height of the action, now sat up and quietly logged "Resolution: pending."

Finnian, for the first time all day, let himself hope.

But outside, in the morning blue, a crow cawed three times. Then three more. Then three more, precisely on the mark.

Finnian watched the clock in the bakery window. Its hands, though running backward, moved with a slow, relentless certainty.

He had a creeping sense that the world wasn't finished with him yet.

There was a stillness in the air, a hush so absolute it felt like the world had put itself on tiptoe to see if the disaster had really passed. The clocks in the shop all ran in reverse, but with an elegant, almost casual rhythm—tick, tock, tick, tock, like a heartbeat that had chosen to march backward, but didn't mind doing so. The tension that had vibrated in Finnian's bones now released, replaced by a fuzzy numbness, as if the aftermath of panic was gentler than the panic itself.

He exhaled. Even the air felt easier to breathe.

Jen slouched against the counter, arms folded, wearing a look that was half-respect and half exasperation. "Are you going to reset the clocks, or just leave everyone telling time like they're walking backward?"

Leota, pale but less haunted, pressed her palm again to the Grandfather Clock's face. "It's quiet," she said. "Like it's napping."

Finnian smiled, small and proud. He glanced at the Synchronizer, now dormant on the bench. The diamond at its core was barely glowing, the spring fully run out, and the linked wires lay slack like the aftermath of a cat's midnight raid.

He allowed himself a moment to imagine a future in which people would say, "Do you remember the day time went backward?" and they would laugh, and then have a pint, and then someone would fix it and life would go on. It felt good. He let the shop embrace him, the soft ticking, the faint smell of oil, the comfort of his tools where he'd left them.

But the world has a way of circling the drain, and Finnian noticed, even before the others did, that something was wrong with the way the clocks were running backward.

Not just the clocks. Everything.

A faint, acrid scent stung his nose. He looked for its source, and saw that the brass gear in the moonstone timer—his favorite, the one he'd built with more care than he'd ever admit—had begun to... deform. Not tarnish, not age, but rather... melting? He squinted closer and realized it was decomposing into its component elements.

"Jen, look," he whispered, gesturing.

Jen pushed off the counter, craned in. "Is that—?"

He reached out, pressed the gear with a pin. It crumbled, soft and friable, the metal coming off in blue-green copper dust that left a cold streak on his skin. He scraped at the edge and watched a wave of dullness spread through the rest of the timer, the teeth blunting, the balance wheel beginning to wobble on its post.

"That's not supposed to happen," Finnian said, voice too calm.

Jen touched the rim of the nearest wall clock. Her finger came away streaked with gray, and a fragment of enamel flaked onto the floor. "Is this... all the clocks?" she asked, already knowing the answer.

Leota drew back from the Grandfather Clock. A crack that had run the length of the case now widened, the polished flaking off, the underlying wood growing lighter in color. The glass in the face, once bright, became wavy, then foggy, then grainy, as if it remembered a time before it was ever melted and cast.

Even the light in the shop seemed to fade, the sharpness of the morning blurring to the muddy, hesitant gray of dawn.

Finnian looked at the Synchronizer. "I thought I was slowing the clocks, not..." He trailed off, unwilling to say it.

"Not unwinding *everything*," Leota finished, her voice brittle.

Jen stepped to the window. The bakery across the green was dark. She squinted, and said, "Is that—Makota's kits? They're smaller? No. Younger."

Finnian reached for the door, then hesitated. The wood of the knob had gone rough, splintery, almost bark-like. He turned it with care, and the metal spindle inside let out a sound like a wet cough. The door opened onto the town square, and the first thing he saw was the bread.

Makota's bread, always arrayed in the window like a promise of comfort, had turned slack and gray. The crusts were soft, the loaves smaller, the dough pocked with unrisen bubbles. Finnian stared, stomach turning, as a loaf collapsed on itself, regressing from baked perfection to the sticky, half-formed glob of a morning batch.

On the green, the grass was longer, thicker, more wild than it had been at dawn. The benches had lost their paint, their slats reverting to rough pine. The clock in the town hall tower, visible above the rooftops, spun in reverse, faster than the others, as if trying to outpace the rest of the world.

He looked at the sky. The sun, which had been past the bakery roof just a minute ago, now hovered lower, the light colder, more diffuse. Finnian blinked, and the clouds thickened, as if a full hour had just run in reverse.

He ducked back inside, heart pounding. "It's not just the clocks," he said. "It's everything. We're pulling time backward."

Leota's face was grave. "How long until—?"

He grabbed a notebook and scribbled a calculation. "If it stays at this pace, the whole town's going to be reset. A day, maybe two."

"Reset to what?" Jen said.

Finnian didn't answer. He stared at the Synchronizer, the innocent way it sat on the bench, all its mischief spent.

He thought of the way the device had acted, the way it had overpowered the other clocks, the way it had imposed itself on the world.

It was more than a clock—it was a command. And the command, unopposed, was still going.

He felt sick.

He knew, with the certainty of every engineer and maker who'd ever built a thing that worked too well, that if he didn't stop it soon, the process would accelerate. The world would keep reversing, peeling away the hours, the days, the years.

He turned to Leota. "Is there any magic you can use? Anything to break it?"

She shook her head. "It's not a spell anymore. It's a rule. The whole town's running on it."

Jen looked at him, eyebrows raised. "Then what do we do?"

Finnian stared at his hands, the clever fingers that had made this mess. He closed his eyes, forced himself to think, to see the error in the gears.

"There's only one way," he said, and already hated himself for it. "I have to unwind it. I have to destroy the Synchronizer. Ot fix it. But it's not just the device—it's every clock I tuned into it." He paused. "I can fix it. I just need to reduce the friction in the main escapement, use a smaller regulator, maybe an—"

Jen interrupted. "You can do that?"

"I think so," he said. "But I need to hurry."

He turned to the bench, hands trembling, and reached for the Synchronizer.

As he did, a crow cawed, loud enough to shake the window glass. The sound echoed, then doubled, then tripled, until the noise was so thick it felt like the world itself was repeating, frame by frame, unable to move forward.

He looked at the clock in the wall. The hands now spun in a blur, minute and hour undifferentiated, the numbers peeling away from the face in a spiral of painted dust.

He felt the panic, but forced it down. He breathed, and in that moment, made a vow:

He would fix this, or he would see the world erased in the trying.

He reached for his tools.

twenty

. . .

FINNIAN'S FINGERS darted for the tool tray, knocking over a bottle of jeweler's oil that promptly re-corked itself and slid in a perfect reverse parabola back onto the shelf.

He swore under his breath and yanked the Synchronizer off the table, cradling it like a rabid stoat. The casing already vibrated with an unfamiliar heat. "Come on, come on, hold," he pleaded, his voice a snarl of technical desperation. "If you can just stabilize the mainspring—"

"'Stabilize the mainspring?'" Leota's voice lanced through the air, sharper than the edge of a new file. "Springdale, you're not tuning a carriage clock. The town's magic is already unstable. You're feeding it more chaos."

Finnian did not look up. His focus was all on the device. "If I can get the regulator to interface with the quantum, uh, fudge factor, it should balance the feedback loop. The negative vector of time is only strong because the original event was so synchronized. If I can just add a little… drift…"

He trailed off, because the world outside the window was now blinking, not fading: the afternoon sun jumped from one angle to another, casting the shop into a strobe-lit nightmare of light and dark.

He watched as the blue enamel in his favorite wall clock lost its shine, then color, then simply peeled away, leaving behind a raw, pitted brass like the aftermath of a fire.

Leota groaned. "This is why they banned chronomancy. It always looks clever until you accidentally invent negative bread."

Finnian glanced, just for a second, at the side table where Makota's rolls had once sat. The bread was no longer bread. It was a pale, gummy mass, collapsing into a puddle of yeast and flour and regret. The label—stamped "Freshest This Side of the Lake!"—slid off, the ink first paling, then vanishing.

Finnian muttered, "Not even my worst morning has gone this bad," and twisted the Synchronizer's casing with both hands. The diamond governor at its heart gave a high, whistling whine, as if protesting the indignity of being made to work overtime.

He thought, for a moment, that he had it. The whine steadied, the blue glow in the diamond pulsed with something like a heartbeat, and the minute hand in the Grandfather Clock slowed its mad dash.

Then, with a snap that reverberated through the bench, the Synchronizer's mainspring detonated—spring steel fractaling through the air like a slinky possessed. A gear rolled off the edge of the workbench, bounced, and unrolled itself all the way back to the tray where it had been cut hours ago.

Finnian let the device fall to the table, hands burning from the friction, and bit down a scream. He wanted to cry, or punch the wall, or maybe just curl up on the floor with the negative bread and try to bake himself into a roll. Instead, he found himself laughing, high and sharp and just on the edge of breaking.

Leota stepped over, her face the color of curdled milk, her eyes black and bottomless. "Are you done?" she asked, voice gentler now. "Or should I call in the Púca again to audit the failure modes?"

Finnian tried to answer, but all that came out was a helpless, wracked snort. He wiped sweat from his brow, or tried to—the sweat had retreated, the skin already gone cold and dry. "I thought," he said, "that if I could get every clock in town to sync, I could shut them down all at once. Instead—"

Instead, the entire town was being unwound like a badly wound watch.

Leota sighed, and her expression softened just a fraction. "Finnian, you're good at what you do. But sometimes, the best solution is to stop cranking the mainspring. Just let it run down."

He shook his head, breath shuddering. "No. If I stop, the momentum carries the whole thing past the zero point. You saw what happened to the bread. If the cycle keeps going, we'll wind up before the town was even founded. Before the lake filled. We'll reset the valley to nothing."

A silence followed, punctuated only by the gentle, chilling sound of the clocks all agreeing on the next mark.

Leota regarded him for a long moment. Then, quietly: "So what's your plan?"

He wanted to lie. To say he had a plan. But in that moment, looking at the blinking blue sun, the devolving bread, the shop's walls turning from neatly whitewashed to raw, wet pine, he could only offer the truth:

"I'm out of ideas."

He said it quietly, but the words landed with the force of a cracked anvil.

A piece of the ceiling plaster dropped onto the floor, then uncrumbled itself and floated back up into the corner, restoring a patch of mildew that hadn't been there all season.

Finnian closed his eyes and pressed his fists against them, hard. He tried to focus on the feeling of pain, of presence, of the here and now. But even that felt unanchored, as if his own life were being subjected to fast-forward and reverse at the same time.

He looked at Leota, desperate. "I just—wanted to fix it."

Leota did not respond immediately. She crossed to the Grandfather Clock, the most stubborn piece in the shop, and placed her palm against its fractured case. The wood thrummed under her touch, and she closed her eyes, listening.

When she spoke, her voice was soft and certain. "Let's break it more," she said.

He blinked. "What?"

"We've been trying to fix the system. But the town never ran on perfect time. It ran on mistakes, and accidents, and the drift between one hour and the next. The magic wants a little chaos, Finnian. Let's give it a lot."

She said it so matter-of-factly that Finnian felt his hope restart, if only for a moment.

He looked at the ruin on his workbench. "What do you propose? Smash every clock in town?"

Leota shook her head. "Just the important ones." She grinned, small and grim, and added, "Start with yours." She reached for the nearest regulator, yanked it from its shelf, and, with all the satisfaction of a woman who had never been allowed to break things in his entire professional life, hurled it against the stone floor.

The case split, the glass face shattered, and, as if in protest, every other clock in the shop stuttered. The blue light in the Synchronizer hiccuped, dimmed, then—hesitated.

She smashed a second clock, then a third. Jen joined in, and within seconds, the workshop was a battlefield, clock corpses and springs and hour hands littering the floor.

It felt, for the first time in hours, like the world had a chance.

As the chaos mounted, the clocks began to lag. Some stopped altogether. The tick-tock became a muddle, a musical cacophony of imperfection. The sun outside the window lingered, then moved forward, then back, then stilled.

For a moment, the world held its breath.

Then the clocks, everywhere, started again.

Backwards.

But at least more slowly.

Leota, hands on her knees, laughed once, short and wild. "We've got it by the throat. Jen, get some help."

Jen, a tiny gear flying out of her braid, threw open the shop door. The effect would have been dramatic, except that the way was immediately blocked by the sternest Security Guard Púca Finnian had ever seen. It was not much taller than Finnian's own knee, but compensated with an official's sash, a hat festooned with more badges than the average general, and an aura of resolve that seemed to radiate for several feet in every direction.

"Access restricted," it intoned, a voice that landed somewhere between a squeak and a gavel. "No entry, no exit. All persons must remain within the perimeter until the incident is resolved or properly documented."

Behind it, in a wedge formation, came Cole, Warren, and Galhani.

The Security Púca stepped sideways, pivoting on one shiny black boot, and planted itself in front of the door like a living turnstile. "Identification required. State business."

Finnian, still cradling his stinging hands, started to answer, but Jen rolled right over him. "Emergency protocol," she barked. "They're here to fix a clock problem before it becomes a town-wide disaster."

"Denied," chirped the Púca, unmoved. "Risk of collateral damage exceeds authorized parameters for civilian intervention. Please remain calm, hydrate, and wait for a licensed Response Team."

"I'll Response Team you—" Jen muttered, but Leota touched her arm and gave the Púca a look that Finnian recognized as "witchy," though not in any magical sense. It was the look you gave a stubborn child, or a mule with an advanced degree in paperwork.

Before they could escalate, another voice piped up from behind the standoff.

"I think you'll find that exceptions can be made under the Common Towne Charter, provided the problem is, and I quote, 'urgent, existential, and demonstrably the fault of a currently present party.'"

Galhani, the gnome, stepped forward. She was so quick and light on her feet that the floorboards didn't even squeak. She bustled through the Púca perimeter and perched on a stack of boxes beside the door, hands folded, bright eyes shining. Her entire body radiated cheerful mischief; she wore a tea-stained apron and had a dab of flour on her cheek, as if she'd paused in the middle of a baking marathon to save the world.

The Security Púca gave her a withering glance, then reached into its satchel for a rulebook. Galhani watched, delighted, and, before the Púca could open to the right page, launched into a rapid-fire stream of ceramic-sounding clicks and pops—the Púca language, if Finnian remembered right, though he could never catch more than a word or two.

The Púca's ears twitched. "Objection noted," it said, then glanced at Jen. "Counterargument?"

Jen shrugged. "Either let them in, or we do this through the window. I don't care which."

Warren, never one to linger when things needed fixing, simply stepped over the Púca and beelined for the Synchronizer, which still trembled and spat sparks at the edge of the bench.

Galhani leaned in and smiled at Finnian. "Hi! The time is coming apart outside, by the way. I saw the bakery sign go from 'Best Since 4 Years Running' to 'Opening Day Special' in about five minutes. Very creative, but probably not sustainable. Need help?"

Finnian blinked, still a little shell-shocked. "You speak Púca?"

"Everyone in my family does," Galhani said. "It's mostly legalese and snack recipes." She beamed. "But I'm best at the legalese."

The Púca, meanwhile, and Galhani had escalated their debate to a full-on rapid-fire exchange. The sound was less like conversation and more like a pair of bone china chess sets attacking each other. "Section 4, paragraph 3!" Galhani sang out, waggling her fingers for emphasis. "Chronological emergencies override all other perimeter protocols."

"Subclause D, Line 7," countered the Púca, "which stipulates—"

"That's only if the event is less than thirty-two seconds long. You want to time this one?" Galhani grinned.

The Púca frowned, consulted its watch, and glared at Finnian, who tried to look innocent.

In the background, Jen and Leota had already set to work. Rather than tinker, Leota grabbed the Synchronizer with both hands, gritted her teeth, and twisted. The frame groaned, then burst, unleashing a blizzard of cogs, screws, and hair-thin springs that caught the lamplight like glitter. Jen swept the table with her arm, knocking a tangle of half-assembled regulators to the floor. The air filled with the sound of things being taken apart and the kind of gleeful cursing usually reserved for the aftermath of a plumbing failure.

For a moment, all was chaos: Galhani and the Púca bickering like rival law clerks; Jen and Leota demolishing years of careful work with the joy of a pair of children given permission to break every toy in the box.

Finnian watched, a little in awe. This was not the orderly disassembly of a craftsman, but a campaign of creative ruin. Jen pried off the back plate of the Synchronizer with a butter knife. Leota yanked out the diamond governor and threw it over her shoulder, where it bounced, rolled, and disappeared down a crack in the floor.

Leota, caught up in the moment, bellowed, "WITCH SMASH!" and brought a heel down on the largest gear, reducing it to a glimmering pile of brass teeth. Gears pinged off walls and landed in teacups. A cloud of fine, glittery debris drifted through the air, settling on every surface.

For the first time in a long while, Finnian felt himself smile without reservation.

He joined in, grabbing the half-formed moonstone timer and slamming it flat with a rubber mallet. The device gave a little whimper of escaping air, then lay quiet and still.

Within minutes, the Synchronizer was not just dismantled but obliterated. The springs had all unwound, the cogs had been bent and twisted into abstract art, and the housing had gone from "sturdy" to "barely identifiable." Even the Grandfather Clock, in a moment of inspired sabotage, had its pendulum yanked loose and suspended from a hook in the ceiling, where it swung like a battered lantern.

Jen dusted her hands, grinning. "That's more like it. If we're going to live in a broken world, at least let it be our kind of broken."

Leota nodded, her smile less wild but no less real. "Magic feels better already."

Galhani, having declared victory in the legal debate, curtsied to the Security Púca and stepped into the shop, her feet crunching on a layer of shattered glass and clockwork detritus.

The Púca regarded the devastation, consulted its incident checklist, and wrote something Finnian couldn't see. Then it saluted Jen, fixed Galhani with a look of deep respect, and stood to the side.

The world outside still shimmered and flexed, but through the front window, Finnian could see the sun holding steady, the bakery sign returning to its usual cheerful promise, and the crows once again arguing among themselves in the gutters.

He looked at the mess, the battered crew around him, and, for a moment, felt lighter than he had in days.

Sometimes, the best fix was to let things stay a little bit broken.

As the last battered minute hand spun to rest on the floor, Finnian's panic memory kicked in. His arm shot out, snatching for a runaway gear as it arced off the bench—a reflex as old as his trade. "Wait—" he started, but Jen, barely breaking stride, caught his wrist and set it back on the table.

She gave him a look, half stern and half fond. "We can, and we should. The mess of a life lived slowly is better than a perfect, regulated void. That's what you always told me, remember?"

Finnian blinked, then tried to reclaim his hand. Jen held on for a beat, then let him go with a little push, and resumed her campaign of tactical mayhem.

Leota, meanwhile, had stopped smashing and simply cradled a broken carriage clock in her hands. She looked at Finnian, her face softer than he'd ever seen it, and said, "Feel it, Finnian. The town doesn't want to be regulated. Not now, not ever."

The words hit like a slap, but in a good way.

He looked around: at the dust drifting in the shaft of afternoon sunlight (itself now holding steady, no longer stuttering or flickering); at the random heap of clock fragments on the floor; at Jen and Leota, faces sweaty and triumphant. Even the Púca Security Guard, who'd been muttering about protocols just moments before, had settled onto a crate and was regarding the chaos with the small, grudging admiration of a bureaucrat who'd seen something truly impressive.

Finnian reached for another clock, this one an old favorite with a hand-painted lake on the dial, and—heart pounding—twisted the faceplate off. Instead of pain, he felt a strange, deep relief.

Jen, noticing his hesitation, said, quieter now, "You're doing the right thing." Then, more quietly, with the corners of her mouth fighting not to smile: "Witch Smash."

Leota did her best to stifle a laugh, which came out as a snort.

Within a few minutes, the shop was a graveyard of timepieces, and the only clocks that survived were the ones that ran a little slow or fast on their own. At the center of the workbench, the Synchronizer lay in a puddle of melted solder and bent wire, completely inert.

Jen and Leota wasted no time. Together, they began picking through the debris, plucking the least-wounded clocks and setting them on the shelves with deliberate care. Each timepiece was set a few minutes off from its neighbor. Some ran fast, others slow, and a few (for old time's sake) simply refused to keep time at all.

"Go on, Galhani," Jen called, waving a hand at the door. "Tell everyone—set their clocks however they want. Tell them it's for the public good."

Galhani gave a little salute, then zipped out, her voice already rising into the street in a stream of joyful, efficient instructions. Finnian watched her go, then looked at Jen and Leota, who were methodically destroying any clock that threatened to fall in line.

And, as they did, he noticed something he hadn't felt in days: the air in the shop was warm. The light was rich and forgiving. The world outside had gone back to its subtle, organic ebb and flow—the sun creeping across the window, the gentle hush of wind through the green, the far-off thump of the smith's hammer, not quite in rhythm with anything but itself.

Leota set her hand on the battered Grandfather Clock, then smiled. "I can feel it again. The town's magic—divine, if you want to call it that. It's breathing. Not pushing."

Jen nodded, rolling her shoulders. "I can feel my gift, too. The peace is back. Or at least the inclination toward it." She fixed Finnian with a sly look. "I'd better get out to the trade road. No telling what kind of chaos has broken loose there."

He nodded, and suddenly realized he'd been waiting for her to say just that.

"Thank you," Finnian said, the words a little raw but very real. "I couldn't have done this without you."

Jen shrugged, grabbing a bent spoon from the floor and tucking it into her belt like a trophy. "Don't mention it. It was fun." She winked. "Let's not do it again."

She left in a blur of boots and blue sash.

Leota lingered a moment, setting a battered, off-kilter wall clock just so on its hook, then dusting her hands. "Go on, Finnian," she said. "Let the town drift for a while."

He watched her go, then turned to face the glorious mess.

One by one, he went to the clocks and set them all differently: some two minutes off, some ten, some running backward. The sound, when he finished, was not a discord, but a harmony—a living, breathing song.

He sat at his bench, looked out at the world, and smiled.

For the first time in memory, Finnian Springdale was perfectly, gloriously, and forever late.

twenty-one
. . .

FINNIAN SPRINGDALE HAD NEVER BEEN SO PERFECTLY, gloriously, and unrepentantly late. In the wake of yesterday's crisis, he took his time with everything: slept past dawn, wandered his kitchen in slippers, let the bread burn just enough to give it character, and if the clocks on the wall disagreed with each other about the hour, well, that was their business, not his. He relished the friction of a world finally off the rails, the freedom in every unhurried step. Even the shop—now more museum than marketplace, its shelves littered with the war-wounded relics of yesterday's rebellion—seemed to sigh in relief at the slow pace.

He was winding a regulator at the bench, sipping a mug of tea that had cooled to near-absolute zero, when the shop's bell jangled. Finnian's first thought, characteristically, was to ignore it; whoever came through that door was probably just seeking refuge from the fresh chaos outside, and he'd resolved to let the town settle into its own rhythm before he set hands to it again.

But the voice that followed was a brisk, clipped staccato: "Time audit, portfolio review, and lost person's report. Is this the establishment of record?"

Finnian set down the regulator and rolled his eyes, but he couldn't hide the smile. The Púca were back.

This one was not like the others. He wore a trim, midnight-blue suit with white piping, and his beard was clipped into a point so sharp it could have served as a drafting instrument. His spectacles glinted with suspicion, and his voice came with the polished efficiency of a professional disaster mitigator.

"Portfolio Manager Púca," the little man announced, flashing a card the size of a postage stamp. "I am tasked with rebalancing the temporal assets of North Pointe, effective immediately."

He strode up to the counter, his boots giving sharp, efficient clacks that set every clock on the shelf to vibrating in faint irritation. The air around him crackled with a faint, ozone tingle—a sure sign of fresh time-magic in the making.

Finnian, unfazed, poured a second mug and offered it across the bench. "Morning. If you're here to repossess the shop, I'd ask you to wait until I've finished my tea. I hear it's easier to evict a man after he's had his tea."

The Púca sniffed. "Your sense of humor is noted. Unfortunately, we are not in a humorous situation." He produced a sheaf of papers from somewhere inside his jacket—Finnian couldn't begin to guess at the logistics—and tapped them against the counter. "As of last evening, all timekeeping in this quadrant is showing unacceptable variance. The clocks in your shop have been flagged for excessive individualism. There is also," and here the Púca's voice dropped to a scandalized whisper, "a Project Manager missing in action."

At this, Finnian's attention snapped back to the present. "Yes."

The Púca bristled. "Project Managers do not simply go missing. They may go absent, temporarily unaccounted for, or otherwise displaced in the flow. But not lost. Please refrain from spreading rumors."

Finnian bit his tongue to keep from laughing. "Noted. But if you're looking for someone, you're a bit late. Things have already been put back to—" He searched for the word. "Not normal. But tolerable."

"'Tolerable' is not a compliance metric," said the Púca, and began to scan the shelves with a practiced eye. "Is the Grandfather Clock operational?"

Finnian glanced at the corner. The clock still loomed, its casing cracked, the pendulum suspended from the ceiling on a bit of twine. But even in this half-mutilated state, the minute hand crawled forward with grim determination, ticking at its own unrepentant pace.

"Operational might be generous," Finnian said. "But it's alive, yes."

Portfolio Manager Púca nodded, making a note. "We were told you might be difficult. I see the reports were accurate."

Finnian, who would have agreed if the insult had been phrased with a little more wit, just shrugged. "If I'm difficult, it's only because the world seems to need more of it lately."

At this, the Púca paused. He actually looked at Finnian, as if seeing him for the first time.

"Difficult is not always a deficit," he said, and for a second, Finnian saw a flicker of kinship behind the bureaucratic mask.

But just as quickly, the moment was gone. The Púca straightened, plucked a pen from his pocket, and turned to Leota, who had appeared in the doorway as silently as a ghost. She looked marginally healthier than yesterday—her skin had lost its haunted, paper-white quality, and the black dress she wore actually seemed to absorb a bit of the morning sunlight.

"Leota Harbinger," she said, not waiting for a question. "If you're collecting confessions, I have none to give."

The Portfolio Manager bowed, stiff and precise. "I would not presume to interrogate the town witch. But I am required to ask: have you seen Project Manager Púca? He is described as—" (here, the Púca flipped through three pages of forms) "—of average height for his kind, red vest, blue notebook, and an overwhelming sense of urgency."

Leota grinned, sly. "You just described half the Púca in town, friend."

Finnian interjected. "He was drawn into a portal. If I had to guess, I'd say he's probably stuck in the same place as all the missing seconds, minutes, and hours. Somewhere between here and the next best thing. Or possibly he's simply traveled to wherever his destiny awaits—that's what happened to everyone else who went through one of the portals."

The Portfolio Manager did not smile. "Thank you for your assistance. If you see him, please advise him to report to the nearest timekeeper." He clicked his heels together, then performed a crisp about-face, scanning the shelves for evidence of malfeasance.

Leota, watching him go, whispered, "That one's wound tighter than your springs, Finnian."

"He's still a step up from the Safety Inspector Púca," Finnian said. "At least this one's got a sense of irony."

They both turned to the Grandfather Clock, which, despite being thoroughly unwound, had somehow accelerated its ticking to a near frenzy. The pendulum jerked in brief, agitated sweeps. Finnian felt the hairs on his arms prickle: it was not supposed to move like that, not even in the aftermath of a crisis.

Portfolio Manager Púca noticed, too. He returned, fixing the clock with a steely glare. "Why is it doing that?"

Finnian shrugged, but even as he did, the truth dawned on him. "It's not broken. It's just—" He hesitated, searching for words that could capture what he felt. "Trying to get somewhere. Like it has unfinished business."

Leota stepped closer, black eyes locked on the dial. "Or maybe it's trying to tell you something."

The room fell silent, the only sound the desperate tick-tick-tick of the clock. Finnian found himself holding his breath, waiting.

The minute hand jerked, then stopped—dead center on the hour.

A faint electric pulse fizzed through the air. The ozone smell was now strong enough to taste.

Portfolio Manager Púca, who had just opened his mouth to offer a bureaucratic remedy, snapped it shut. His white beard quivered with the effort.

Finnian took a step forward. "It's me," he said, his voice just above a whisper. "It wants me."

Leota nodded, as if this was the answer she'd been expecting all along.

The Púca scribbled a note. "Inadvisable," he muttered. "Never interface directly with a corrupted temporal anchor."

Finnian ignored him. "This is my journey," he declared, and for once, the words felt right. The world had always wanted him to be the fixer, the maker, the one who solved things. Maybe, for once, he'd let the clocks do the same for him.

He scanned the shop, searching for the right tool. His eyes landed on the battered, copper-plated teakettle in the back room—the Mark I Brewer, source of so many happy failures in the early days. He'd always meant to fix it, but somehow it never seemed urgent enough.

He fetched it, cradling the warm metal in his hands. The kettle's brass fittings shone, even under years of tarnish. He set it on the workbench beside the Grandfather Clock.

Leota watched, arms folded, but didn't interfere.

Finnian moved with uncharacteristic care. He opened the clock's casing, exposing the delicate gears and the ghost of the pendulum's former anchor. He positioned the kettle just so, aligning its spout with the cavity in the clock's heart. Then, with a practiced twist, he activated the kettle's steam valve and waited for the hissing pressure to build.

The shop filled with the smell of old oil and scorched air. Steam curled in lazy arcs, beading on the glass of the clock face. Finnian turned away, determined not to watch.

"There's no joy in watching the tea be made," he said, loudly, to the room at large. "I'm just trying to get it done as efficiently as possible."

The Portfolio Manager Púca frowned, sensing a trap but unable to name it. He stepped back, notebook at the ready, just as the Grandfather Clock's ticking grew louder—louder, and faster, until the sound filled the entire shop, then the street, then the world beyond.

The brass face of the clock shimmered. For a moment, it looked like a sun, or maybe a full moon caught behind clouds. Then, with a sound like silk tearing, the face irised open into a perfect circle of gold and blue light.

A portal, neat as a pin and twice as sharp, yawned open in the middle of the shop.

Portfolio Manager Púca gasped and dropped his notebook. Leota, caught off guard, steadied herself against the workbench, her dress fluttering in the sudden wind.

Finnian just smiled, and stepped forward.

Passing through the portal felt less like stepping through a door and more like being pulled, squeezed, and reconstituted by a very particular kind of bureaucracy. Finnian's eyes watered; he blinked once and found himself floating in a void so dense with possibility that every breath stung his tongue with the taste of copper wire and old batteries.

There was no up or down. Or rather, there was every up and every down at once: the world was a churning, infinite expanse of clockwork, rendered as if by a child's dream and an engineer's fever. Gears the size of wagons whirled past, unmoored to any axle, gnashing their teeth at nothing in particular. Springs uncoiled and recoiled in slow motion, their voices a low chorus of metallic ping!s that resonated in Finnian's teeth and the tips of his fingers. The very air shimmered with a blue-gold haze, and each inhalation carried a static charge that made his hair stand on end.

Far below, or perhaps above, or perhaps everywhere at once, chains of pearls and orbs drifted on invisible currents. At first, Finnian thought them stars, until he realized each orb glowed with its own internal label, visible even from this distance: "Makota's Bakery, Grand Reopening"; "Cole Coleson, Birthday"; "Alred's Return"; "North Pointe, Midnight Storm." The orbs flickered, dimmed, brightened, and shuffled themselves in response to forces Finnian could not name but instinctively understood.

He turned, and the world tilted. Now the void resolved into a kind of... plaza? No, that was too solid. A gathering place of pure potential, a market square for the intangible. In its center hovered a desk, and at that desk—frenzied, his red vest flapping like a banner in the wind—was Project Manager Púca.

The Púca had not noticed Finnian's arrival. He stood on a stack of paperwork nearly as tall as he was, waving his blue notebook and barking orders to a squadron of spectral, clipboard-wielding subordinates. Each of these subordinates moved with the nervous energy of a startled hare, darting from one floating gear to another, re-aligning cogs, jotting notes, and re-inking the air with precise lines of what Finnian could only guess was policy.

"Section five, line three!" barked the Project Manager. "If you'd just adhere to the schedule, we could have a smooth transition—no need for these improvisational disasters, thank you very much! Oh, and for the love of the Founders, will someone untangle the Regression Springs on the left vector before the whole quadrant snaps back to infancy?"

A chorus of "Aye, boss!" echoed, high and squeaky, through the non-space. Finnian watched as a half-dozen ghostly Púca zipped to the left, where a snarl of springs threatened to implode. With coordinated, hyper-efficient movements, they sorted, re-coiled, and polished each one, leaving behind a row of perfectly ordered, perfectly dull springs.

"Good, good," muttered Project Manager Púca, making a tick mark on his clipboard. "We're on track. Ahead of schedule, even. That's the way to do it."

The clockwork world responded in kind: with every successful fix, the chaos around the plaza lessened. The gears slowed, synchronized, and began to mesh with each other, forming great chains of interlocking wheels. The orbs re-ordered themselves, aligning in straight lines, then in a grid so perfect it made Finnian's vision blur. The pendulums, which had once swung wild and free, now fell into sync, their motion uniform and utterly devoid of surprise.

Finnian felt a shiver run down his back.

He looked for a means of escape, but the portal had vanished—or, more precisely, been replaced by a hatch marked "Egress Point: Do Not Use Unless Authorized." The sign hovered in midair, bristling with small print and amendments. Finnian snorted, and the sound echoed for miles.

The Project Manager finally noticed him. "Ah! There you are! Finnian Springdale, right on time—no, wait, you're three minutes late, but we'll call it a rounding error. Come in, come in!"

Finnian floated closer, his boots finding purchase on a platform of solid paperwork.

Project Manager Púca leaped down and pointed at him with a

stubby finger. "You, sir, are the cause and, if we're lucky, the solution to all our problems. Do you have any idea the scale of the crisis you've created?"

"Only vaguely," Finnian admitted. "It seemed to be escalating, but I think it's sorted, now."

"That's putting it mildly!" said the Púca, shaking his notebook at the heavens. "You see, every time you introduce a flaw, a deviation, a... spontaneous adjustment to the schedule, it doesn't just affect North Pointe. It ripples, echoes, and resonates throughout the entire domain! The system craves order. It demands regularity. When you smash a clock, that's one thing. When you reset a dozen clocks out of phase—well, then you get this!"

He gestured at the world, and it all made sense to Finnian. The acceleration of order. The hunger for efficiency. The reason the shop had started to feel like a railroad timetable and less like a home.

Finnian watched as the plaza grew even more organized: the floating gears arranged into lattices, the orbs of potential locked into spreadsheets of light. Even the air lost its fizz, becoming crisp and dry, like a winter morning in a bank vault. The Púca's subordinates scurried to and fro, always ahead of the next disaster, always perfecting, never satisfied.

In the midst of it all, Finnian understood: the world wasn't being destroyed. It was being optimized.

It was a world that had forgotten how to drift.

Project Manager Púca looked at Finnian, and—for the first time—his bravado faded. "You know, I never wanted to be a Project Manager," he said, voice trembling. "I wanted to be a tinkerer, like you. I wanted to build things that worked, but not so well that you couldn't find a way to make them better." He gazed up at the now-rigid sky, where a massive clock face had replaced the sun, ticking away the moments with a grim, mechanical certainty. "But here, everything runs on rules, and the rules hate to be broken."

Finnian, feeling the pull of the clock above, nodded. "I know the feeling. I've spent my life making things work, but the best moments were always when they worked a little less than perfectly. That's where the living is."

The Púca brightened, just a touch. "Then you see it? The only way to win is to lose. We need a little chaos. A smidge of error. Without it, the world grinds itself down to nothing."

Finnian grinned, and his heart pounded—not in fear, but in anticipation. He realized, with absolute certainty, that this was not a place for fixing. It was a place for breaking.

The Púca's voice dropped to a whisper, just for Finnian: "If you can break the cycle, I can send you home. But you'll have to be quick—the system is always correcting itself. And if it catches you—" He didn't finish, but the glance at the clock overhead said everything.

"Where do I start?" Finnian asked.

The Project Manager pointed: "Over there. The Archive of Possible Worlds. If you can introduce a bit of uncertainty, a little randomness, the whole place might shake loose. If not—well. At least you'll have given it a proper go."

Finnian nodded, rolled up his sleeves, and launched himself across the plaza, boots crunching on a surface of crystallized ledgers and old meeting minutes. He could feel the order of the place pushing back, trying to correct his every step. But for the first time in his life, Finnian Springdale had no intention of being corrected.

And the world, sensing his intent, trembled.

The Archive of Possible Worlds was a library in the same sense that the universe was a book: infinite, unreadable, and prone to being reshelved by unseen hands. Finnian approached it in cautious, sliding steps, the floating paperwork underfoot crumpling only when he absolutely refused to place his boot where the world wanted it. The air here was so still, so vibrantly blank, that he felt like every movement was a transgression against the very concept of tidiness.

The Archive itself was built of nothing but neatness. Shelves assembled from interlocked cogs stretched in every direction, populated by crystal globes and obsidian cubes and little brass filaments that spun in circles, whispering possibilities to each other. Every item had its place, and every place had been catalogued and cross-indexed by generations of diligent, probably underpaid, cosmic clerks.

Finnian stepped up to the nearest shelf. He eyed a perfect row of labeled springs—each was stamped with a date and a micro-engraved description of its purpose. The springs flexed ever so slightly, just to show they could, but otherwise kept still.

He let his hand hover. For a second, he thought of his father's workshop—how the old man had made Finnian polish every tool, keep every surface free of even a single speck of oil. "Order is what makes the machine run," his father used to say. "The world loves a system."

Finnian, in his rebellious youth, had always found a way to introduce a little error. A backwards screw. A gear filed just off true. A regulator set to drift by a quarter hour, just for the joy of it. Looking now at the springs, at the perfect order of the Archive, Finnian's heart ached for the beautiful, necessary mess of it all.

He smiled, and with a mutter—"This has to break"—he grabbed the first three springs off the shelf and tossed them, one after another, into the void.

Instantly, the shelf glowed red. An alarm shrilled somewhere. Project Manager Púca appeared, clipboard in hand, face a mask of purest horror.

"What do you think you're doing!" the Púca squeaked, genuine panic in his voice. "That inventory took hours—no, decades—to perfect! Put those back, immediately! There are forms for this sort of deviation!"

But Finnian only grinned wider. He turned to the next row, this one full of glassy spheres, and gave the shelf a good, hard kick. The globes tumbled out in a chain reaction, bouncing from shelf to shelf, each one releasing a faint spark as it collided with another. The sparks flitted through the air, gathering in clouds, then raining down on the plaza like golden confetti.

"Stop it!" cried the Púca, flailing at the chaos. He tried to snatch the springs out of the air, but they twisted and spiraled away, each one unwinding just a fraction faster than the last. "You're undoing centuries of—oh, blast it, why do I even bother—"

Finnian waded into the heart of the Archive, arms wide, knocking over stacks of ledgers, flipping pendulums out of phase, and whistling the most off-key version of "Ode to Joy" he could remember. The subordinates attempted to rally, but the moment one put a ledger back in its place, Finnian had already replaced it with a bent spoon or a stick of sealing wax. The entire system fell behind by more than a minute, then an hour, then an era.

Even the sky was affected: the grand clock face that had replaced the sun started to spin, first wobbling, then lurching backward and forward with the unpredictability of a drunk bumblebee. The pendulums overhead crossed in beautiful, catastrophic patterns, their ticking now a raucous, polyrhythmic riot of noise.

The more Finnian broke, the more fun it became. He started improvising. He set up domino runs with crystal cubes, knocked them over with gears, used the falling cubes to disrupt shelves halfway across the plaza. He sang louder, and the Púca's cries of despair only encouraged him further.

At one point, he stood perfectly still, arms folded, and just let the system catch up for a moment. The Archive, sensing a lull, tried to reestablish order: the shelves snapped back into straight lines, the orbs tucked themselves into neatly numbered slots, and a brief, almost smug silence fell.

Finnian took a deep breath, then jumped straight up, flapping his arms and legs like an uncoordinated moth. The shockwave set off another round of anarchy. Now, orbs collided in midair and exploded in little puffs of glitter. Gears ricocheted, springs snapped, and the ledgers, finding themselves ungoverned, started rewriting their own entries at random.

"Enough!" screamed Project Manager Púca, climbing to the top of a pile of undulating paperwork. "You're going to unmake the whole quadrant!"

Finnian, now sweating from the effort, leaned against a spinning gear. "That's the point, friend."

And then, just as suddenly as it had started, the world froze.

Every orb, every gear, every spring hung in perfect suspension.

A sound, like a thousand clocks striking midnight all at once, rang out. It was deafening, but beautiful: a chorus of error, a triumph of the unscheduled.

A wave of golden light swept over the Archive. It hit Finnian first, then the Púca, then radiated outward. Where the wave touched, chaos became energy; the energy resolved itself into new patterns—strange, unpredictable, but alive.

Finnian felt the change before he saw it. His body tingled, his vision blurred, and then—

He was tumbling, end over end, through a tunnel of light and sound. Project Manager Púca tumbled with him, screaming the entire way.

They landed, together, in a heap of clock fragments and tangled wire. Finnian's shop. The floor was warm, the air filled with the scent of burnt ozone and, faintly, the sweet perfume of cinnamon rolls from across the square.

Leota crouched over them, concern flickering in her eyes. Jen, boots muddy and expression unimpressed, stood behind her with arms crossed.

"Nice of you to drop in," Jen said, deadpan.

Finnian tried to sit up, but the world spun sideways. "Did it work?"

Leota helped him up. "The town's clocks are back to their old, disagreeing ways. I'd call that a win."

Finnian looked at the wall. The clocks all ticked, none quite in time with the others. Even the Grandfather Clock, battered and twisted, swung its pendulum with a lazy, happy indifference to the hour.

"Perfect," he whispered, and actually meant it.

He turned to Project Manager Púca, who was dusting himself off and trying very hard not to cry in front of the big people.

"Sorry for the mess," Finnian said.

The Púca sniffed. "Order will return, eventually. It always does. But—" He looked around, and a grudging smile tugged at the edge of his mouth. "Perhaps a little mess is tolerable, if it keeps the world interesting."

Jen clapped the Púca on the back, nearly knocking him over. "That's the spirit. Come on, you two, the bakery's just opened a new batch. Let's see if time tastes any sweeter now."

The four of them staggered out into the morning. The street was alive: children darted between benches, the crows cawed at the hour in complete disagreement, and the bells from the trade road competed in a happy, uncoordinated chorus.

Finnian watched it all, and for the first time in his life, let the world run without his intervention.

He stood with friends, ate fresh rolls, and let the clocks tick as they pleased.

It wasn't efficient.

But it was, finally, enough.

twenty-two

. . .

THE FIRST THING FINNIAN NOTICED, waking in the half-light, was the ticking.

He lay still a moment, eyes closed, and let the silence unfurl around him. There was no creeping sense of doom, no itch of impending regulation—just the warmth of flannel, the faint sweetness of old pine beams, and the soft, aimless clatter of a world finally left to its own devices. The clocks on the wall offered up a confused patter—some slow, some fast, all at odds—but none in a hurry to impose their will.

He allowed himself a full ten minutes, maybe more, before sitting up. The light through the bedroom window arrived at an oblique, dishonest angle, and Finnian, for once, refused to check its accuracy. He pulled on his thickest socks, ran a palm over his crown to tamp down the tufts of white, and padded to the kitchen.

Even here, the clocks squabbled. One chirped the half-hour at the precise moment another rattled out the hour, and a third, mounted above the pantry, played a brief, tinny melody that Finnian did not recall arranging. He poured tea, ignoring the minute hand's erratic march on the stove clock, and opened the shop door with the gentle push reserved for mornings where nothing urgent was meant to happen.

The shop looked exactly as he'd left it—beautifully ruined.

Clock faces gaped open, revealing their brass and bone innards. Wires and gears littered the benches, a fine layer of filings turning every surface into a diorama of last night's adventure. The battered Grandfather Clock loomed in its corner, its pendulum still swinging on a length of garden twine, and somewhere above, the faint rasp of a crow reminded Finnian that the crows, at least, had never cared for time in the first place.

He crossed to the workbench, his slippers whispering over the dust, and surveyed the day's first problem.

The Toast-Buttering Machine stared back at him, or would have, if it still had both eyes. The leftmost dial was loose, spinning freely without intent; the right had popped out altogether, and now hung by a wire like the world's saddest monocle. The arms—designed to butter two slices simultaneously—were frozen mid-stroke, one knife up, one knife down, as if engaged in a lifelong duel with itself. A faint glisten of congealed butter marked the end of the left blade, and Finnian felt a paternal twinge of disappointment.

He set the mug down, rolled up his sleeves, and set to work.

He began as he always did, with a gentle touch. A clockmaker's hands were never in a hurry. He coaxed the casing free with a careful wiggle, then tapped the offending dial back into place with a bone-handled mallet. He plucked the monocle from its tether, inspected the gear housing, and found—yes—a gummy plug of hardened butter clogging the action.

"Always the same story with you lot," he murmured, and set the monocle aside.

Inside, the mechanism was more complicated than he remembered. What had started as a clever linkage to spread the butter evenly had, over the years, grown three extra cams, a pair of tension springs, and a strange, redundant piston that did nothing but vibrate when the machine was on. Finnian shook his head, the faint smile on his lips betraying affection more than regret.

He dismantled the extra bits, lined them up on the bench, and considered their fate.

"Too clever by half," he told the piston, then dropped it into a jar marked 'Interesting, Useless.'

He repeated this procedure with the rest of the machine: strip, inspect, discard, save only the pieces that did honest work. In the end, the Toast-Buttering Machine was reduced to a body, two arms, and a dial that, while now a touch wobbly, no longer spun out of control.

Finnian dusted his hands, took a sip of cold tea, and looked up at the wall.

He'd done the same, over the years, to every device in the shop. What started as a tidy lineup of clockwork had, by increments, become a kind of menagerie: a spaghetti-twirler that doubled as a nutcracker; a teapot with a built-in timer that shrieked at the precise moment the leaves were steeped, then kept shrieking until someone sang to it (a hack suggested by Galhani, who'd claimed the noise encouraged promptness in gnomes); a salt mill that dispensed exactly one grain at a time, for those who liked to argue over seasoning.

The shop was, in short, a catalogue of every bad idea Finnian had ever dignified with brass and enamel. Each had a story, and, more often than not, a lesson in humility.

He set to work, not with the aim of perfection, but with the honest intent to make things a little less embarrassing. Every time he picked up a device, he thought of what Leota had said—about letting things run down, about the magic wanting a bit of chaos.

He started with the shelf of "automated companions." The Egg-Peeler was first. It had three arms: one to hold, one to tap, and one to peel. The original design was meant to give the user more dignity at the breakfast table, but the result was always a shell-shower and, on two memorable occasions, the spontaneous launch of a peeled egg across the room.

Finnian unscrewed the base, unspooled the tension spring, and snipped the rubber bands that had once powered the arms. He kept the shell-tapping hammer—clever, in its way—and set the rest aside for parts.

Next, the Tea-Leaf Sorter. It was a disaster of cams and buckets and delicate wires, all designed to select for the perfect leaf. He couldn't remember why he'd made it; likely, someone had made an offhand comment about the quality of tea in the Capital, and Finnian, with the bitterness of a lifelong provincial, had sworn he could do better.

He could not.

He disassembled it piece by piece, relishing the way the tension left his shoulders with every part consigned to the "Maybe Someday" bin.

It went like that for the next hour. He moved along the shelves in a slow, meditative circuit, dismantling the excesses of his own genius. Now and then, a familiar pang would rise up—a stubbornness, or a prideful twitch of the fingers—but he let it wash over him and pass. The shop, for the first time in memory, felt neither like a stage nor a prison. It was simply a place for work, and for a while, that was enough.

He reached the Variable-Timekeeping Timer last.

It sat at the end of the bench, looking, as always, innocent and faintly amused. It was meant to run at random, the escapement modulated by a sack of tiny, polished stones that shifted at every tick. No matter how many times he calibrated it, it ran unpredictably: sometimes it would chime in an hour, sometimes in seven minutes, sometimes it would skip a whole day's worth of ticks and then catch up in a blur.

Finnian picked it up. The casing was warm, almost alive. He flipped it over, loosened the back plate, and looked inside.

The stones were still there—each a different shade, some bright as berries, others dull as ash. He fingered them gently, letting them click and tumble. He could feel, in the pads of his fingers, the friction that made the clock what it was. The friction that made it fun, and maddening, and useful in precisely zero professional contexts.

He considered simply putting it back on the shelf. But something in him, something he hadn't listened to in years, said: no.

Instead, he dumped the stones, counted them, then set them back in at random. He swapped two gears for lighter ones, and, just for mischief, replaced the hour hand with a feather from the crow that lived in the roofline above the shop. The clock, when he wound it, ticked out a slow, lazy beat, then shivered, ticked three times fast, and then went right back to lazy.

He set it on the counter and grinned.

He realized, only then, that he'd built it not for Leota, but for himself. A lesson in error, hidden in the trappings of a gift.

He poured a new cup of tea, this one hot, and leaned back to savor it.

The shop had changed.

Where before the air had been thick with fate—visions of futures racing by in staccato flashes, as if every clock predicted a thousand possible outcomes—now it felt like a fog had settled in. The future, once so clear and insistent, was soft around the edges. If a customer were to walk in, the shop would offer up a vision, but only a brief, gentle nudge. A sense of direction, not a destination.

He liked it better this way.

He took a minute, or perhaps five, to sweep the shop. It was not tidy—nothing in Finnian's life ever stayed tidy—but it was honest. The parts he'd stripped from the morning's work were sorted into little bins, some by type, others by the simple criterion of "stuff that might come in handy." The clocks on the wall drifted, unconcerned, each marking time in its own, errant way. The old Grandfather Clock, still battered, ticked with the deliberate, loping rhythm of a dog napping in the sun.

He'd just sat down to mend a pair of spectacles (his own, though he'd never admit to needing two pairs), when the world outside the window flickered with motion. Finnian looked up, tea mid-sip, and watched as a young man, hair in disarray, peered through the window with the forlorn expression of someone who desperately needed to know what time it was, and couldn't trust the answer.

Finnian raised his mug in greeting.

The man hesitated, then stepped inside. His boots made a crisp, deliberate sound on the threshold, the kind of step meant to announce a presence before the rest of the body had time to catch up. Finnian, who'd been setting lenses in the bridge of a stubborn old spectacle frame, looked up without hurry.

The young man blinked at the chaos of the shop—rows of clocks all out of phase, the fine dust of a morning's worth of de-invention still glittering in the air, a sweep of oddities populating every flat surface. He seemed almost ready to turn on his heel and leave.

Finnian offered his best welcome: "Come in, unless you've got a moral objection to honest disorder."

The traveler hesitated, then grinned. "It's—livelier than I expected," he said, and the way he said it suggested a man familiar with at least three other types of disaster.

"Livelier's the point, I think." Finnian gestured at the workbench. "How can I help?"

The man crossed to the counter, eyes roving everywhere but never settling. Up close, he was not so young—maybe Finnian's age, if one measured by the lines at the corners of the eyes instead of the color of the hair. His coat had the battered trim of a long-haul postman or a field scientist, and the faint lines of old spectacles marked the bridge of his nose.

"I'm told you have alarm clocks," he said, like someone asking for a delicacy that might be illegal in certain circles. "The kind you can pack in a satchel."

Finnian nodded toward a shelf, where a dozen travel clocks, no two the same size or shape, jostled for attention. Some were classic: bell-on-top, windup in back, a smile in the way the numbers lined up. Others were more Finnian's own invention—one with a phonograph needle meant to play a barked 'WAKE UP' at the appointed hour (Finnian had borrowed the voice from Sam at the Claw, with her permission and three mugs of stout), and another that catapulted a small rubber ball toward the sleeper on a spring-loaded arm.

The customer surveyed the array, brow furrowed. "Do any of them… actually work?"

Finnian cackled, which made the customer grin despite himself. "They all work. They just don't always do the same thing twice. It's an honesty issue. These clocks are made for travelers who live in the world as it is, not as it's supposed to be. If you want something infallible, best go to the capital. They'll sell you a regulator that'll ring on the second, even if you're dead."

"Dead is exactly what I'm trying to avoid," said the man. "Last week, I missed a sunrise by three candlemarks. Woke up in a hayloft, sun already above the bakery, and every decent loaf sold out by then. The wagon crew threatened to leave me."

Finnian raised an eyebrow. "And they didn't?"

"They tried, but I caught them at the bridge. Ran half a mile, breakfast in hand." The man seemed proud of this, though it clearly pained him to admit it. "But if you have something reliable enough to give me a fighting chance, I'll pay in coin or favor."

Finnian pretended to weigh this. "What about you makes you so prone to sleep through a day?"

The customer shrugged. "Work. Road travel. And I've a fondness for reading at night, which sometimes blurs the line between one day and the next."

Finnian selected a clock from the shelf: a sleek oval, its hands bright red, with a brass bell that promised honesty but not cruelty. "This one's my favorite," he said. "It runs a little fast on cold mornings, and a little slow if the air is heavy with salt, but otherwise it keeps decent time."

He wound it, set the alarm for one minute from now, and placed it on the counter.

"Watch," he said, and sipped his tea.

The minute hand ticked forward at a stately pace, but Finnian could already see the telltale signs: the ever-so-slight drag in the gear, the way the minute hand quivered as it passed the half-way mark. He took out his watch and set it next to the alarm, grinning as the two hands drifted apart by a hair, then two, then back together again as the clock worked through its eccentricities.

When the bell finally rang, it wasn't sharp and shrill, but bright—like the opening note of a festival morning, or a polite but insistent reminder that the world could always use another cup of tea.

The customer smiled at the sound. "That'll do," he said. "May I?"

Finnian pushed it across the counter. "Take it outside, if you want to see how it fares against the real sun."

The man did, and Finnian watched him through the window as he set the clock on the stoop, squinted at the sky, and ran his own calculation. He returned, satisfied.

"How much?" he asked.

Finnian named a price, lower than most would, and the man paid it without haggling. He seemed to relax, now that the business was done, and let his eyes wander the shop more freely.

"Never seen so many clocks," he said, picking up the phonograph model and giving it a once-over. "Were you always a clockmaker?"

Finnian considered this. "Started as a tinker. Became a clockmaker by accident. Found that people will forgive all sorts of mistakes, as long as you can make them on time." He shrugged. "But lately, I think they just want someone to make them feel less alone with the minutes."

The customer's face softened. "That's true enough."

He held the clock in both hands. "This may sound strange, but—if you had to say what a clock is for, what would you say? Not just the waking, or the making of meetings, but the point of the thing."

Finnian took his time with the answer. "A clock is for forgetting, mostly," he said at last. "You wind it, and for a day or a week, you don't have to think about what comes next. When it's done right, you don't even notice it. You live your day, and the clock does the counting for you. At worst, it's a reminder of all the things you've missed, but at best, it's a promise that you have more to look forward to."

The man nodded, as if he'd known the answer already but was glad to hear it said aloud.

He pocketed the clock, and for a long second, simply stood in the middle of the shop, soaking in the riot of ticking, the uneven sunlight, the smell of brass and tea.

"Thank you," he said, almost formal now. "I feel better just having seen this place."

Finnian smiled. "That's the other point of a clock. Makes it easier to leave, when you know you can come back."

They shook hands, the man's grip firm and warm. As the contact lingered, Finnian felt the faintest prickle at the back of his neck—a sign, in this town, that a vision was being born.

It wasn't the flash of possible disasters, or the tangled, infinite branching of futures he'd once glimpsed. Instead, it was a brief, quiet certainty: the man, rising before the dawn, eating a warm roll in the predawn chill, the new alarm clock ticking beside his head, and the light in his eyes a little brighter than before.

Finnian saw, too, a vision of himself: standing behind the counter, tea in hand, watching another customer—maybe a child, maybe a stranger—pick up a clock, set it for themselves, and carry the promise of a new day out into the world.

The vision faded, leaving a warmth that lingered in Finnian's chest.

He watched as the customer stepped into the street, checked the time against the bell tower, and then strode off toward the bakery with purpose.

Finnian, alone in the shop, looked at the shelf of clocks. Each ticked as it wished, and not one asked his permission to do so.

He grinned, poured another cup of tea, and let the day drift as it pleased.

twenty-three
. . .

AT FIRST LIGHT, the town square of North Pointe was still a hush and a haze. The air was blue as a swallow's wing and smelled of damp stone, frost-wet grass, and the faint, rising tang of yeast from the bakery. Finnian Springdale stood on the stoop outside his shop, boots planted in the dew, and let the day—his first free of crisis in what felt like a lifetime—unspool around him.

He listened, as he always did, for the tick of the world. Not the grim, relentless tempo of a few days before, but the softer, looser rhythm of a place relearning itself. It was everywhere, if you cared to hear it: the chime of the bell tower off by a handful of seconds, the click of a postman's cane against uneven flagstones, the chorus of children shouting (not in unison, blessedly) from somewhere behind Makota's bakery.

He stepped down, feeling the familiar crunch of gravel under his heel, and wandered toward the heart of the square. The public clocks —four of them, perched at the cardinal points on the town's green— ticked like a set of mismatched teeth. The north clock was a hair ahead, eager for the sun; the east ran slow, possibly out of spite; the south was stopped altogether, its glass face reflecting the sky and nothing else.

No one seemed to mind. A pair of retired salt-spicers, arms linked and coats buttoned up to the chin, ambled beneath the northern clock and paused to argue about the merits of candied versus fresh ginger. A newsboy—still new to the job, Finnian guessed by the size of his hat—stood at the crossroads, cawing the hour and the headlines in a wavering voice, getting both wrong more often than not. The old men at the benches had traded their usual competitive timekeeping for chess and unhurried complaints about the morning's cold.

Finnian smiled. He couldn't recall a day where the green had looked so alive.

He moved, not with purpose, but with the gentle drift of a man in no hurry. The shop doors along the square—once snapped open at the mark of the hour—now woke at their own pace. Finnian tipped his hat to the grocer, who replied with a grin and a bag of yesterday's bruised apples, and to the tailor, who fussed over her window display, her spools of thread as riotously misaligned as the clocks.

At the bakery, Makota was already at her post behind the counter, ears perked and tail swaying as she rang up the morning's first customers. The smell inside—warm sugar and melting butter—hit Finnian like an old friend. He joined the queue, which wound around a shelf of sweet rolls and up to a blackboard menu dense with corrections, cross-outs, and the scrawled notes of Makota's kits.

When it was his turn, Makota gave him a look that mixed relief with open mischief.

"Sleep well, clockbreaker?" she asked, voice purring with pleasure.

Finnian leaned on the counter. "Better than I deserve. Looks like the world survived."

"Barely." Makota flicked an ear toward the ovens. "We ran two batches of sourdough last night, and both of them turned out different. Sora says she guessed the second rise by 'feel' and got it perfect. We haven't seen that in a while." She boxed up a half dozen rolls and slid them across. "You want the truth? I think the clocks were making us worse at guessing. Now, we just watch and hope."

Finnian took the box, weighed it in his hands. "There's more magic in guessing than people give credit."

Makota grinned, exposing the sharp tips of her incisors. "Tell that to the Multi-Timer you made. Sora keeps it for special occasions, like when the holiday cakes go in. Otherwise, we just trust our noses."

Finnian laughed, the sound easy and bright. "It never worked quite right, anyhow. You were always better off with instinct."

She plucked a roll from the tray and took a bite, chewing with visible delight. "You know, I do like that machine. It made the whole place feel measured."

"That's what passes for progress," Finnian said, then more softly: "I'm sorry if I ever made you feel like you had to run on gears."

Makota shrugged, licking the sugar from her fingers. "If you hadn't, I wouldn't know how much I liked doing without." She fixed him with a look that was as much challenge as affection. "Go on, then. Take your mess to the next disaster."

He bowed, a little more formally than necessary, and carried his rolls into the street.

The sun was up now, sharp against the bakery's brickwork and blinding off the iron crossbars of the green's benches. The south end of the square was already lively: Warren, the town's ogre-smith, had set up a temporary forge near the statue of Old Captain Yarrow. Smoke from the coal fire snaked up, then dissolved into the clear blue, and every so often Warren would let out a booming "MORNING" that startled birds and humans alike.

Finnian watched as Warren's son, Darby, ran laps around the anvil with a pair of tongs, each pass accompanied by a whooping sound and a shower of sparks. The townsfolk, who would once have clucked at the "danger" and the "loss of order," now just laughed or offered advice. Even the town bell, which tolled the hour at the north end of the square, seemed to ring just to give Darby more time to play.

Finnian strolled to the forge and found Warren mid-argument with a Púca in a safety vest.

The Púca had a clipboard nearly as big as himself and gestured at the forge with the intensity of a lawyer cross-examining a witness. Warren, for his part, folded his arms and bared his tusks in a smile that could curdle butter.

"I think you'll find," the Púca squeaked, "that the manual specifically prohibits the operation of forgework in public spaces without a designated, pre-certified timepiece. Not only does this breach open-flame guidelines, it also—"

"OGRE FORGE IS TIME," Warren bellowed, "AND TIME IS NOW."

He rapped the anvil with a hammer for emphasis, and Darby echoed the gesture, which set off a round of applause from the onlookers. The Púca glared at Finnian as if seeking a co-conspirator, but Finnian just shrugged.

"Can't argue with the result," Finnian said. "The town looks better with you out here, Warren."

The ogre grunted, but his face softened. "Clockmaker's right. The green's meant for hammer and play. Not for hiding in sheds with ticktocks." He winked, then lowered his voice. "Besides, it gives Darby something to chase. Keeps him from chasing the cats."

Finnian nodded toward the work-in-progress on the anvil: a blackened ring, not yet closed, with spurs of molten metal radiating from its center. "What's that one for?"

Warren picked up the ring, turning it in his massive hands. "It's a gift for the town hall. Cole suggested it, but I made it ugly on purpose. So they'll put it up and everyone can make fun." He set it down and dusted his hands. "What about you? Making more clocks, or just fixing the broken?"

"Neither," Finnian said. "Just... watching. Seeing how everyone gets along when time's their own again."

Warren nodded, solemn. "Is good. Town feels lighter. Maybe you did magic, too."

The Púca, not to be ignored, stamped his boot and declared, "If you're not going to address the safety violations, at least sign here to confirm you accept full liability for all consequences, direct or indirect!"

Warren took the clipboard, bit off the top of the pencil, and signed with a flourish that covered three lines. The Púca, momentarily defeated, stomped off, muttering about appeals and the collapse of civilization.

Finnian stifled a laugh and traded a sweet roll for a chunk of

Warren's fried potatoes. "You ever think the town would let you run a forge on the green?"

Warren shrugged. "Truly no point. Better breezes out here."

They ate in companionable silence, the only clock in sight the north tower, ticking off the hour with a proud disregard for the south and east. The world was, for the moment, exactly as it should be: slightly behind, a little ahead, and stubbornly imperfect.

Finnian made his way toward the edge of the square, where Wilem was already at work beneath a wagon. The cartwright's back end stuck out from beneath the chassis, boots splayed in the universal sign of a man doing a job he'd rather not, but his hands worked with the care and confidence of a master.

"Morning, Wilem," Finnian called.

Wilem's boots jerked, and his head appeared from under the wagon, white hair wild and eyebrows thick with grease. "Finnian! Tell me you didn't bring more clocks. I've only just got last week's out of the bearings."

"No clocks," Finnian promised. "Just passing through."

Wilem wiped his hands on a rag and stood, creaking like a century-old hinge. "Good. Nothing personal, but the trade road's got enough problems without every wagon running on a different minute. That last batch of timers you built? They kept time so well we had a dozen wagons collide outside the bakery—everyone showed up at the exact same second, and no one would give way. It was a proper mess."

Finnian laughed. "I heard. Makota said the whole morning was a parade."

Wilem grunted, but his eyes glinted. "You know, it's better now. The drivers come and go as they please. Some are late, some early, but everyone gets their turn."

He bent and retrieved a step-counter from a tool bin. "You see this?" he said, holding up the odd contraption. "It's a counter, but I set it for 'about' instead of 'exact.' It lets me know when it's probably time to stop for lunch." He slipped it into his pocket, as if hiding a guilty pleasure. "Don't tell the Púca, or they'll make me calibrate it."

"Your secret's safe," Finnian said. "I think we all needed a reminder that 'about' is good enough."

Wilem smiled, sudden and bright. "About is where all the best things live." He ducked back under the wagon, leaving Finnian with the scent of axle grease and honest sweat.

The rest of the morning, Finnian wandered.

He watched a cluster of children build a fort out of milk crates and old banners, timing their attacks by the shouts of whoever claimed to be captain, and never once glancing at the clocks. He watched the grocer haggle with a trader over apples, the argument drifting from prices to politics to the relative merits of pie versus crumble. He watched Jen—her boots muddy, her blue sash askew—marshal a group of teenagers for what looked like a litter-pick, but rapidly devolved into a snowball fight.

He felt a warmth, soft and unhurried, spread in his chest.

He returned to his shop just as the second chime from the bakery clock sounded—slightly off from the bell tower, but exactly in time for the batch of afternoon rolls. He unlocked the door and let himself in.

Inside, the shop was as he'd left it: parts bins sorted by whim and not by logic, dust floating in the sunbeams, the clocks on the walls each in a different mood. He set the box of rolls on the bench and read the new labels he'd made last night, just before bed:

FOR DREAMING, read one, with a little sketch of a moon and stars.

FOR BOILING EGGS, read another, the letters looping like a child's handwriting.

He arranged the clocks accordingly. The first, a grand, brass-bellied beast that drifted in and out of time, he set in the window, so passersby could see its slow, loping hands. The second, a squat tin number with a painted rooster on the face, he set next to the kettle. He wound them both, and listened.

The world, now, was not a series of demands, but an invitation.

Finnian sat behind the counter and watched the light move across the shop. He watched customers wander in and out—not for repairs, but to talk, to laugh, to see what the clocks might do today. He greeted them all, and if they asked for the time, he gave it as best he could, but always added, "or thereabouts."

As evening approached, the town slowed even more. The shops

closed when their owners felt like it; the children, tired from snow and mischief, drifted homeward. Even the crows on the bakery roof, those eternal skeptics of progress, seemed satisfied.

Finnian poured himself a cup of tea, strong and dark, and took the last roll from the box. He ate it slowly, savoring every grain of sugar and cinnamon, every second the world refused to hurry.

He looked up at the clocks.

Some ran, some slept, some ticked with the languor of a summer day.

It was perfect.

And in the quiet, Finnian heard the future: not as a race or a chain, but as a long, slow note, sustained and sweet, echoing from one end of the green to the other.

He closed his eyes and let the time pass, not marking it, but living in it.

And when the last of the sun left the square, Finnian Springdale, for the first time, thought to himself: this was a day well spent.

epilogue
...

THE TEA HAD GONE from hot to comfortably warm. Finnian Springdale cupped the bowl-shaped mug in both hands, letting the last rays of the day slide over his knuckles and turn the clear brown liquid into a prism of gold. He sat cross-legged on the step of Galhani's porch, which—true to its owner's vocation—overflowed with potted herbs and oddments: spiky rosemary, round-leafed marjoram, a pot of nasturtium blazing orange, and even a little twisted tree that smelled sharply of lemon whenever the wind nudged it.

Leota Harbinger perched beside him, one long leg stretched down into the grass, the other bent up to brace her cup on her knee. Her black dress blended with the shadow under the porch rail, but her hair gleamed blue-black in the sun, and the pale of her wrist flashed when she tipped her cup to her lips.

Inside, through the wavy glass of the tea shop's window, Finnian could see Galhani bustling from jar to jar, her gnome-sized frame barely clearing the counter as she re-shelved a rainbow of dried blossoms and bark strips. Every so often she glanced their way, and if she caught their eye, she'd grin like she was in on a joke and then vanish into the back for more organizing.

On the little table between Finnian and Leota, a battered teapot steamed gently over a ceramic stand. It was a perfect match for the place: slightly askew, patched in three places, and painted with a cheerful sunflower that had lost half its petals to age or accident. A plate of walnut biscuits, mostly eaten, was pushed to one side, close enough that Finnian could grab another if he got ambitious.

For the moment, he was not ambitious.

He breathed in. It was all there: the green, musky sharpness of thyme and basil; the mellow, roasted scent of grain from the bakery down the lane; the ghost of sweetness from the dried fruit in the biscuits; and underneath it, the cool bite of river air that always slipped into town just as the sun started to angle west.

Leota caught him mid-sigh. "You're thinking," she said, "about how the world got so quiet."

Finnian smiled, not looking away from the sunlight on the grass. "I was thinking about nothing at all, and it's been so long since I managed that, I thought it deserved a moment of respect."

Leota grinned into her cup. "That's the best kind of thinking. I suppose it takes a world on the brink to teach a man how to sit still."

"You'd think so," Finnian said. "But I tried sitting still before. The clocks wouldn't allow it. My bones wouldn't allow it. Something about the town, too."

Leota stretched, spine arching like a cat's. "Now you have no excuse but to idle."

"I'll need to practice," Finnian admitted.

"Practice is overrated." She took another sip, then set her cup on the table with a clink. "But I will say this—" Her eyes slid sideways, mischief glinting. "Tea tastes different when you don't rush it."

Finnian rolled the cup in his hands, letting the warmth bleed out and in. "I used to drink it so hot it burned the skin off my tongue. Never even considered waiting."

Leota chuckled, low and dry. "You were the only clockmaker I ever met who refused to wait for time."

Finnian shrugged, pleased with the way his shoulder loosened rather than tensed. "You can always borrow time, if you know how to return it with interest."

Leota raised her brows. "You think that's what we're doing? Returning time?"

"Seems fair," Finnian said, and tipped the last of the tea into his mouth, savoring the way the flavors had unfolded rather than simply arrived.

At the foot of the porch, on a small three-legged stool, Project Manager Púca sat with a stack of parchment forms on one knee and a minute quill in hand. He wore the same blue vest as always, though the shine had dulled since the last adventure. Every so often, the Púca muttered under his breath, scribbled furiously, and then signed with a flourish that made the page curl from the enthusiasm.

Finnian watched him out of the corner of his eye.

The Púca scowled at the paper, clicked his tongue, and recited, "Unscheduled Leisure Time Report, Section Five, Subclause Three, Observation: Two hours and seventeen minutes spent in inefficient relaxation protocol. Estimated productivity loss: variable. Enjoyment metric: unquantifiable." He paused, looked up at Finnian and Leota as if expecting an apology, then returned to his paperwork.

Leota smothered a laugh behind her knuckles.

Finnian leaned over the porch rail. "Is there a form for 'time well wasted'?"

The Púca glared, but with a practiced air, as if he'd endured worse slights from a thousand other offenders. "Every moment can be accounted for, if one has the proper ledger. The system expects a report. The system always expects a report."

Finnian sipped the dregs of his cup. "Seems to me the system could use a cup of tea and a nap."

The Púca sniffed. "You mock, but I assure you: unscheduled leisure is a leading cause of metaphysical drift. This entire quadrant could slide back to pre-dawn if you're not careful."

Leota refilled her cup from the battered pot and held it out. "You want some, Finnian? Or are you waiting to see if the world unravels before you pour again?"

He grinned and slid his cup forward, letting her fill it to the brim. "I'm learning patience, remember? I can wait."

She passed him the cup and, with a gesture, flicked a sprig of mint off the table and into the grass. "Practice, then. See how long you can hold out before you drink."

Finnian set the cup between his hands and tried, he really did, to resist. He lasted a minute and a half, then gave in and took a sip. The flavor was new—thicker, bolder, with a slow-spreading heat that crept up his tongue and stayed there.

He made an appreciative noise.

Leota raised her brows in a "See?" motion.

"Best cup I've ever had," Finnian said, and even the Púca looked up as if to mark it for the record.

They sat like that, a little trio of misfits, as the light eased down the front steps and into the square. At some point, Galhani came out with a fresh tray of fruit slices and more biscuits, which she set between them with a wink. "If you don't finish these, I'll make you count the poppy seeds," she said, then bustled back inside before anyone could protest.

The fruit was perfect, sharp and tart and soft enough to bruise under a thumb. The biscuits were sweet enough to demand a second cup of tea, so Finnian obliged, pouring for himself and Leota both.

After a comfortable silence, Leota set down her cup and turned, her voice dropping a note. "You're not worried at all, are you?"

Finnian thought about it. "No. Which is a new thing for me. I usually have at least three concerns on simmer, two on boil, and one threatening to overflow."

Leota laughed softly. "Maybe that's the point of the world, after all. You get your disasters, your emergencies, your dramas—and then you get a little peace."

Finnian stared out over the green. "I think I could get used to it."

The Púca finished his form with a decisive dot, then stacked it on the pile and began the next, muttering, "Potential for disorder: High. Counterbalancing benefit: To be determined."

He continued, quill scratching and tongue clicking.

Finnian leaned back on his elbows and stretched his legs, the tips of his boots brushing the tips of the overgrown thyme. He closed his eyes for a moment and let the sun warm his face. For a heartbeat, he imagined the world as a gigantic, slow-turning clock—one with a lovely, honest drift. It didn't matter what hour it was, or even what day; what mattered was the people on the porch, the smell of the herbs, the warmth of the last light.

Leota nudged him with her toe. "You drifted off."

He shook himself and grinned. "Only for a second."

She arched a brow. "You want to go inside and see what kind of mischief Galhani is up to?"

Finnian watched the gnome through the window, now stacking tins with what looked like deliberate randomness. "If I had to guess? She's building a display that will only make sense after dark."

Leota stood, stretched, and offered a hand to Finnian. He took it, let her pull him to his feet. He looked back at the Púca, who was now deep in debate with himself about which subsection best described "excessive porch idling."

"Come in when you're done with your paperwork," Finnian called, and this time, the Púca managed a small, rueful smile.

"We shall see," said the little man, and made a note on his form.

Inside, the air was even warmer, the light richer and thicker. Galhani greeted them with a laugh and set them to work tasting every blend she'd invented that week. Finnian lost track of time, and didn't mind at all.

As the sun slid behind the western rooftops, and the square outside faded to blue, Finnian realized he could not remember the last time he'd felt so perfectly, gloriously unhurried.

The conversation had wandered from the best way to dry basil leaves to the curious color of the watercress flowers when the porch boards creaked with new weight. Finnian glanced up, expecting another neighbor in search of tea or gossip, but saw instead the constable's blue sash and the iron badge glinting like a second sun.

Jen came from the direction of the trade road, boots clicking in a cadence she could never quite break. She paused at the edge of the porch, boots rooted square to the step, and looked down at the little gathering.

"Afternoon," she said, nodding to each in turn. Her voice was as clipped as ever, but there was something unhurried in the way she set her jaw.

"Afternoon, Jen," said Leota. "Tea?"

Jen shook her head. "On duty," she said, but there was a ghost of a smile in her eyes.

Galhani, who had emerged to refill the tray with almond cakes, offered a wink. "We can make it decaf."

"Still a no," Jen replied, but less firmly. She studied the group, as if checking for signs of trouble. Finding none, she allowed herself a moment to lean against the rail, arms folded.

"Just making my rounds," she said, addressing the porch. "Wanted to let you know the clocks are back to their old ways. North and east tower disagreed by six minutes this morning. Baker's is already two ahead, and the south one's dead as a stone. Town seems content to use whichever one makes them happiest."

Finnian felt a warm spread of satisfaction, like good whiskey or a new roll of beeswax. "And the world hasn't ended?"

"Only if you count the fishmonger missing his first delivery in a fortnight," Jen said. "He blamed you, Finnian, for getting him 'hooked on leisure.' Said he's never seen his nets so empty, but he's never enjoyed the waiting so much, either."

Leota snorted. "I'll take that as a win."

Jen shrugged. "No one's complained. Some said it was nice, walking into the bakery and not knowing if it was time for breakfast or lunch. People started talking again—used to be, everyone just marched from appointment to appointment, heads down." She cocked her head at Finnian. "You did a good thing, clockmaker. Bartram said he hasn't sold this many shoes in a sennight since the town was new. People keep losing track of time and staying in his shop to chat."

Finnian grinned. "Did he grumble about it?"

"Loudly, at first," Jen said, the corner of her mouth quirking. "Now he's the one opening early and closing late. Told me he might take up a second trade in storytelling."

Galhani clapped her hands in delight. "I knew he had it in him! You give a man time, and you find out what he loves most."

Jen's gaze shifted to the sky, where the sun had begun its long slide behind the bakery roof. The clouds, thin as a glaze of sugar, went first gold, then a color Finnian could only call apricot, before deepening to the bruised rose that promised a perfect dusk.

"Suppose I should get on," Jen said, pushing off the rail. "But I like to see a porch with friends on it. It's the right sort of order, if you ask me." She nodded to Finnian, then Leota, then—after a moment's hesitation—to the Project Manager Púca, who had not looked up from his forms.

"Stay out of trouble," Jen said, and walked back toward the heart of town, badge catching the last blaze of sun.

Finnian watched her go, feeling the easy sense of things in their place. He refilled his cup, now only lukewarm, and cradled it in his lap. The porch had gone quiet, save for the hum of bees on the thyme and the scratch of the Púca's quill.

Leota stretched her legs, her boots bumping against his. "Content?"

"More than," Finnian said. He took in the view—the town green, the drifting children, the bakery windows glowing, the wagons pulling in at their own uncoordinated pace. The world was loose, but not unmoored. It was, if anything, more itself.

He let his mind drift. There was no next crisis to solve, no second hand ticking down, just the slow dissolve of day into night and the knowledge that tomorrow, and all the tomorrows after, would come when they came.

At the end of the porch, the Púca looked up, as if sensing the weight of the moment. He eyed the sunset, made a small, neat notation, and sighed with theatrical resignation.

He wrote, in careful block letters: "Sunset Appreciation: Duration, Indeterminate. Joy, Excessive. Resolution, Pending."

Finnian laughed, loud and full, and the sound seemed to carry across the green, reaching even to where Jen strode, boots kicking up little clouds of dust.

He sat back and watched the sky unfold, colors rippling and changing without any clock to dictate how long they should last. He let the tea cool in his hands, his fingers relaxed, his mind at ease.

He did not care what time it was.

The journey, at last, was all the point.

afterword

I began outlining this novel on the first day of my retirement from my "day job." As you can probably imagine, my state of mind probably had a significant impact on that outline! The first few weeks of retirement were a daze, as I kind of moped around and wondered what to do with myself. Suddenly, I saw inside Finnian's mind: the need for structure, the emphasis on deadlines and precision, the detailed mapping of the moment-to-moment day. I'm not saying that I lost track of the journey in favor of the destination all the time... but... maybe sometimes, at least a little. Then one morning I woke up and thought, "I have nothing to do today, and *that's just fine*. I think I'll go sit and watch the wood stove with my dog on my lap."

That was a big day, and it was a bit like Finnian's own revelation. Complexity for fun is fine, but for the day-to-day stuff, simple wins. The journey is often more important than the destination. And life may be short, often too much so, it's still long enough to enjoy the empty moments.

So!

This is Book Nine in *Tales from the Broken Claw,* and I've Book Ten mapped out. It focuses on Dexter's story. Remember him? He doesn't

Afterword

pop up much, but when he's needed it's like he was there to begin with. Almost preternaturally fast, you might say.

After Book Ten, I actually do have more mapped out—twenty books in total, if you can credit it, giving one book to each of North Pointe's shops. But I'd really love to hear from you if you'd like to read them—even a quick email to don@donjones.com can be more inspiring that you can imagine. And you'd have some say in which order those stories come out! So please, if you'd like to visit North Pointe a few more times after Dexter… let me know. I will probably be taking a bit of a break regardless, to work on other projects, but if you're up for a return trip, I'm up for taking you there!

I also urge you to "follow" me on your favorite bookstore website, book review website, or whatever. My website, DonJones.com, has convenient "follow" buttons right on the front page. That'll make sure you know when I have a new novel out, and it'll make sure your email address stays with the websites you've already given it to. Of course, I do have a newsletter at DonJones.com/signup that you can opt into, if you'd like to hear about new releases from me directly.

Until next time, I hope you have a cozy day :).

award-winning fiction

Daniel Scratch: a story of witchkind

- Kirkus Starred Review
- Winner, American Fiction Awards—Best Fantasy (2023)
- Finalist, American Legacy Book Awards—Best Fantasy (2024)

Clara Thorn, the witch that was found

- Winner, American Fiction Awards—Best Young Adult (2023)
- Runner-Up, American Fiction Awards—Best Fantasy (2023)
- Finalist, American Legacy Book Awards—Best Fantasy (2024)
- Finalist, American Legacy Book Awards—Best Young Adult (2024)

Award-Winning Fiction

Find these books and more at DonJones.com

about the author

Don Jones spent two decades writing tech books before he finally penned his first sci-fi novella, *A History of the Galactic War*. His well-reviewed and award-winning novels span fantasy and science fiction, with a focus on world building and relatable characters.

Connect, get free novels and short stories, and learn about upcoming releases by visiting Don's author website at DonJones.com.

also by don jones

stories of witchkind®

<u>Age of the Adherents</u>:
Daniel Scratch • Master of the Tower • The Fifth Axis

<u>The Order</u>:
The Order of Some • The Conspiracy of One • The Truth of All

Clara Thorn

Clara Thorn, the witch that was found

Clara Thorn, the witch that fought

Clara Thorn, the witch that won

Endless Sky®

Truthsayer • New Worlds • Old Bones

Tales from the Broken Claw

Pubs & Pegasi • Anvils & Avatars

Volumes & Villainesses • Teas & Tribulations

Watchers & Windstorms • Stitches & Snake Oil

Peacekeepers & Púca • Cuts & Catastrophes

Gears & Gateways • Bandages & Banshees

The Never: A Tale of Peter and the Fae

Bob Constantine (no relation)

———

Find more at DonJones.com, including a free fantasy trilogy, a free superhero duology, two collections of short stories, and even more short stories and flash fiction.

Sign up for the author's newsletter at DonJones.com (click the "Freebies" link) for notifications of new novels, and ample opportunities to get free ebooks by becoming a beta reader!